Lost and Found

Lost and Found

Louis M. Fink MD

ISBN:	Softcover	978-1-4990-7767-4
	eBook	978-1-4990-7766-7

This is a work of fiction. Names, characters, places and incidents either are the product of the author's imagination or are used fictitiously, and any resemblance to any actual persons, living or dead, events, or locales is entirely coincidental.

This book was printed in the United States of America.

Rev. date: 10/06/2014

To order additional copies of this book, contact:
Xlibris LLC
1-888-795-4274
www.Xlibris.com
Orders@Xlibris.com
672799

CHAPTER 1

They were her children now. Maria thought as she caressed the red leather bound passports. She had found an Austrian forger and had him prepare identity documents for Tomas and Robe. Their Christian names were unchanged but their surname Havas was erased and replaced with her maiden name. They were now Maria, Tomas and Robe Gutta. She kept her certificate of marriage to their father Rolfe Havas but she put it in an envelope separate from their passports.

Arriving in the Vienna Sudbarnhoff she held five year old Robe with her right hand and seven year old Tomas with her left hand. As she went to step down from the train carriage Robe squirmed. Maria lost her balance and started to fall. She let go of the boys' hands.

A hand reached out and grabbed her. His arms lifted her like a powerful derrick.

"Shalom" he whispered into her ear as he hoisted her to her feet. While he was lifting her, she felt knotted silk strands and a small leather box the size of a match box beneath his shirt sleeves. He was wearing a black coat extended down to his knees and had on a black felt brimmed hat. His face was covered by a long straggly brownish beard and curled sideburns. As he raised her, he tucked a small bag into her pocket.

When she regained her equilibrium she murmured "bitte"

She felt a caress as the man released his tight grip from her. His touch gave her a feeling of familiarity. She wanted to continue holding on but the stranger let go and disappeared into the crowded terminal. The encounter did not last longer than twenty seconds. She was so startled that no words came out. Maria straightened up and searched for the face of the bearded stranger. He was gone as if a ghost.

As a blast of steam blew out across the platform from the boilers of the locomotive they were enveloped in a warm gray cloud. Maria pulled the boys to her and brushed them off. She wiped their faces with a tissue from her pocketbook.

The boys walked along side of Maria. As they entered the station's rotunda, Maria felt a bulge in her coat pocket; her fingers stroked a leather purse that had been placed there. She was afraid to remove it out in the open station.

All the benches were occupied so Maria had the boys sit on their suitcases while she went to find the W.C. She removed two sandwiches from her pack and gave one to each boy. They promised not to move from under the four faced bronze clock hanging from the center of the rotunda's dome.

Inside the dirty white tiled lavatory sat a fat old woman. Her grey hair was covered by a babushka that was tied below her triple chin there was a trace of a mustache above her upper lip. Her eyes seemed shrunken and her cheeks had brownish dirt smudges. The palm of her hand extended from the torn sleeve of her patched overcoat. It was open and waiting for a coin.

Maria shut and bolted the door to the toilet stall. She removed the suede purse from her worn long leather jacket. She twisted the metal snaps open and found a wad of Austrian shillings and a sealed envelope. She pried open the envelope and read silently mouthing the words. It was the twenty third psalm; The lord is my shepherd I shall not want........ It had been torn from a prayer book. She felt the serrations from where it had been ripped from a binding.

Why would a Hassidic Jew secretly place this purse in her pocket.

She was confused.

She didn't understand why someone would give her a copy of the Lord's Prayer but she was elated because her funds for travel to return to Budapest were almost gone. She thought maybe it was an accident or a mistake. Perhaps he mistook her for someone else.

She put the purse back into her knapsack and left the toilet stall. At a basin she washed her face and hands. Looking into the cracked mirror she pushed her blonde hair into place. She applied a coat of lipstick using a gold tube that her husband Rolfe had given her on their brief honeymoon last year. She felt her forehead and looked to see if there were any new wrinkles.

Upon leaving she dropped ten pfennigs into the pocket formed by the apron between the stubby legs of the matron attendant.

As she reentered the crowded station she turned her head like she was a camera rotating during a panoramic shot. She could not see anyone resembling the bearded Jew. She looked again and there was still no sign of him.

Tomas and Robe were where she had left them. Each of them wore woolen sweaters and caps. Tomas had on long pants and Robe had short pants with long socks that reached almost to his knees. They were still eating the pieces of pumpernickel and cheese. She packed what was left of their food and brushed the crumbs off of them.

They went to the agent and purchased one way tickets to Budapest.

Out of compulsiveness she checked the blackboard for the train schedule. Maria with one boy in each hand marched to the platform where their train could be boarded. Again she scanned the station again for the stranger who had helped her. Maria rechecked the tickets and their identity papers. They found their third class coach compartment. They got seated and settled. The train started with a few lurches and gathered speed. Maria pulled the window up to keep out the black carbon soot. The clanging of the wheels on the tracks had a soporific effect and soon the boys fell asleep against her, one on each side.

She closed her eyes and thought about her husband Col. Rolfe Havas. With her thumb she and turned her gold wedding band. She wondered whether he was alive or dead. She prayed "please God let him be alive and let him return to me and his sons."

She fantasized that the stranger who had kept her from falling in Vienna was an incarnation of Rolfe.

During the trip she felt as if someone was watching her but she never saw anyone.

Because of the occupying Russian and American troops and the border- crossing, the trip, which could have been done in three hours, took almost ten hours. When they reached Budapest it was two in the morning and there were no taxis at the station. Maria awakened the boys and buttoned their jackets, and they walked almost three kilometers to the home of Maria's aunt. The apartment consisted of only one room and Maria knew that she would have to find another place for them to live as soon as she could. They slept in their clothes on the hard wooden floor that night.

CHAPTER 2

Rolfe called his men to gather around him. He knew most of them, if not by name, by sight. Some had been under his command for over five years and some were only with his unit for the past several months. The new soldiers were much younger than the regulars who had fought on the Eastern Front with him. Some seemed barely adolescent. He wondered how well they would fare without an officer or a parent to tell them what to do.

"Find what is left of your homes and families" he said to his men and "May God be with you."

He watched as groups of what was left of his former battalion started to walk away from the railroad yard. Only his lieutenant and five of his NCOs' stayed. These were the men who had been with him since he had been commissioned as an officer in the Hungarian Army.

He was a gambler and always said "The dice are in the hand of the thrower."

This time he was wagering with his future and his life.

"Wait for me here" he said to the small squad of men who had remained with him.

At the telegraph office he asked the operator "How far away are the Russians? How far are the Americans?"

The operator answered "the Russians are just outside of Vienna and the Americans are south of Munich."

Rolfe calculated that Salzburg would be occupied within twenty four to forty eight hours.

Rolfe gave an address and a message to the telegraph operator. A series of dots and dashes spelled out "delivery tomorrow evening."

He gathered his remaining men and a train crew of two and led them to a small brick warehouse adjacent to the freight loading platform. It was padlocked. He commanded "smash open the locks, pile the load on the flat car and cover it with a canvas tarpaulin." They used dollies to move the load of heavy sealed metal canisters, trunks and wooden crates onto the single flatbed train car at the rear of the loading dock. While they did this, Rolfe studied a set of maps carefully and planned the trip south

There was a steam locomotive, a coal car and a flatbed car. The cargo was tons of treasures. The soldiers did not know the exact nature of the sealed cargo but most had some suspicions. There were oils by Monet, Rubens and Cezanne, gold challises, ruby laden goblets, handwritten Torahs in sculptured ornate silver carved covers, thousands of gold wedding bands and dental fillings melted into bullion. The loot had come from the shuls, homes and bodies of wealthy and poor Jews from Budapest to Kiev. It had been awaiting shipment to Germany. Rolfe had heard about the cache when he was billeted with several generals from the Wehrmacht. He had other plans for the loot.

Rolfe told his men that he would slow the train along the route so that they could jump off and head home to Hungary.

As they departed Salzburg Rolfe could barely make out the silhouette of the walls and turrets of the castle, the Festung Hohensalzburg high on the ridge above the city. The train headed south. Rolfe rode in the locomotive cab. He studied the rail markers and the detailed maps. They weren't far out of Salzburg when he told the engineer to slow the train. He signaled the crew and his men to jump off.

It was only fifteen kilometers to Hallein. When he saw the station in the distance he began to gently brake the train. When the train coasted to a stop it was right at the platform. The place was deserted except for a bearded monk. He was wearing a dark brown frock with a hood that was tied and lay across his back. A polished wooden cross hung on a thin leather strap from his giraffe-like neck. His eyes seemed to squint as if he was trying to focus without glasses. His full beard blended into closely cropped sideburns. His bald head was partially covered by a skull cap. The monk ordered several of his colleagues to move the load from the train to the waiting wagon. When the job was done he climbed up onto an buckboard. He extended a hand to help Rolfe up to the seat next to him. He placed the reins in his hands and shook them to get the horse to move. It was a twenty- two hand remnant of a large Clydesdale-like horse. This work horse had probably hauled thousands of kegs of beer to mountainside guest houses. This was probably its last trip since there little else for the horse to pull and was no other food left at the monastery.

Brother Simon had instructions from the Bishop to bring the Colonel and the wagon to the monastery. They traveled over a wooden planked bridge crossing a stream partially covered with water carved ice structures. Rolfe imagined that he could see a kneeling figure with folded hands in front of her bowed chin and breasts, as if praying.

The route took them twelve Km to the southeast of the Hallein station. The rutted dirt road was bounded by snowdrifts and pine trees some of which had been felled or partially cut for fuel. The Salzach River's raging roar slowly blended into the silence of the night. The overhead moon played hide- and- seek with the clouds resulting in a sensation of movement even when the wagons came to rest in front of a brick white portico.

A piercing owl-like shriek from Brother Simon signaled a hidden sentry to peel the leaves of a three meter iron gate apart. They entered a courtyard and pulled to the entry to the Monastery. Rolfe gazed at the massive bronze doors covered by an oxidized greenish patina. The only place he had ever seen anything like this was on his first honeymoon trip to Florence in 1932. If they were not the Gates of Paradise by Ghilberti they surely were an excellent forgery. The Gates were reliefs that decorated the door of the Baptistery. They had been cast in 1425. Each of the ten panels was an image from the Hebraic stories of The Old Testament, starting with the Sacrifice of Israel in the upper left panel.

Brother Simon was relieved by a tall thin priest in a black garb. Hanging below his chin was a silver cross on a silver chain. On his right hand was a gold ring set with an emerald that was larger than his incisor teeth which appeared in his mouth when he grinned. The priest said "velcome we have been expecting you."

The walls of the monastery had gaps in the stucco façade revealing an underlying base of reddish brickwork. The central cathedral still held stained glass windows between the flying buttresses. The serenity of this compound in this Bavarian setting was in marked contrast to the maelstrom devastating the collapsing German Empire. There was anger and confusion throughout most of Europe.

Rolfe was told that he must go no further. The monk took the wagon up the road. It led to an orifice in the rock carapace adjacent to the church. The horse, wagon and steel drums disappeared as if they had been swallowed. The entrance was sealed by huge steel doors that were bolted. Dirt and rocks hid the doors. The Priest said that it "reminded him of the Red Sea's flooding after the Exodus and that the code for the cache should be the plagues of the Passover."

Rolfe went to the rectory and composed a letter to Maria. In the letter he told her that the story of Exodus would be important in his family's survival. He said that he would see her in "another world." He sealed the envelope and addressed it to an aunt of Maria's in Budapest. He asked Brother Simon to mail it for him when he felt that mail service was restored. He took a worn copy of the Old Testament and tucked it into his pack.

He knew that he too must disappear. He closed his eyes and made a mental imprint of every detail. His and his family's future and fortune would depend on how well he could store the events of this night.

CHAPTER 3

Rolfe was a little disoriented when he left the monastery complex where he had delivered the valuables from his "gold train." He didn't have a plan. Previously, even when his dreams collided with reality, he had been able to quickly adapt and restrategize. When he heard about "Crystal Nacht" (night of the broken glass) in 1938 and the proposed extension of the Nuremberg Laws forbidding marriage and sexual relations between Jews and non-Jews, he had made plans for Julia, his first wife and the mother of his sons Tomas and Robe, to divorce him and escape to Palestine. Her family fortune and his family's aristocratic background facilitated a divorce and passage from Bulgaria to Cyprus and on to Jerusalem. Julia had cried "I do not want to go and leave you and my children behind." She said "I would rather die than leave."

Rolfe said "We will be together in a new world".

Julia's roots were embedded in Budapest. Julia's family the Gluckes were descendants of the Cohen tribe of Jews. They had stopped their gypsy-like wandering and peddling of bicycles to found a motorcycle factory, three generations ago. The plant was a sprawling complex on the outskirts of Pest that was managed by her brothers after her father's death in 1931. Her father had never been orthodox, but he attended the synagogue on Yon Kippur and Rosh Hashanah and contributed to the congregation. His social life was with the Sephardic Community. He had never disassociated himself from his faith. The memories of past "Pogroms" still scorched his soul. Julia and her brothers, were tutored in Hebrew by the Rabbi and they brought tzedakah, charity, for the less fortunate congregation members. They were exposed to all the Sabbath and holiday rituals but asked for assimilation and acceptance into Budapest society. Out of respect Julia waited. The year after her father's death, Julia married Baron Rolfe Havas. Because they came from different religions there was a compromise. They eloped and were married in a small shul in Florence. With their background of money and power, few of their friends or relatives ever dared openly discuss the intermarriage.

~~~~~~~~~~~~

In the forest near the monastery Rolfe came to, as if out of a stupor, and realized that he had better extricate himself from his precarious position. If the Red Army coming from the East found him, the consequences could be fatal or he could face an indeterminate imprisonment in a Stalag in Northern Russia or Siberia. His records would show his participation in the German invasion of Russia. The alternative, capture by the Allies could lead to a trial and unknown retribution or imprisonment. Neither of these was his decision. He had been a gambler most of his life and his intuition had usually led him to success. Out of chaos often came solutions. "Where was the most disorder," he thought. The Ebensee concentration camp was twenty kilometers away, and if he shaved his head, carved and imprinted a tattoo onto his left arm like those he had seen on Auschwitz camp prisoners, his emaciated body could allow him to act the part of a confused disoriented Jew from the concentration camps. He knew his former brothers-in-law well and even resembled the younger brother Ted Glucke. He had also listened to enough conversations with the Glucke family, his in-laws, so that he was almost fluent in Yiddish. It had been easy for him to learn Yiddish since most of the words were similar to German.

That night he shoved in the wooden door on a little schoolhouse where he found an inkwell. With his penknife, a quill, and black ink, he carved a triangle and the numbers 10416 on his left forearm. He managed to remove enough clumps of hair with his knife so that he appeared slovenly shaven. He reconnoitered the sleeping village and found tattered pants and a shirt in the bedroom of an empty cottage. He changed into these old clothes and shed his uniform. In a deserted cabin, he built a small fire and burned his wallet, his identity papers, and his uniform. He loaded his metal insignias, helmet, ribbons, medals and pistol into his pack weighted with stones. He threw all this into a nearby deep glacial lake.
~~~~~~~~~~~~

He headed east towards Ebensee where there was a small concentration camp, and after a day and a half of hiking he was taken on May 14, 1945, by the advancing 90th division of the US Army. He was briefly interrogated, fed and given an olive woolen blanket, a set of fatigues socks and sandals. The soldiers seemed to be preoccupied and other than asking Rolfe what camp he had been in, they wanted to know if he had heard anything about "Nazi Gold." They had orders to find a trainload of Nazi loot before the Red Army could get to it. Rolfe told them that he had seen Germans unloading heavy containers near Merkers, southwest of Uln, two nights ago. Rolfe was taken back to a hastily constructed displaced prison (DP) camp near Hallein where he slept for the next 12 hours. He awoke while dreaming about his wife Maria and his sons Tomas and Robe.

Maria had a serene attractiveness. Her light coloring and large deep-set brown eyes gave her the contrast characteristic of platinum/palladium photos. Her beauty had simplicity so basic that cosmetics or other adornments could only detract from her allure. She wore only a dark rouge lipstick. She moved so smoothly that her tall, pale silhouette was almost camouflaged in the sunlight and she might have passed unseen except for her shadow. Maria's physical inconspicuousness and demure gave no hint of the complexity and depth of her mental musings. She would have been the quintessential poker player.

After completing her undergraduate studies at St. Charles University, in Prague, she enrolled in the Doctoral Program in Budapest where she began to study the new science of Psychology under Professor Sandor Ferenczi, a disciple of Sigmund Freud, who was called the "mother of psychoanalysis" Maria had wanted to go to Vienna to study with Freud and had planned to go to London to study with him Dreams had fascinated her since childhood. She had been accepted by Freud, but his buccal cancer, caused by his passion for cigars, had put him in poor health, and she had to find another mentor. It was not clear how a doctoral degree in psychology would provide an occupation, but Maria thought that the understanding of human emotions was the epitome of knowledge. Ferenczi died in 1933 so she continued her studies with Michael and Alice Balint until they fled to England along with the Freud family.

In order to afford to continue her studies, Maria sought out part-time employment. She was hired by Julia and Rolfe Havas to take care of their two sons.

After the hurried divorce and departure of Julia from Hungary in 1939, Rolfe entrusted the care of his sons to Maria. She adapted to her maternal role willingly and naturally. She suspended her studies at the University to devote all of her efforts to caring for and raising the two boys.

Rolfe's unit became part of Operation Barbarossa and departed for the invasion of the Soviet Union in June 1941. During a short leave from the Eastern Front, Rolfe returned to Budapest to find that Maria had taken on the role as head of the household. She had matured under the pressure from these duties, from a free spirited student to a conscientious homemaker and mother.

At first Rolfe fought the sexual attraction between them. One night they accidentally collided in the hall after she had put the boys to bed. They literally fell into each other's arms. Both were engulfed with passion, Rolfe was Maria's first real love.

Her devotion to him and his family prompted Rolfe to ask Maria to marry him. When Rolfe asked her to marry him she sensed that he had not given up his great love for Julia, but she was overcome by her love for the two boys and her passionate love for Rolfe. She agreed. The wedding was in a civil court with only a magistrate and two witnesses. After the wedding, Rolfe packed Maria and the boys for a trip to one of his family's vacation homes near Lenz in Austria because he felt that they would be safer there. Provisions and money were sequestered. Maria was to wait for him to return from his assignment in the Ukraine.

CHAPTER 4

It was 1974 and Robin (nee Robe) Goode peered out of the porthole of the 747, the fog appeared to hug Manhattan at the edges of the river confluence at the Battery. A green arm with a torch and the tip of a head with a crown rested in a white snowy cloud drift. The dark blue waters filled the spaces between the clouds. The windows on the tall buildings reflected the eastern sunrise. The plane banked off to the right, flew back toward the Atlantic and circled to land at Kennedy International Airport. As they taxied toward the jetport, they passed the new sleek, needle-like proboscis, of the Concorde SST on the tarmac and Robin promised himself that someday he would fly on that plane.

The passengers were herded through the cylindrical tunnels at the TWA terminal to the immigration booths. Robin counted the cycles of the wait-stop light that signaled his line to move. The gray uniformed officer beckoned him to come to his counter. He presented his Austrian passport and visa and she asked "what is the nature of your visit to the USA." He had been asked this and related questions a hundred times when he had applied for his green card in Vienna. He answered "for medical studies." She asked, "Have ever been a member of the Communist Party." He answered, "No." He was asked why he had an Austrian passport since his place of birth was listed as Budapest. Robin had been prepped to answer clearly and succinctly without anger. He told the officers "I fled Hungary and had been allowed asylum in Austria and given Austrian citizenship." The sound of the stamping seal of the USA on his passport resounded inside his brain. His suitcase, somewhat scarred from his journeys, was on the circular baggage carousel. The customs agent ran her gloved hand around, randomly lifting underwear and unwinding balls of socks and asked him, "Are you carrying drugs or agricultural items?" When he said "no" she motioned him through the metal-pillared barrier.

Robin restrapped the buckles on the worn calfskin bag, walked outside and let the gentle rain of America wash the old world off him. He had only $100 in US dollars and had instructions on how to take the airport shuttle bus to the IRT subway and how to get to Second Ave. and 73rd Street in Manhattan. But he decided to splurge and hailed a taxi. He gave a slip of paper with his destination to the cabby. During the ride he was comforted by the recognition of remnants of the 1964 World's Fair. The taxi walkie-talkie crackled with Arabic, the taxi license from New York had a picture of a bearded man who was NO 10139 Mohammed Mufti. Mo, as he designated himself, wove through the traffic lanes, funneled into the single file and through the tollbooths into Queens Midtown Tunnel. The fare was $8.50 and with tip it came to $10.00. Mo said, "Welcome to the Big Apple" as he handed Robin his bag.

The rain had stopped. He looked up and could see a deep blue sky and sunshine, but he was in the cool shadow of the 20 and 30 story buildings. Seventy-two twenty-nine (7229) was quarters for residents and fellows at the Cancer Center, which was so close that even on the coldest days one could dash the 129 meters in a light jacket without a chill. In the vestibule was a panel with what seemed like hundreds of names and buttons. On top was a button and telephone receiver. Robin called the manager who took him to his room on the eleventh floor, 1111. The room was a studio with a small bed that had two pillows and doubled as a couch, a frig, a two-burner stove, and a closet-sized room with a shower stall, sink, and toilet. Robin raised the shade and looked out at Flexner Hall at Rockefeller Institute and the Queens Midtown Bridge. If he stood on the right and strained left, he could see the light gray white brick of the Cornell Medical Center.

The next morning Robin rose at 6 a.m. and walked to the hospital. He was feeling elated and excited. He had planned and prepared for coming to the US to train in oncology for the past two years. He was confident in the area of his medical studies and he had also absorbed American culture and idioms from his girlfriend Rose, a southern belle from Richmond, Virginia. Rose was working with the CRA (Commission for Recovery of Art) with appointments with the USIA (United States Information Agency), the NARA (National Archives and Records Administration), and NATO (North American Treaty Organization) in tracking the source and dispersion of plundered loot during the rise and fall of the Nazi's. Rose from Richmond was a beauty; her appellations could not have been more appropriate. Her vermilion lips, areola and vulva contrasted against her blue eyes and her pale white skin symbolized American beauty as much as the red, white, and blue of "Old Glory". Rose had transformed Robin's English from the sterile somewhat Oxford English dialect he had acquired from college instructors and textbooks to Americanize comfortable from Boston to 'Bama. She had tutored him so well on how to fit in that an outside observer would have had difficulty in discerning whether he was a "Kennedy at Hyannis" or a "Mac Enroe at Forest Hills." He could have been the prototype character for Dr. Ben Casey or Dr. Kildare. Both men and women found him appealing. He could be crude and rude, sophisticated and polite, masculine or femininely sensitive. The only people who ever disliked Robin were envious of his perfection. Even they, almost always became seduced admirers.

Robin reported to the Hematology office on the 12th floor of the Cancer Center. After medical school, he had stayed on the house staff at Gratz and spent two years in general internal medicine and one year in hematology. He had solicited and gained a fellowship to specialize in treating blood cancers. The secretary led him into Dr. Max Bluda's office. The office was mahogany bookshelves floor to ceiling with journals and three large desks with piles of reprints and manuscripts. Dr. Bluda, as Robin was to be reminded repeatedly over the next several years, had authored over 1000 papers in the last 30 years, a prodigious rate of 3 papers per month. He had even been nominated for a Nobel Prize several times. Dr. Bluda had emigrated to the US from Prague and had studied or collaborated in virology on studies with Peyton Rous, the discoverer of viruses causing cancer in chickens, Avery and McCloud, the discoverers of DNA as the main component of genetic material, and L. Old the father of tumor immunology. This pedigree marked Dr. Bluda as a thoroughbred in the New Medicine. The office had the aura of great revelations.

Dr. Bluda was best known for his studies on immunological protection of animals against viral induced leukomogenesis. The difficulty was in showing that his seminal work was a paradigm for human cancer. He held on to his beliefs that nature was a continuum, and he remained committed to a viral etiology for cancer. His belief of the theories on immunoprotection was so intense that he prepared human tumor extracts and inoculated patients with advanced cancers. Occasionally, the patient would show regression however, almost all eventually succumbed to the disseminated metastasis or pernicious side effects of the tumors or the chemotherapy.

Dr. Robin Goode stood before this slight bowed gray Teutonic giant. His huge acromegalic-like jaw opened, showing his tobacco stained widely spaced teeth. He extended his huge paw-like hand and bellowed, "Welcome to the USA". When their palms touched, a bond was formed between mentor and student that seemed supernatural. Robin was escorted by his mentor to the Hematology-Oncology wards where they discussed each of the current 21 in patients with lymphoma or leukemia. The resident reviewed the history, PE (physical exam), ROS (review of systems) lab, pathology, x-ray reports, progress notes, diagnosis, plan of treatment, and orders. Twenty-one patients may not seem like a large amount but the process seemed only perfunctory when at 11:30 p.m., thirteen hours later, they had finished this, the first of many rounds. Robin felt unfulfilled because he knew about the patients, but he felt they were depersonalized; he knew nothing about who these people were. Dr. Bluda told Robin to get something to eat and to rejoin him in the pathology laboratory at 7:00 a.m.

Robin's head hit the pillow at 1:00 a.m. after he reviewed the chapters on leukemia in Wintrobe's Textbook of Hematology. In the brief few moments before the stupor of sleep, he thought he could feel Rose entwined in his arms and legs gently caressing his exhausted body. She sucked the fatigue from his body and mind as he passed into deep sleep.

Five and a half hours later a gray New York mist shielded the sun rising over Queens from casting shadows. After a glass of juice, Robin ran to the hospital and headed to the basement where a trace of formaldehyde fumes guided him past the morgue and the histology laboratory where tissues taken at surgery or autopsy were processed and sent to a reading room where there was a microscope with eight binocular extensions. The scope reminded him of a giant centipede. Robin pulled and lowered a stool so that he could focus the lenses on the oculars. Dr. Bluda and the Hem-Onc resident were already seated at the scope. A pathology resident, Dr. Knife, placed the glass slides on the microscope stage. As he focused, the pink and blue patterns of the biopsies came into view. Dr. Knife described the salient features both negative and positive that formed a Gestalt pattern, which determined the diagnosis. Dr. Bluda often asked for a systematic rationale for selection from the differential diagnosis presented. At one distal portion on the multi-headed scope nicknamed "caput medusa" was Dr. Vicary Minutiae who seemed to know every known fact about tumor morphology. Whenever he could interject he would pontificate, not only on the anatomic features of the case understudy, but on trivia related to the early Coptic art of Egypt or the Battle of Ulundi during the Anglo-Zulu War in 1899 when 1500 Zulus were slaughtered by British troops in South Africa. What came to amaze Robin was the vivid description of these places and events that was given by someone who had never left the US. He had never ventured further than the reach of the Rapid Transit System of New York. He was petrified by the fear of travel. All his descriptions were engineered by his fanciful imagination; his exhaustive reading, his photographic memory and his eloquent articulate oratories. It would take courage to contradict him even if you were a native who had been present and participated in the historical event under discussion. You had better check your own data if you doubted his diagnosis. He was better at describing death and disease than at living life. His friends nicknamed him "Vicary", short for vicarious.

The ensuing few months was exhausting. Dr. Bluda would quiz Robin on any and every practical or theoretical aspect of the cases and diseases they saw. Robin learned that he was never to render a diagnosis or treat a patient without personally reviewing the biopsies, the x-rays, or having personally interviewed and examined the patient. The pathology and radiology departments became his second homes. The autopsy room was not unfamiliar to Robin. He came from a background of medical training where the autopsy was a revered part of medicine. The final diagnosis rendered by the dissections was only the beginning of his thoughts on how to improve his diagnostic acuity and how to provide better therapies.

After a year as a fellow, Dr. Bluda asked Robin to join the staff of the Cancer Center as a research associate so that together they could begin clinical trials of combining tumor immunization with transplantation therapy. There was no lack of volunteers. The protocol was to remove and process the cancer cells to create a dead cell preparation. Killer lymphocytes would be obtained by inoculating a family member with the preparation; these killer lymphocytes from the donor could be engrafted into the patient where they would attack the tumor cells. This approach was radically different from other research groups who had either tried to develop tumoricidal antibodies in animals, in cell culture systems, or in immunized volunteers. There were inklings of tumor regression with antibody therapies, particularly at Stanford in Palo Alto, but the tumors eventually became resistant. Also, experiments at the NIH with the cytokine IL2 (interlukin-2) had produced transient tumor lysis. Dr. Bluda and Robin were well aware of the rumors of an unexpected transplantation of a tumor, a melanoma, from daughter to mother in an upstate cancer center. This had been caused by an inadvertent transfer of live tumor cells in an inoculum presumed to be "fixed" and incapable of cellular growth and replication.

They rationalized their approach based upon success in animal models and the fact that medicine had no better alternative therapies. A similar justification was used by their colleagues who would concoct chemicals to kill cancer cells. They would alter the chemotherapeutic drugs by modifying compounds that had been shown to cause tumor lysis. They injected the drugs into cancer patients with widespread incurable tumors in order to check whether the toxicities to non-tumor tissue could be minimized or abrogated. Often these drugs went from synthesis to syringe for *in vivo* testing. The surrogate testing on *in vitro* cell cultures could not provide the toxicity information. Animal tests were often not appropriate because the metabolic alterations and detoxification pathways were often somewhat different in humans. The approach chosen by Dr. Bluda and Robin was riskier and was certainly "cutting edge".

In May 1977 Robin examined a frail 27-year-old Caucasian male, Rod Ranger, who presented with severe weight loss and cachexia. He had lost 75 pounds in the past four to five months. He had had severe diarrhea and loss of appetite. The 90 pounds that was left of him revealed the remnants of a good-looking male with fine delicate features. There were marble to golf ball size protruding rubbery lymph nodes in his neck region and his groin. Upon further examination, Robin found that Rod had been working as an airline steward flying between New York, Paris, Morocco, and North Africa. During his layovers in New York he had set up a studio in the East Village and had become an artist. He had become good enough that he was selling his works and had shows in several galleries in Soho. His burgeoning success prompted him to quit flying and focus on sculpting. He would force a smile from his frail body and say to Robin, "Not bad for a kid from Teaneck, New Jersey".

Robin felt that Rod's disease was associated with some sort of infection. He checked for every parasite he could think of, especially because of his history of travel to third world countries. He hydrated him, and tried hyperalimentation and empirical antibiotic therapy to stem the wasting. Rod's weight stabilized and he regained some muscle strength but his lymph nodes grew larger. During this time Rod's mother would come in from Jersey to visit. She was a fiftyish woman, a loving, robust, doting mother, who brought morsels of deli food for the nurses and Robin. She would spoon feed Rod as if he were a rebellious two-year old. When she left the hospital room she would silently weep in the visitor lounge and wait until she could talk with Dr. Goode.

Mrs. Lucy Ranger told Robin that Rod's father had abandoned them when Rod was an infant and that she had raised and supported him alone. He was her essence for living. She had worked as a housekeeper and office maid to provide not only the necessities for Rod, but music and art lessons. She was disappointed when Rod turned down a scholarship to study at Bard College, in order to see the world. She was helping to support him in his studio while he began his career as a sculptor. She told Dr. Goode "I love my son, Rod, more than life and I will do anything to prevent his death."

During rounds, Robin had the new fellow present Rod's case to Dr. Bluda. After the review it was decided that one of the lymph nodes from the axilla, under the armpit, would need to be biopsied. Robin went to Rod's bedside with Dr. Slaughter, a general surgeon. He explained that a small sample of tissue was needed for a definitive diagnosis. A brief description of the surgical procedure and the unlikely complications was presented. The day shift nurse held Rod's hand to steady him while he signed consent forms.

The next morning under local anesthesia, an almond sized pale pinkish piece of tumor was removed. It was cut into halves, revealing a rubbery consistency and a smooth cut surface. One-half went to the pathology laboratory and the other half went to the Tumor Immunology Laboratory where Robin and Dr. Bluda did their experimental work.

It was on the eighth floor and separated from the main hospital by two sets of electronically controlled doors. The air pressure gradient kept a barrier between the laboratory and the hospital. Just outside of the first door was a plaque dedicating the laboratory as a gift from the Hershel family in memory of their loving daughter whose short life was prematurely and abruptly ended at age 12 by leukemia.

The tumor was placed in a petri dish in a sterile hood and minced by Dr. Goode. The cells, free of host defenses were now free to divide and multiply.

The other half of Rod's tumor was taken to Dr. Knife in the pathology laboratory. Frozen sections 6 microns thick were cut and stained. The remainder of the tumor was fixed in formaldehyde, processed and embedded into a paraffin wax. On a guillotine-like microtome, sections were cut, placed on the surface of a water bath, and floated onto glass slides. The supporting wax was removed and the tissue was stained with dyes. The tissue was covered with Canadian Balsam and a rectangular thin glass coverslip entombed the tissue as it hardened. The slide was ready for microscopic examination.

Dr. Knife fine-focused the objective lens of the Zeiss multiple headed scope. He quickly saw the sea of blue ovoid nuclei. Most of the cells were larger than normal lymphocytes and the normal architecture of a lymph node was gone, "effaced" was the descriptive term he used. He dictated his gross and microscopic descriptions along with his presumptive diagnosis of lymphoma. After consultation with the Attending staff pathologist, Dr. Minutiae, he ordered special tests to see whether specific antibodies bound to these cells. The results with immunostaining of sections from the frozen tissue showed that the tumor cells were B-lymphocytes. The report was amended and called to Drs. Bluda and Goode who were seated at the scope a half-hour later.

The tumor cells in culture were pipetted out of the swirling spinner flask and a membrane protein preparation was made. Dr. Bluda and Robin debated whether to treat with the enzymes DNase and RNase to destroy all possible genetic material but they elected to omit this treatment. Mrs. Ranger was waiting for her son's doctors in a treatment room just off the nursing station on the ward where Rod was being treated. She had signed the consent forms blanking out all possible untoward side effects that the inoculation of her son's tumor cells could cause. Whether she would participate in this attempt to generate tumoricidal immune cells seemed to have little or nothing to do with her concern for her own welfare.

The injections were given twice with a 12-day interval. The mixed lymphocyte studies combining Mrs. Ranger's lymphocytes and Rod's lymphocytes, which had been removed prior to immunization, showed little reaction and suggested that they were related enough to prevent rejection of Mrs. Ranger's donor cells. In fact, their tissue types and blood types matched so well that she could have been an organ donor for her son.

Because the injection contained fragments of cells, Mrs. Ranger was pretreated with an antipyretic and an antihistamine. Steroids were not used because they might blunt her immune response. The injection into the veins of the forearm was performed slowly over a period of 25 minutes, during which time her pulse, blood pressure, and temperature were monitored constantly. The insertion of the butterfly catheter went easily. Mrs. Ranger had prominent veins on her muscular forearms from years of mopping and the labor of her janitorial work. She tolerated the two procedures well and was instructed to return in two weeks for further testing. During this time, she prayed "God give me strength." She was not religious and did not completely understand the rationale for her injections, but she knew that if it were to work, she would have to supply some ingredient that Rod was lacking.

The tumor cells isolated from Rod's tumor were tagged with radioactive chromium and incubated with blood cells isolated from Mrs. Ranger. Whereas there had been little killing and release of chromium prior to the immunization, there was extensive tumor lysis with the lymphocytes removed seven days after the second inoculation. Dr. Bluda and Dr. Goode seemed encouraged and made plans to obtain large numbers of lymphocytes from the mother. They infused them into her son, Rod.

Over the ensuing weeks, Rod's tumor nodules seemed to remarkably regress, but he developed a rasping cough, and difficulty breathing. The chest x-rays showed a "whiteout" of his lung fields consistent with the presence of a pneumonic process. He was treated with antibiotics and after the cells obtained from bronchial washing showed the presence of cytomegalic inclusion virus (CMV), he was treated with antiviral agents. Nevertheless, the lung destruction and loss of function became so great that Rod died four weeks after the immunotherapy began. Mrs. Lucy Ranger was at the bedside to say goodbye to her son. She was lost to follow-up soon after.

CHAPTER 5

Lucy Ranger lay on the cold steel autopsy table where she had been heaved by the deniers. Water was washing under the horizontal slats supporting her cold rigid body. Her gray hair draped down over the rubber tee supporting her head at a slightly lower angle than the same apparatus that holds footballs for the kick offs. She was K-77-531 at the New York Medical Examiner (NYME) on 12/13/77. She was the first autopsy of the day for Dr. Knife who was moonlighting at the Manhattan medical examiner's office.

Knife remembered his first day at the NYME office, the City Morgue. They, the regulars, told him to join their "rounds", which down here was a rapid decision-making review in front of refrigerated bodies, rolled out on steel gurneys for a short history. They knew only the few facts on the police reports which usually contained the name, location of death, and a few recorded facts from the site of death. In minutes, a decision as to whether an autopsy was necessary had to be made. All unattended deaths, all therapeutic misadventures, all homicide deaths with criminal implications or related to health and welfare of the New Yorkers were candidates for study by the forensic pathologist at the ME office. In the entry foyer of the ME's building, carved in marble, was the quotation, "So that the living may live."

There were 200 refrigerated cabinets, many containing corpses. When they got to the third case, Dr. Basin, Senior Fellow in the forensic program turned to Knife and asked him for a differential diagnosis on a nude male body with a roughened, reddish head denuded of skin. Knife, whose only experience was in hospital pathology, had never seen a body in this condition; he answered, "R/O (rule out) exposure to extreme acid, lye, or other caustic solutions, unusual burn, or thermal injuries." The "Pros" laughed and teased Knife because he had not seen the ravages of roaches before. This man had been a dope dealer who had OD'd on uncut heroin in his triple locked and dead-bolted flat. Based upon the history from his tenement neighbors, he had been dead at least ten days before the rotting odor brought the police and health department. This case served to remind Knife that the geosocial facts, sparse as they may be, had to be melded with the anatomical, chemical, immunological and genetic analysis of the cadaver. The integration of these facts could have significant legal, monetary, or scientific impact. These cases, because of the sparse, scanty, histories often required more study and scrutiny and suspicion than cases dying in hospitals where there were numerous labs, x-rays, nurses' notes and other studies.

Dressed in greens, decked with a rubber apron and thick rubber gloves of the type used for industrial cleaning, Dr. Knife read the sheet labeled Lucy Ranger. He matched the number on a tag fastened to her toe with that of a data sheet on his clipboard. She had been found dead in a cardboard box cut out from a GE refrigerator carton in a lot where homeless squatted near the Manhattan end of the Brooklyn Bridge. The neighbors told the police that Lucy had lived there for the past weeks and that she was so ill that they brought her soup and coffee. At first, she had coughed so loud that the inhabitant's adjacent box huts told her to get to a hospital because she kept them awake. She had refused as her coughing became weaker, punctuated by occasional wrenching. The quietness was disturbed only by the rattling of the cars on the off-ramp of the bridge and was pierced by an occasional staccato bleep of an automobile horn. The officers from the ME office cut away the side of the carton and placed the stiff rigored body on the stretcher. Her face was a dusky blue and there was a bubbly foamy froth on her lips. The body was wrapped in a white shroud, tagged and placed in the ambulance for a short ride uptown.

After reading the police record, Dr Knife decided to wear a mask during this case as a precaution against TB or other infectious organisms.

CHAPTER 6

March 28, 1942, the lights were out all over Brooklyn as the ships headed east crammed with military hardware and personnel. Jacob Knife walked light-footedly and rapidly along Shore Road Blvd. Up from 69th St. where the Staten Island Ferry had taken him to work for the past ten years. He looked out at the camouflaged olive-gray stripped destroyers and cruisers loaded with his colleagues and former students. He felt much of his world was answering the call to stop the Nazis and leaving him behind. His deafness had stemmed his musical career, aborted his PhD dissertation and had put him into the 4F classification. Each night, as he walked along the Narrows, he would hear the muffled voices in the defective crystal in his hearing aid, which now acted as a radio receiver. He thought he was going mad until his wife, Paula, put the hearing aid to her ear and heard the same voices. Together, they figured out that he was picking up transmissions from the tugboat captains in the NY harbor

Tonight, even with all his sadness and problems he was happy. He was on his way to Paula to be with her as she gave birth. He had feared that his progeny would have the hereditary otosclerosis that afflicted his six brothers and sisters. He boarded the 69th St. bus and rode to 13th Avenue and entered Doctor's Hospital. In the delivery room, he arrived just after the placenta was delivered and the cord was clamped. They named the baby Mark.

The baby cried and cried. Jacob and Paula tried to comfort him. The pediatrician called it colic and told them that he would outgrow it. They lived in a two-story house and the owners, an old Italian couple who owned the house, nicknamed the baby "Caruso" because of his wailing serenades.

After the war, the Knife family had to find another home when the son of their landlord returned from military duty. Many families were moving away from Brooklyn, but Jacob and Paula taught in the public schools there and wanted to remain close to their jobs and to the libraries, museums, and theaters in the city. Jacob was afraid to drive a car because of his deafness. Paula drove for several years, but in 1950 they gave their 1939 Chevy to a nephew and used only public transportation. In a rare emergency they phoned for a taxi.

The Knifes moved several times and eventually found a stucco duplex house off of Ocean Parkway and Avenue I. From here there were buses, subways, and trolleys that took them to almost any part of the city except Staten Island. The family lived simply. They planted trees with apples and pears; they grew grapes on vines up the brick walls of the adjacent apartment house. As a teenager, Mark paved the sidewalk paths and built concrete fish pools and a barbeque pit. When relatives and friends came to visit they commented, "Trees really do grow in Brooklyn." The population of Brooklyn was three and a half million, and it was the melting pot for immigrants from Europe. It was fast becoming a concrete jungle. Brooklyn of the 1950's was not only home to gangsters of the Mafia; it was the spawning grounds for enormous numbers of achievers in the arts and sciences. There was an environment of competitiveness, epitomized by the Brooklyn Dodgers. Roy, Gil, Jackie, PeeWee, Carl, Billy, Duke, Preacher, Don and Sandy were like family. The twang of a Brooklyn accent often marked a person as aggressive. The street corners, often filled with teenagers singing or fighting, gave rise to "Rock and Roll." The first real Rock and Roll concerts were at the Brooklyn Paramount Theater with WINS and Alan Freed. Jacob would not allow Mark to go because there was fear of violence fermented by the lively music and the ethnic turf gang battles.

The Canarsie Tigers, the Ditmas Dukes the Hawks SAC (Social Athletic Club) ruled the schoolyards sporting their black leather or red silk jackets emblazoned with their logos. Their hair was greased and met in the rear to form an upturned vee of DA (ducks ass). Mark avoided the violence as much as possible; occasionally there was no escape from confrontations. In shop class, Mark was grazed by a .22 caliber bullet from a Zip gun being assembled from a broken car aerial barrel mounted on a cap gun, and he had his front tooth smashed by a teen waving a yard metal ruler in shop class. In order not to be a total wimp, Mark practiced lifting weights and became very muscular. This kept him out of most fights and made him feel good with the girls. He wore pegged pants with triple saddle stitching, a four inch high rise, a pink belt and a pink turtle neck. He was a sight to behold in 9SP2, a class for the "intellectually gifted" at Montauk Jr. High.

In 1956 Jacob and Paula announced that they had saved enough money to take a trip to Europe; Mark tried to refuse going because he was in love with the girl next door. The problem was that she hardly knew or cared. Secondly, the tickets on the Queen Mary sailing on June 30 were not refundable. The trip across the Atlantic, even on the 72,000-ton Queen was rough and Mark was seasick for three of the five-day voyage. He watched the crew gamble and drink until early in the morning. At Le Havre they took a train to Paris. They checked into the Regina Hotel across from the Tuileries. Mark was given a small hotel room down the corridor from Jack and Paula. At about ten in the evening, Mark dressed and went out. He walked to Rue Montmartre where he had been told the ladies of the night were to be found. They were easy to spot in their flashy dresses sauntering, stopping to look in the shop windows and survey the street in the reflections for potential clientele. At first the women ignored this teenage boy, but then one asked "Voulez-vous une femme?" Mark, in his mentally practiced junior high school French asked, "Combien?" She answered "dix dollars." He replied, "J'ai seulement huit dollars." She led him to a dark alley and up to a small room. After he came, she rolled him off. While she sat on the bidet, she asked "was this his first time." Fifteen minutes later he was rushing back to the Regina Hotel thinking, "That's all there is to it?"

In the morning, Mark told his father nonchalantly that he had used his allowance to "buy" a woman. When Jacob relayed this to Paula, she almost fainted. When she recovered her composure she and Jacob made Mark take a scalding hot soapy scrub in the bath. They could not think of any other course of action, but for the rest of the summer at each hotel a cot was brought into the room so that Mark could not stray. In Nice, while Jacob and Paula went into a hotel to ask for directions, Mark waited with the luggage. A young woman approached Mark; this was observed by Paula. Before the woman could address him, Paula rushed out from the hotel lobby and shrieked like a mad woman "You leave him alone, he is a minor."

When they traveled to Mallorca they relaxed by the pool. A young man struck up a conversation with Jacob and Paula. He told them that he had just graduated Summa Cum Laude from Harvard. He was traveling around to try and find out what he could do for a career with his degree. He had majored in "social" sciences. It was then that Mark decided to become a physician. That summer in Europe was indelibly imprinted into Mark's memories. He came home with a Van Gough reddish beard and a swagger.

In the fall, Mark went off to Boston to the university. The course work was relatively easy. The studies that Paula had made him do in preparation for their touring in Europe was harder than most of his class work. Most of his effort was devoted to his pre-med science course work and to dating. He managed to date a whole floor of women in the Charlesgate Womens Dormitory. By Mark's senior year he found his territorial reach extending to Wellesley and Pembroke colleges. It was only the voluminous amount of memorization for the classes in medical school that impinged on Mark's libido.

By the second year in medical school, Mark was desperate for female attention. He had little time for the rituals of dating. He had become interested in research and had begun to spend all his spare time in the new human genetics laboratory. On a trip home from a conference in Boston, Mark sat in the rear of a Greyhound bus. A young woman boarded and sat in the seat in front of him. Inadvertently, Mark put his foot over the footrest and accidentally clicked it upward. He was trapped with his foot clamped to the seat in front of him. He tapped the young woman in the seat in front of him. She ignored him at first. He finally pleaded with her to move her seat forward so that he could remove his shoe. At first she was standoffish but soon realized that he sincerely needed her help. At the end of the bus trip they exchanged telephone numbers. He invited her to his apartment for dinner. She found that he could barely boil an egg. Within months she took over the mundane tasks of his everyday existence. He enjoyed the freedom and used it to spend more time doing his research projects. Six months later Toby and Mark were married and six months after that he became a father. His wife asked him what he loved more, his research or her. He answered, "There was no comparison." This same question was asked over and over. The non committal response was only answered years later after they parted.

CHAPTER 7

Dr. Mark Knife, the pathology resident, was always running. His 50-inch chest commanded its space at the caput Medusa multi-headed microscope in the sign-out room of the Cancer Center. His 17-inch biceps were indented by the cuffed edge of his short-sleeved shirt. It was clear that he was pumping iron. As Robin got to know Dr. Knife he realized that Knife's whole life was spent running on a treadmill. In contrast to Dr. Minutae, Mark had use not only for knowledge that helped solve puzzles, but frequently lived in an abstract world where facts and fantasy combined to form static images that blended into sculptured forms. When he wasn't on surgical pathology, or doing autopsies, he was across the street at the Rockefeller Institute with his colleagues trying to work out how chemical carcinogens perturbated the structure of genomic DNA, a change that they thought would result in the loss of control of cell division and cell death. On a weekend, when Knife wasn't covering at the Cancer Center, he would rise early, run to the lab at Rockefeller, start his experiments and then grab the Second Avenue bus south to 23rd Street. Here at the NYME office under the tutelage of the renowned forensic pathologist, Halperin, he would probe the cause of death (COD) of those who died unattended or in nefarious situations. It was gruesome work but the inquisitive forensic nature of the work appealed to him, and he needed the extra money. He was living with his wife and two infant girls in a housing project south of Essex Street. However, the extra money was rarely used for necessities. It was to provide the occasional opera at the Met or bottle of Don Perrignon served when friends came over to blow smoke. A cadre of scientists and artists met frequently, often apologizing for having to go home at 3 a.m. or 4 a.m. Robin attended these sessions several times but his rare relaxation time was not to be satisfied by philosophical musings. Knife and Robin respected each other.

After Knife completed the autopsy on Lucy, he took the bits of tissue and snapped them into plastic cassettes in a jar of formalin fixative. He took this to the laboratory and marked it ASAP. If he didn't do this, it could take several weeks for the slides to be made because of the large number of cases processed. Since he was a part-timer, he left his phone number and a message for the histology technician to call him when the microscopic sections were ready.

Two days later Knife was at the microscope in the ME office studying Lucy's tissues. There was no evidence of cancer. The lymph nodes were enlarged and hypercellular but the basic architecture was intact. The major findings were in the lungs, which showed a collapse and obliteration of the alveolar air spaces. The cells lining these centers for exchange of oxygen and carbon dioxide were swollen with viral inclusions. Some of the cells were sloughed from the walls into the alveoli, which also contained copious pink proteinaceous fluid that had inhibited vital gas exchanges.

There was a striking similarity to the findings Dr. Knife had observed when he had autopsied Rod, Lucy's son. Dr. Knife was perplexed but considered the observations unlikely to be fortuitous. He thought about Occam's Razor, the guiding principle in diagnostic medicine. You were taught that when a complex set of findings had a previously described common relationship, a unified composite known or unknown causality was a more likely explanation. He wondered whether the experimental inoculation, performed by Dr Bluda and Robin, of tumor fragments could have caused Lucy's disease. He could not eliminate the possibility of both mother and son having been exposed to a common infectious agent, or the possibility that their similar genetic composition made them susceptible to a common etiological agent. He discussed the case with the pathologists at the ME office and was given permission to report on Lucy's autopsy at the Cancer Center.

The administrators, Dr. Bluda, Dr. Goode, and Dr. Minutiae were gathered in the conference room. The gross and microscopic photos of the autopsies performed by Knife on Roy Ranger at the Cancer Center and on Lucy Ranger at the ME were projected in the darkened room. Knife reviewed the history of each case and, as he postulated that the causality of the mother's death was related to her role in the treatment protocol, there was silence. Dr. Bluda's face became plethoric. He stood up and blurted, "B….S…" and stomped out. Knife and Robin then went to the pathology lab to further study the slides and to plan on how to further test Knife's conjecture. The hospital administrators reconvened that afternoon and after three hours of debate, they issued a memo:

"Although we cannot scientifically implicate the infusion of cell fragments in the causation of disease in the recipient, there is sufficient uncertainty to suspend further clinical trials until the safety and efficacy of the procedure can be validated."

Dr. Bluda read the memo carefully. He could not tell whether the intense pain that seared through his left chest was heartache and anguish from embarrassment or resentment. It felt like a burning steel pipe had been rammed through the sternum to the scapula. He sat down in his warm leather chair, bit down hard on his pipe stem, hoping he could neutralize the chest pain. He collapsed forward onto his desk, with a gasp, his hand landing onto an unfinished manuscript and died.

The funeral for Dr. Bluda was held the next day and it was attended by some of his distant cousins. The services were held in a small chapel on West 83rd St. across from the Museum of Natural History. The eulogy was delivered by a reformed rabbi who had to be briefed on what words would best describe Professor Bluda. The benediction was held in English, except for the Kiddish Prayer. Several young physicians and scientists who had studied under Dr. Bluda had great admiration for the deceased, but only Robin had tears welling in his eyes. His voice failed and he could not respond with the words of remembrance. His fiancée, Rose had flown all night to be with Robin. She clutched his hand trying to transmit her strength to Robin, who, for the first time that she could remember, seemed drained and limp. It was the first time she saw Robin without control of his emotions. She now knew that beneath his calm and cool veneer was a loving caring man. That night he felt her strength. He wanted her by his side. He proposed and she accepted.

Shortly after the funeral Rose and Robin were married in a simple civil ceremony at the Manhattan Court Building. The only friend present was Dr. Mark Knife. The threesome celebrated by having dinner and toasting each other at Tavern on the Green in Central Park. He knew that Rose would provide him with the emotional support and family that he had not had while growing up. In his slightly inebriated state he kissed Rose so fervently that she was breathless. Knife looked into his glass and blushed. He was slightly jealous and envious.

CHAPTER 8

Leaving New York City was hard for Robin. The East Side had become his habitat except for an occasional jog in Central Park, or a jaunt to Lincoln Center. Work at the Cancer Center had consumed ten to twelve hours daily for the past five years. There was brunch on Sunday at the Recovery Room Restaurant, a rare date, a few furtive Friday forays on the Second Avenue Bar scene, and reminiscences of rare one-nighters with a neurotic Brooklyn Jewess whose sexual education from spring breaks in Fort Lauderdale overshadowed her Fine Arts Degree from Barnard. This was the "Seventies," and if you were young and without sex, you were weird. Robin tried a few drags on the lids of grass, clipped in roaches, passed down the line at a Simon and Garfunckel concert in Strawberry Fields, but his only high seemed to be in the successes in his work. The elation of peer approval and acceptance satisfied him more than an orgasm. The applause after his presentation at the American Society for Oncology at Haddon Hall in Atlantic City, to an audience of 2000 dwarfed the satisfaction felt even on the best of nights when he and Rose made love. He was a "wonderkind," a new Brahman in the war on cancer. The country was trying to refocus from the Viet Nam fiascos. There was a mandate from Nixon to turn centers of biological warfare into citadels for the fight against cancer. The success of the US in World War's nuclear bombs, and a race to the moon, was to be harnessed and directed to the conquest of cancer.

Coming down from the "highs" of research was for Robin like the addict trying to go "cold turkey." He had shakes, sweats, and hallucinations of being engulfed and smothered by amorphous amoebic protoplasm.

Robin and Rose were moving to Birmingham, the remnants of the Pittsburgh of the South. They had visited for several days in May and were on their way in early June. The most lasting impression was that of the cast-iron statue, the Vulcan, built in 1904 for the St. Louis World's Fair by Guiseppe Moretti. It towered from its pedestal on Red Mountain, and conjured up thoughts of the Colossus of Rhodes. This statue was their landmark and acted as their Polaris in orienting themselves.

Over the last five years, while Rose and Robin had been dating, Rose had flown back from Austria with increasing frequency. She stayed with Robin in his studio apartment. They grew to be a couple separated by 4000 miles. Neither had wanted to end their work so they stayed apart. Rose had become obsessed with making order out of the chaos left after the war and muddied by the Iron Curtain. Her focus was on the tracking of stolen treasures. She calculated the loot and entered it onto a special sheet from IBM using punch cards, which were used to collate the bits of data.

The major repository for the loot was at Uln where there was approximately 2.2 billion dollars worth of Nazi gold and other artwork. Her investigative units had found strong evidence that a cache of several million had not been found. She had evidence that this was at the border of Germany and Austria. She donned lederhosen and a knapsack and hiked the mountainous region. She put on a jumpsuit with leather patches over her buns and slid down long polished chutes into the bowels of the salt mines. She crossed underground lakes in rowboats listening to the echoes of singing tourists. She asked in German, everyone she met about the rumors of unfound Nazi loot. Some of the natives were rude and cursed her in idiomatic pejoratives they never expected her to comprehend. Her eyes donned a quizzical look so that she could gather unstated information. Some of these remarks came together like the glass in the stained windows of a cathedral. One night as she stood before a monastery outside of Hallein, she knew she was close.

Rose stayed in the youth hostel just off a small lake. Exhaustion and the cool crisp mountain air caused her to sleep until 9:00 a.m. She awoke to the splashing of stoic swimmers frolicking in the glacial fed lake.

After a brunch of onions and brockworst, she walked to the nearby monastery, knocked at the large doors and was met by a priest who appeared to be about 40 or 50 years old. She thought that this would have made him about 15 or 20 at the end of the war. The unusually large emerald ring on his left hand caught her eye.

He invited Rose to walk through the exquisitely tailored gardens. After a while, they sat on a concrete bench. They looked out over the small cemetery, which contained a few small vaults, toward a shaft opening in the rocky mountainside.

She was very direct in her conversation and asked the priest whether the rumors about war treasures hidden in the salt mines adjacent to the monastery were true. The priest was shy and silent at first, wringing his sweaty hands while twisting the large gold ring. His face was almost devoid of expression and seemed very pale against his black vestments. He turned, stared at Rose and after several minutes of silence he answered.

"Yes, there had been crates of gold and artwork stored in the cavern beyond the cemetery." He had even been working at the monastery when they were delivered by an officer of the Wehrmacht in 1945, but he added "The crates were no longer here." A deal had been cut. When messengers with the agreed upon codes returned, the loot would be surrendered. The codes were from the story of Exodus. The ten plagues described as God's retribution for the Pharaohs mistreatment, torture, enslavement, and detention of the Jews. The plagues were: blood, frogs, gnats, dog flies, murrain or cattle plague, boils, hail, locusts, darkness, death of the firstborn son of the Egyptian families.

Only a dozen gold bars and one painting were left as a gesture and recompense for the storage. The details were sketchy because most of the contact was between the former Bishop and the bearded men. There were six men and they talked to each other in a language that sounded German but was not German. The priest was enlisted in loading a large canvass covered truck. The cargo was heavy and often the crates required two people to lift and stow them on the trucks. Occasionally he heard bits and pieces of conversation that had Hungarian words.

Rose thought, "Who were the people the priest was describing?" It was unlikely that they were German or Austrian military. She needed more clues. Perhaps the stolen painting left as payment would help. Rose asked the priest what happened to the painting. He said "it is hanging in the vestry." Rose asked to see it. Together they walked to a small stone structure adjacent to the church. Rose was escorted into a darkened room lit only by a candelabra, behind which there was a large oil canvas set in a gold gilded ornate frame. The picture was at least 6 x 10 feet. The flickering flame of the nearby candles barely illuminated the painting, but it was a scene with flowers, lilies in a pond. Rose's mind flashed up a slide from her introduction to art appreciation during her freshman year at college. Her skin tingled and she wondered whether she was truly seeing a Monet. For a minute she was frozen and almost in shock from the excitement but she quickly regained her composure. She endorsed two fifty dollar American Express Travelers checks and handed them to the Priest as a donation to the church. She was already making her next plans for tracing the loot.

CHAPTER 9

Rose walked back to the guesthouse, gathered her few items of clothing, maps, passport, and money and packed her satchel. She paid the bill and walked to the railroad station. She was so excited and elated that she inhaled the crisp mountain air and surveyed the scenery of snow-lined Alpine meadows on the surrounding peaks. Walking past the Domplatz in Salzburg she reminisced about the Passion play 'Jedermann', by Hofmannsthal. Her parents had dragged her to in 1956 when they visited Salzburg for the commemoration of Mozart's 200th birthday. She thought of her mother's devotion to culture and of her father, Jon Thor a professor at Emory, who had treated her as an intellectual even before her teens. Her parent's love of truth and beauty led them to skimp and save so that they could travel with their daughter throughout Europe each summer when they were not teaching. Each evening after dinner they would sit and study the history and topography of the town or city they were exploring. These trips gave Rose an education and flavor for the continent that no college curriculum could ever equal. The excursions were always exciting with the result that her whole youth was an adventure, a probing into the evolution of western culture. Her parents were gregarious and multilingual, speaking fluent French, German, Spanish, and bits of Russian. They frequently engaged the native residents or fellow travelers in conversations that revealed a flavor and depth of appreciation for folklore and oral history. During these years Rose was not only imbued with a self-assuredness and inquisitiveness, but also with the confidence that she could travel alone and comfortably engage strangers in social intercourse. It was as if she was a human "lie detector." She could gage the truthfulness and commitment of people better than most instruments measuring physiological responses. She had almost x-ray vision of the psyche.

Rose systematically re-analyzed the conversation and events that had occurred last night at the monastery. She was convinced that the priest had told her at least some, if not the whole truth as he knew it. As they spoke in German he remembered a few neoGermanic words from the men who had come for the treasures in 1947. There was no doubt in Rose's mind that it was Yiddish. This was her first clue. During her travels with her parents they had on several occasions traveled with other couples whose command of German was only from their Yiddish heritage. She had a recollection of meeting an Israeli acquaintance of her mother who had spoken in both German and Yiddish.

The second clue was the use of the ten plagues as code words. Rose remembered them well from the Hagadah she had read with the Katz family at a Passover Seder in Jerusalem as they recollected and celebrated the Exodus from Egypt. Julia and Myron Katz, made the analogy to their own Exodus from Hungry in 1939, the year before their son David was born.

The third clue was the priest's reference to some Hungarian markings on the crates, which had been crossed out and covered over by German labels. This, along with his recollection of the few Hungarian words interspaced in their conversation, suggested that Hungary might have been the origin or destination of the treasure seekers.

The last clue was the painting. There was both a chilling and thrilling feeling when Rose recognized the painting. She remembered seeing that painting or one extremely similar to it on three separate occasions. The first time was at 8:00 a.m. Intro to Western Art at Wellesley when she sipped bitter black coffee to wake her from the boiler banging headache and hang-over acquired after a frat party in Back Bay at Boston University. The punch had been spiked with ethyl alcohol, and she had ended up in the sack with her date, Mark something or other. The second time was on the written exams for her qualifiers when she was working on a MA. The question was "describe how a malady can influence art." She had answered in depth how the cataract development in Monet had either caused or allowed the painter to see the light and colors and of the lily pond at Giverny, in a manner different enough each time, to present almost an evolution of nature's beauty. The third time she had seen a photograph of the lilies was in the CRA list of missing art. It was considered to be part of the pillage by Nazis in their plan to make Hitler's art collection out rival the spoils and acquisitions assembled at the Hermitage, the Louvre, the Met or the British Museum. After all, Hitler considered himself an artist, a painter and connoisseur.

The flyers listing unrecovered art, even at 30 years after the end of the war, still listed between 1300 and 1500 major works as unrecovered. There was no certainty as to whether the missing works of art were destroyed, hidden, or sequestered into private collections. Battles were raging over pieces, which had been purchased for exhibition by reputable museums. Some of the owners of this art had either perished in the Holocaust or died subsequently. Did their heirs have dibs on the treasures of Western civilization? This was not an issue in Rose's mind. She was most concerned with the information on who and where the owners of this painting were prior to its theft by the Nazis. She telephoned the Frankfort office of the CRA and asked that a full text description of the painting and the addresses of prior owners and present claimants be sent to the American Consulate in Vienna. Rose purchased a ticket for the trip to Vienna.

This excursion into the field was a new approach for Rose. She had worked in Frankfort in an office tracking artwork and monies stolen and hidden during WWII. Most of her work was dealing with Swiss banks, Archives in Berlin, Prague, Warsaw, Budapest, Nuremberg, and Washington, DC. She had been chosen for the job because of her training in fine arts, her linguistic skills and her knowledge of travel and customs in Europe. The fact that her father had been recently appointed Undersecretary of State did not hurt her application.

Rose had few vacations from her work. Was a trip to the Aaland Islands in the Baltic Sea off the coast of Finland to see where the ancestors from her mother's family originated. It was here that she learned of the bleeding disorder that afflicted many of her relatives. Perhaps the same gene caused the severe blood loss from the monthly periods that Rose experienced.

Rose's second vacation was to Gratz in Austria. Here she met Robin Goode a Hungarian immigrant who was studying medicine at the University. Because her work required extensive travel and her reports could be filed electronically, she requested and was allowed to have a virtual office. She moved her clothes, tape recorder, camera, and typewriter to a guesthouse on the bank of the Mur River. Soon Robin and Rose became a couple.

Rose thought Robin was a statuesque Hungarian. He had large facial features, thick eyebrows and a heavy thick head of hair. He was well proportioned and athletic although he shied away from most sports. His athletic prowess was evident when they skied the steep expert trails at Cortina where the Olympics had been held in 1956. Stamina on their long hikes in the Bavarian Alps and in their bed, where they would frolic for hours, was his strong suit. What Rose found most fascinating was his intensity and intellect. Robin was almost totally consumed with his studies on the clinical and molecular aspects of cancer. While Rose had focused on the arts, Robin had pursued the sciences.

When Rose got the facsimile, she read it carefully and was not surprised to learn that the missing Monet had belonged to a wealthy Hungarian Jewish family. The fax also showed that after 1947 there were no more inquiries about this missing art. Also interesting was that the original listing as the rightful owner was filed from Palestine by a Julia Katz. She had originally filed on four paintings, two pieces of sculpture, and six items of jewelry. The date and place of the alleged Nazi theft was May 1942, by order of Adolf Eichmannn to Laszlo Baky. The description of events stated that six uniformed officers came to Julia Katz's brothers' home on Kazinczy U. in Budapest with orders to remove any objects of art or jewelry. A handwritten receipt for the confiscated property was presented and the objects were loaded into a personal carrier. The address for Julia Katz was 20 Hertzel Place, Tel Aviv. Rose remembered that she had had dinner with a Julia Katz, but this had been in Jerusalem not Tel Aviv. Two Israeli Julias. It was probably a coincidence, after all Katz was a common Jewish name.

Rose boarded a hydrofoil, which sped down the Danube River to Budapest. On the adjacent banks there were hills dotted with "Fellegar" the remnants of forts and castles, baroque cathedrals, and Gothic churches from medieval times. She languished in the sun's rays on the open aft deck of the boat and thought of the storybook settings while the waters sprayed her face. The river was not quite the blue described in song but had chopped foamy spray against blue-black sun specked surface. They docked for a customs check as they crossed eastward from Austria into Hungary. As the hydrofoil approached the city, the boat switched to conventional navigation. The hills of Buda contrasted with the flatter Pest. Ornate bridges connected the two cities. The baroque architecture was spectacular.

Rose's travels had not previously taken her to Hungary, so she had purchased a Michelin guidebook in Vienna which contained a foldout map and a brief description of some of the tourist sites. The turreted towers of Budvari Palota on the Buda hills were easily identified. Its role in defense of Buda during the Turkish siege in the 16th century was noted. She thought of Robin and wished that she had made him talk more about his childhood and his memories of Budapest and Hungary. Rose had missed Robin but had not written or telephoned him in the past few weeks. She always found the eight-hour time differential and Robin's intense work schedule made telephoning inconvenient and difficult. She had not told him that she was going into Hungary for several reasons. He would be nervous about her going behind the Iron Curtain even if it were a satellite to the USSR, because of her government and NATO affiliations. Secondly, she wanted to surprise Robin, she wanted to identify with the roots of the man she loved and planned to marry. She hoped a spinoff of this mission would be the ability to understand and feel closer to Robin who almost never revealed memories of his childhood and adolescence. Given her intense and intimate relationship with her parents, it was difficult for her to understand how she could love a man about whom she knew so little. All her intimacy with Robin was in the present; the past was like a blurred black box. Perhaps this trip would act to give her the keys necessary to unlock his inner self. There was no doubt that Robin was a giving person and was always concerned with the welfare and well being of others, but when it came to intimacy he was stone cold. Was it a protective posture, had he been taught that solitude served as strong armor? She wanted to be inside him, inside his conscious and unconscious mind probing deeper than their physical relations. She wanted the oneness experienced physically during sex to extend deeper. No other man had so eluded her psychological probing.

Dressed in a loose woolen black skirt, black V-necked blouse, covered by a black sweater worn over her shoulders with black open-toed low heeled shoes, half carat diamond studs in her earlobes, a Movado MOMA watch with tiny diamond flecks as hour markers for the gold hands, a Leica M3 and a black Coach bag slung over one shoulder, and a small tan Hartmann leather luggage bag over the other, Rose walked in the direction she thought was the VII district. From studying the maps, she decided the walk should be about 25 minutes. The streets were beginning to crowd with people heading to the parks, sparse elderly women leaving church, and couples strolling behind baby carriages with infants or hand in hand. It was a sunny Sunday afternoon. Most of the people were dressed drably except for an occasional colorful accoutrement. The women had smooth shiny skin with a touch of rouge. It was as if the whole country practiced cosmetology. Rose thought of the Gabor sisters, of their beauty and zest. The men had large moustaches. They walked tall; their physiques evidenced the pervasive physical culture. They had a proud youthfulness with no evidence of subservience to the Russian conquerors and no traces of defeat from the '56 revolution, of which the only remnants were an occasional chipped scarred bullet hole in the buildings, surrounding the National Museum.

Because Rose sensed that her best chances of tracking and finding the paintings were dependant on clues from the Jewish community, even though 800,000 Jews had perished, there was still a community of several thousand who had either been protected by sympathetic Hungarians or had been evacuated to safe places by humanitarians such as Raoul Wallenberg. A few had returned to their homes after the war. The solitude of the neighborhood gave little hint of the heinous history. The few American or British-Jewish tourists had to scratch deep to find memorials. Several residences had been converted into bed and board facilities to accommodate this trade. Rose chose one of these, a three-story gray stone building with a façade of windows protected by fluted metal shutters.

She registered, signed the guest book and presented her passport to the young man behind the desk. He looked at her name and raised his eyes without lifting his head. His eyes seemed to question her. What was Rose Thor, a blonde goyisha bombshell, doing here? She saw the camouflaged black knitted yarmulke, clipped by a bobby pin in his thick black hair. He came from behind the counter and carried her bag up the curved spiral staircase overlooking an ornate crystal chandelier to the first floor and directed her towards the rear section where there were two large doors separated by a bathroom. He opened the door with a large brass key attached by a linked chain to a white golf ball sized sphere with a painted number 3 on it. The room was spacious by European standards and beyond the brass bed was a wall of French doors leading to a small patio. She said "danke" and tipped the young man.

After he left, she pulled the drapes aside, opened the doors and went out onto the small landing lined by ironwork fencing. Across the courtyard she could identify a distinctive Budapest landmark, the Dohany Synagogue. It was undergoing restoration of the central dome but the uniquely carved and inscribed entrance was clearly visible. She pulled her guide book from her purse and read the description of the Synagogue. It was mostly Byzantine but also had Roman and Gothic features. In her pocketbook was a 200-millimeter telephoto lens, which Rose screwed onto the bayonet mount of her Leica. She focused on the western façade, the two polygonal copper domed towers, and the archway with intricate carvings. In addition to taking several shots of it, she traced her impression of it on a pad of sketch paper.

The day had passed quickly and Rose decided that she needed some dinner and a bath. She locked her door and descended the staircase to a small restaurant off the foyer. She ordered a cold borsht beet soup and a portion of boiled chicken, the renowned goulash was not on this menu. She was hungry and ate quickly. She returned to her room, undressed and slipped into a silk kimono, entered the bathroom adjacent to her room. The fragranced bath soap bubbled when the hot water ran onto it. She shed her robe and slid below the layer of suds. The warm water relaxed her muscles so that she was limp and almost sedated by the steamed aromas of the bath oils.

Rose was thinking of Robin when the other door to the bathroom opened. She gasped and reached for a towel to cover her naked breasts. Looking up she saw an elderly man. He was a tall man stooped by age. His face was covered by a grayish beard and he wore rimmed glasses. His hairy chest and arms extended from beneath a white tee shirt. When he saw her, he turned quickly and fled out the door at the opposite end of the bathroom.

CHAPTER 10

Rose was exhausted both from her travel and the excitement of being surprised by a strange intruder while bathing. She managed to calm herself, pull the drapes closed, and lock the doors to the corridor and to the bathroom. As Rose felt the sleep state overcome her, she thought of Robin and promised herself that she would try to call him the next day.

She sipped some brandy from a silvered flask she carried in her travels and fell asleep as soon as her head hit the pillows.

At 8:00 a.m. Rose awakened with the distant sounds of machinery. She drew the drapes apart; a crane on a large steel shaft was rotating into position to deliver concrete from a canister to men atop the dome on the Dohany Street Synagogue. Rose dressed and went to the small restaurant where she had dinner the last evening. She looked about for any sign of the bearded man who had intruded on her bath, but did not see him. For breakfast she ordered a croissant, which came with a rich sweet jelly, and dark rich coffee with milk.

Rose checked her guidebook with its inserted street map and walked around the block to the front of the 180-year-old synagogue. After passing through the police barrier and the metal detectors, she signed in at a guest registry. There was only a family of Americans with two teenage children entering the synagogue. Rose read the brochure which described the building in the 1850s; the synopsis of the temple history described briefly the events and devastation of Hungarian Jews, the massacre and burial of 3000 Jews here, and the rescue of the remaining Jews by the Russian troops in 1945. There was a museum shop off the entry, which sold artifacts, religious items, books relating to Jewish history and several biographies of Theodore Herzel, the founder of modern Israel. Also present was an exhibit with pictures of Tony Curtis, an American actor whose philanthropic organization was bankrolling the restoration of the Dohany Street Synagogue.

Rose peered in at the prayer area; a guard came over and told her in broken English that this was the second largest Jewish synagogue in Europe and showed her where the women's prayer section, separate from the men's, was located. Because of the reconstruction one could not enter under the dome. After she found the signs to the Rabbi's study, Rose asked his secretary receptionist if she could set up an appointment for a meeting with him. The receptionist told Rose to wait. She returned in a few minutes saying that the Rabbi could see her now.

The Rabbi's study was paneled in oak and with built-in shelves housing hundreds of books. On the wooden tables were scrolls partially unrolled revealing Hebraic texts. The Rabbi, in a white shirt and black trousers and shoes, had a black-gray beard; his bald spot was partially covered by a yarmulke. He appeared to be middle age, about 55 years old. He extended his hand to greet Rose and said "Shalom", and he asked her to sit. He called to the receptionist to bring some tea. Rose presented her card, which had her affiliation with the CRA engraved on it, and the Rabbi said "I am familiar with the organization." He asked "what can I do to help you."

Rose recounted her encounter with the priest at the Bavarian Monastery and told the Rabbi that she suspected that the loot had either been rescued or rehijacked back to Hungary. She told him of the suspicion of what other artwork and artifacts might be with the treasures based upon her tracking of filed reports of stolen art. In particular she mentioned Julia Katz's filing from Palestine in 1947.

The Rabbi was intrigued by her detective work and her deductions. He said "I survived the war in Budapest by being hidden in a secret basement. A Christian Hungarian family brought me food. I never saw daylight for almost fifteen months. In 1947 I was asked by a stranger to participate in a clandestine mission but could not go because I had a broken leg. The participants of this group, which called themselves "Golem" after the mythical humanoid artificially created by the sages of the Talmudic era (circa 500 AD) to defend Jews from abuse or oppression. The Kabbalists further describe the Golem as a tool of retribution. Both native Hungarians and some Israelis were members of this "Golem" group. One of the members of this gang appeared by his dress to be a Hassid."

The Rabbi's receptionist came into the study with a teapot and several crackers on a tray. He stopped his story and poured tea for Rose and himself. He cleared his throat and returned to telling his story.

"Included in the group was a pair of brothers from an old and wealthy Sephardic Budapest family. This distinguished them from the majority of Budapest Jews who were Askanazi in origin. The Hassid, who was the leader seemed unfamiliar to the group of Hungarian Jews. Because I was not able to participate in the mission that this group was planning, I only have suspicions as to what their activity was. I do know that the brothers still live in Budapest." He pulled a telephone directory down from a shelf adjusted the bifocals on his nose and flipped the pages, When he found the listing he was searching for he wrote the address on the back of his business card. Rose thanked him profusely and he said "I wish you good luck but remember there is more to wealth than worldly goods. Following the path of treasures leads to incredible stories of people and families scarred by the forces of good and evil. May God guide you in your travels."

The next day Rose had set aside for touring and getting to know Budapest. It was a mild day so she walked over the Erzsbet Bridge to the Buda side of the Danube. She walked down to the riverside and looked at the Rudas Turkish baths, an all male establishment where men went to soak away their aches and troubles. From there she went along the Groza Peter Rakpart over to Castle Hill. She crossed back to Pest over the Széchenyl Lanchid; the chain bridge built in the 1800's to connect Buda and Pest. She was in no hurry and stopped to watch the river barges heading back north towards Vienna or south towards Serbia and on to the Black Sea.

Rose uncapped the lens of her camera to shoot pictures of the Parliament buildings. She noted the similarity to London's Parliament. During her meandering stroll, she had a feeling that she was being observed but it was only a sensation because whenever she turned rapidly or glanced over her shoulder, she saw only the normal flow of pedestrians and a few bicyclists, all of them kept on going without pause or notice when she whipped about. The city gave off an aura of European culture, an austere conservative oldness. It felt like the clock had been turned back, frozen in the late 1800's or early 1900's there were none of the sleek, stark modern glass and steel wonders of a 20th century megalopolis. While walking she wondered where Robin grew up, where he went to school, did he go to church, where did he live, did he play in the parks, what about his family? She knew his father was dead but what about his mother and brother. What were his political beliefs? It seems as if these were never in their conversations and it seemed as if Robin's history began in Austria rather than Hungary. She made a mental note: "Who was the man she loved?"

As her walk took her back to her lodging and the Jewish sector, her thoughts drifted back to her work and why she was in Budapest. That evening she decided to dine in a Bistro nearby, but she went back to her room to get a sweater. After getting the key from the desk she entered her room and found her things ever so slightly moved from where she had left them, perhaps the maid had moved them while cleaning. Nothing was missing.

She changed and went out to eat. At the restaurant she treated herself to a glass of red local Hungarian full-bodied wine and a beef goulash that was spicy but "to die for". The dessert was a spumoni-like ice cream. She sat cross-legged in her cast iron chair at a small wooden table lit by a glowing stub of a candle, sipping a tumbler of Madeira port. When she returned to her room she carefully locked the doors to the bath before slipping into the steamy tub.

The next day Rose set out to find the brothers that Rabbi Levy had described. On Kazinczy U. about 10 blocks from the synagogue she found the address written on the Rabbi's card. The structure was attached to the adjacent houses and was three stories; plain large wooden windows punctuated the rectangular stucco façade. A push on the doorbell was followed by a deep brass chime. A stopped man of about seventy opened the door and waved Rose in as if he had expected her.

The entry foyer was overhung by a large silver chandelier from which dangled hundreds of crystals emitting the electric lights as thousands of prisms with rainbow spectra. They walked through a set of sliding wooden doors into a parlor with several high-backed armchairs, two sofas, and a coffee table. Rose silently gasped as she saw the painting of a sitting woman adjacent to a bath. The colors were striking and vivid; the style so unique that there was no doubt this was a Matisse. It was painted in the 1920s in Paris and the catalog at the CRA listed this work as one of the unrecovered stolen treasures. Rose calmed herself quickly and turned away scanning the rest of the room so as not to divulge her recognition of the masterpiece. She knew she had hit pay dirt; years of tracking the pieces of this puzzle were interplaying for a glimpse into the cryptic solution.

It was obvious when the second old man joined them and introductions were made that Ted and Sig, Theodore and Sigmund Glucke were brothers. Both were tall with silvered black hair and long eyebrows with hairs curling upward. They had dark complected, smooth shaven skin. Their age was evidenced mostly by the stoop of their tall frames. Their noses were prominent and sharp; each had a smothered smile giving them a cheerful contorted look. Rimless continental eyeglasses shielded dark brown pupils. It was Ted who had let her in and who introduced himself and his brother Sig. The brothers looked so similar they could have passed for twins. Sig had slightly more scoliosis and walked with a sleek polished wooden cane. The brothers were both dressed in black slacks and open necked silk blended white shirts rolled up at the cuffs.

Rose reached into her purse for her calling card and handed one to Ted who passed it on to Sig. In flawless English Ted said "we have been expecting you." Her suspicion of being shadowed was not her imagination. The presence of this beautiful blonde bombshell had rippled through the Jewish sector. It seems that she was not watched by one but rather by the community. Her movements were traced like a flashlight beacon in a dark room.

As they sat, Sig brought over an engraved silver tray with a pot of tea, lemon slices, sugar, glasses and small wafer finger cookies. He poured the tea into the glasses. Ted naively asked Rose "Why have you come to see us?"

Rose answered "it is my job to track Nazi plunder and help see that it is returned to the rightful owners." She explained that there was still a large amount of loot that had been unaccounted for and unrecovered. There was strong suspicion that some had gone to safe havens as a potential resource and support for Nazis who had fled in a preplanned Diaspora. Some had gone to South America, some to Mexico, Canada, and even to the United States.

The brothers listened intently and after they poured her some tea she asked them if they wished to tell her their story. It was not abridged and was told in segments by each brother. The family's history could be traced back about five centuries.

CHAPTER 11

Sig began by recounting that their family had lived in Seville. Under the Moors, Spain was a haven for Jews and a center for intellectuals. Beginning with the defeat of the Moors, Christians began to persecute the Jews. After the issuance of the Edit of Expulsion in 1493, Sephardic Jews either became "converses", converts to Christianity, or were tortured, quartered and/or incinerated. A large number fled to distant shores of the Americas, North Africa, Greece, Rhodes, Italy or Turkey. Most of their belongings were confiscated by the state. Those who fled were welcomed in the Ottoman Empire even without their possessions, which they had accumulated since the Diaspora about the time of the Roman conquest of Palestine in 132 CE.

This reverse migration of the Sephardic Jews eastward brought many settlers to the far reaches of the Ottoman reign where they slowly mixed with the local Jewish and non-Jewish populations. During the 18th century in the kingdom of Khazar, along the northern shore of the Black Sea, the royal Turk family of King Joseph had adopted Judaism (the thirteenth tribe described by Arthur Koestler) and many felt safe there. The Sephardim often kept their Ladino language but frequently, particularly when they moved into Eastern Europe, they adopted the Yiddish, which was spoken by the majority of Ashkenazi.

Today Yiddish contains some words that the Sephardic pronounce differently, and certain customs such as the spiced dishes of the Passover Seder are distinctly different. Many Sephardic became so assimilated that they no longer considered themselves Jews. The Hungarian Jews were periodically purged and stripped of their possessions either through taxation or sporadic violent attacks. A smattering of Jews migrated to Palestine in an effort to escape and establish a Jewish homeland.

As industry grew, the Jews of Hungary prospered. There was no opportunity in government or other public positions so the Jews became businessmen and physicians. Although the total number of doctors was only a few thousand, the blend of the heritage of Maimonides and the traditions of rabbinical studies attracted Jewish men. The affluence and influence of Hungarian Jewry shielded them from major pogroms. This safety was occasionally broken by right wing anti-Semitics who tried to synonymize Bolshevism with Judaism. This anti-Semitic element was often aided by church officials who were deeply afraid of the atheism associated with the communist movements arising throughout Europe around the turn of the century. The loss of Hungarian lands and the restructuring of boundaries after World War I fed the fanatical frenzy of anti-Semitism.

"Our family has been in Hungary since the late 1500's. They were "handlers" and peddlers who schlepped house wares of brooms, mops, pots, pans and tools between towns and villages to shetyls where goods were bartered and sold. Travel was their only secular education and served to bring back news and expertise about the rapidly spreading industrial movement.

My great grandparents scrimped and saved to open a store where they built and repaired bicycles. After several years they planned and built a plant to manufacture motorcycles. They hired an engineer from the Ducati plant in Bologna. They coordinated the manufacture of engine block castings using the assembly line process. Their plant manufactured motorcycles, which they entered into professional racing events throughout Europe. At its peak production in the 1930's, the plant employed 1100 workers. Our family had diversified interests in a variety of industries and even became involved in banking. Estates were built at Balaton Lake, a large resort west of Budapest. This town house we are in was the family residence in the city. Substantial contributions were made by my great grandparents for the construction of the Dohany Synagogue."

After the First World War, before the great depression, life had been extremely generous to Ted and Sig. They had been sent to the Sorbonne for an education in the arts and sciences. Ted then crossed the channel to earn a doctorate in economics at Oxford while Sig went to Berlin for a doctorate in mechanical engineering. They both returned to Budapest in 1925. Upon the death of their father theytook over the management of the family's business.

Both of the brothers were welcomed into the society of Budapest and each formed relationships with young women which were furtive because the passage of laws limiting intercourse between Jews and Goyhem.

The brothers were acutely aware of the linkage of the National Socialism party's rise with the resurgence of anti-Semitism and they knew that all Jews had some vulnerability. After the plundering and anti-Semitic riots of Crystal Nacht they feared more for their sister Julia's welfare than their own. They had worked with their brother-in-law, Rolfe, to affect a paper divorce and forge an escape route for Julia. They booked passage for her on the TIGER HILL, an illegal refugee ship that sailed from Romania to Tel Aviv. In 1940, Julia was moved to a Kibbutz 30 kilometers from Haifa in Palestine.

Ted and Sig were able to work until 1944. The Prime Minister Miklos Horthy had little interest in pursuing the extermination policies and did little to enforce them. Jews even were recruited to fight in the Hungarian campaigns against Russia. There was a radical change in policy in March 1944 when Admiral Horthy was in Berlin and Eichmannn came to Budapest to enforce plans for forced labor and extermination. With great efficiency using IBM punch cards, the Jews were stripped of their possessions, herded and hauled on trains to concentration camps.

Sig described the efficiency with which Gestapo agents constructed wooden crates for the masterwork art collection the family had purchased on their travels. He remembered his fear when the cold steel barrel of the Luger pistol was pressed against his temple while he was ordered to open and empty the basement safe. Sig sat, shaking so severely that the officer served him a shot of schnapps, at their family dining table. He was held as a hostage, while the agents escorted Ted to the bank and had him remove the family's gold bars, coins and heirlooms. Upon Ted's return to the house, the brothers were handed a receipt, which stated that these valuables were taken as payment for penalties and delinquent taxes. The list of items taken covered two handwritten pages. An embossed imprint from the local Hungarian magistrate was impressed onto the document copy, and it was initialed by the Gestapo agent.

Most of the material wealth resulting from hundreds of years of work was taken from the Glucke family, but they were alive. The brothers went to the family cemetery plot; some of the headstones had been broken or tipped. Their family's headstones were intact and they placed stones on the top ledges of the markers to signify their attendance and remembrance. At home they gathered their workers and managers and left the house and business in their hands. Ted and Sig selected a few family mementos, placed them in sacks, dressed as peasant laborers and departed to the countryside at a distant sector of their country estate near Lake Balaton that was camouflaged in the dense woods. They walked the paths of their ancestors, not knowing if they were ever to return.

Almost a year later while foraying for food at the edge of the forest, they heard a thunderous clanking of steel belted Panzer tanks in a column heading west towards Austria with their guns and turrets pointed east toward Budapest. The retreating armor prompted Ted to walk the 10 km to the town of Keszthely where he found out that the Red Army was advancing rapidly trying to get as far west as they could before encountering the Allies. The Soviets would leap frog in an effort to pinch off and surround units of the German Army.

It was time to return to Budapest. When they arrived on February 13, 1945, the Russians had just liberated the city and saved almost 100,000 Jews from the carnage Eichmann engineered and nearly carried out when the Red Army took the city. Eight hundred thousand Hungarian Jews had perished. The city was scared by the heavy bombardment. The motorcycle plant was a pile of shrapnel.

The two brothers moved back into their old town home. The windows had been shattered and one by one they covered them with scrap wood to protect the inlaid moldings and ornate woodwork from exposure and from pilfering. Winters were cold and fuel was in short supply. Here they were, without work, without money and short on food. Well, if you want food go to a restaurant. That's what they did. Ted and Sig got work as waiter-busboy- cooks in a small kosher restaurant. The pay was pitiful, but the food was there for them. At the end of the day, they were given a portion of the unsold soup, breads, and occasionally meat or cheese. Anything they could spare was bartered for wooden slats or roofing materials necessary to fix up their home.

All their lives, prior to the past two years, had been spent planning. The past three years were spent existing day-to-day, week to month. It was not a sad time but existing in a collapsed bureaucratic communist society consumed the energy usually reserved for reverie. They thought, if we can get by now, the future will come. Where is God? In the past, present or future? Why didn't God come to the rescue? Was God mean, indifferent, or non-existent?

The first letter in 1947 from their sister Julia, now Julia Katz, rekindled their spirit. They wondered about her first husband, Rolfe Havas, who had been caught in the Hungarian upheaval. They wondered whether he survived and if so, what side of the barbed wire he was on. East or West? Rolfe, Julia, Ted, and Sig had grown through childhood and teenage years in closeness far beyond most family ties. They all loved each other. Rolfe had celebrated the holidays with the Glucke family. Together they sat shiva for their father. Rolfe's two boys were blessed in a briss by a reformed rabbi. They forgave him for his marriage to his au pair after the divorce and bemoaned the failure of getting Julia's sons out before the holocaust upheaval. It had been a time when the fractals of time and place were so independent that one and one exploded into zero, truth was a lie Heisenberg's uncertainty was the only certainty and purgatory prevailed on the face of the earth.

One evening in 1947 a Hasid came into the restaurant where Ted and Sig worked at about 10 o'clock. All the tables were empty but the man chose one in a darkened corner. He ordered tea in a glass with just one lump of sugar. His voice was deep and soft. He asked Sig who was waiting tables to bring his brother Ted from the kitchen where he was swilling the uneaten food from plates into buckets to be traded with farmers for use as animal gruel.

When the brothers joined the Hasid he asked them if they were familiar with the Kabbalah and whether they thought that unlawful justice could act as retribution. The visitor's voice evoked a familiarity without any concrete recognition. The stranger identified himself as Avraham and said, "I have come from Israel with a plan that could only partially rectify some of the plagues and curses that have soiled your family's existence in the past several years." The brothers were taken by surprise and didn't know what to answer at first. They excused themselves from the table with the excuse that they needed to lockup and the promise that they would bring the stranger a plate of biscuits.

While in the kitchen they conferred and agreed that any plan that derailed them from their present daily sustenance strategy was worth listening to. They sensed excitement and they sensed some feelings of honesty and puzzling kinship with this stranger.

All they knew about the mission was that it would involve crossing the Austrian-Hungarian border at an isolated point where the Russian guards would unexpectedly find an unusual cache of 190 proof vodka laced with a soporific agent to assure their inattention while the three forged a stream and crossed the border on a moonless stormy night. Once into Austria they boarded a 6-ton diesel truck "borrowed" from the Allied Forces stationed nearby. They headed westward and kept off the main highways.

They picked up three more men in Eisenstadt. They were all dressed in black with black woolen caps, the type often worn by sailors, and turtle neck sweaters; each carried a leather satchel and a black holstered Walther PP 9mm pistol. The three introduced themselves to Ted and Sig in Yiddish but spoke to each other in Hebrew, a language whose words were only familiar to the brothers from a few prayers.

It was almost one o'clock when they reached Salzburg. At this point the Hassid got out and looked at the mountains, stared at the starry sky and held a flashlight on a crude hand sketched map. Ted, for some strange reason, thought about homing pigeons and migratory birds and how they navigate to their destinations. He wondered when the nature of this mission would be revealed.

The truck passed over a wooden bridge on a dirt road and stopped outside of a monastery. Then the Hassid Avraham entered through a service door at the side of the large polished smooth brass doors at the entrance to the cathedral. He reappeared after about five minutes with a priest and motioned for the drivers to park the rear of the truck as close as possible to the camouflaged entry of a cave in the adjacent hillside.

The combination locks on the steel doors were opened after a short conversation between the Hassid and the priest. Ted could barely make out a listing of:...... frogs, locusts and vermin that reminded him of the festive Seder ceremonies held years ago when their family gathered annually at their estate. He conjured up a vision of his sister Julia in her tiara and sparkling necklace, arm in arm with Rolfe in his ceremonial army uniform, her other hand holding an infant son by her side. Her other son sat in a fancy carriage.

The seven men went into the cave and began loading the heavy steel boxes. These required two men grasping handles on each side of the boxes. The large wooden crates were slipped between the heavy steel crates at the center of the truck where the height from the floor to the canvas was greatest. One large crate was carried by the priest and five men on a dolly to the back of the vestry. After three and a half hours, the load was secured with ropes. Because of the lack of space, Ted and Sig had to ride up front in the cab. They were exhausted but the adrenalin rush of the excitement kept them wide awake.

Only now was there any discussion of the mission and the plans. They headed eastward towards the rising sun. After several hours they turned sharply to the left and northward for several hundred meters where the parked adjacent to a dilapidated wooden pier. The truck was hidden under a canopy of trees among tall bushes. Sandwiches were eaten and three men were posted as lookouts while three slept.

As the sun set that evening, the river was dark and only a rare beacon probed the channel. A low set river boat approached and the heavy hemp looped ropes were slipped over the pylons protruding from the pier. Planks were extended, and the men loaded their cargo. Not all of the crates and steel drums were stowed into false holds in the river freighter. Most of the crates containing canvasses were too large and conspicuous for transport to Hungary. They would be hidden and sold to bidders who cared for their beauty and authenticity but ignored their certificates of ownership. A significant number would be bought by museums for huge amounts of money. Some would eventually hang on the walls of the Berlin National Art museum.

A large portion of the containers contained gold from human dental work, melted into ingots, jewelry or precious stones. These were to be dribbled back across Austria into Swiss Banks controlled by Zionists. Runners nicknamed Schlepers often dressed as Hassid's, would bit by bit bring the money to where it would be used to move DP from holding camps to Palestine. The money was also used for purchases of armaments needed to protect the immigrant Israeli settlers. Ironically, Eichmann had performed a huge funding drive for the benefit of his victims.

The riverboat was unloaded north of Budapest; the cargo was taken to Ted and Sig's house where it was placed in the basement. That is, all except two oil canvasses. One painting was designated for delivery to an address and name unfamiliar to the brothers. It was Maria Gutta on Bathory St. in the 5th district on the Pest section of the city.

When the other painting was uncrated, the brothers each felt a welling of emotion that struck like a lightning bolt. There pulses quickened, their palms sweated, and it felt as if a great vacuum sucked at their chests. They hadn't seen this painting in four years. It was s depiction of God in heaven watching his flock frolicking in the goodness of the lakes and forests done by Raphael. This picture had been bought by their grandfather for Ted and Sig's mother and father when Sig was born. It had hung in the dining room and symbolized the unity, blessings, and prosperity of their family. This picture embodied the spirit and fortune of the Glucke family more than any other possession they owned. The family had been fragmented when the painting had been taken. The brothers wondered how the mysterious Hassid knew the location of these treasures, and how he knew which to return to them. Who was this man? The stranger had disappeared as quickly and mysteriously as he had appeared; only asking that they deliver the other crate.

The brothers scouted the Bathory St. address before delivering the painting. They found that the apartment was occupied by a widow with two young boys. While they watched the house, they recognized an older man leaving. They followed him to a small bakery, where when they stood next to him, they recognized him as having been the manager of the wheel assembly line in their family factory. After shaking hands and embracing, the brothers invited Werner to lunch. They reminisced about the pre-war times, glossed over the hardship, and questioned him about the present. Somehow the conversation got into living accommodations and the brothers got Werner to talk about the tenants in the building where he rented a room. In particular he told them about a fortyish widow whose name was Maria. She lived with her two small children in the two front rooms on the second floor. She had a chiseled beauty; she was intelligent but kept very much to herself and two boys. There was a sadness smothered by her beautiful smile. Her essence of being was in caring for her children.

The brothers dressed as moving men and brought a truck to the house on Bathory St. They knocked on the apartment door on the second landing and told the blond woman who answered that they had a delivery for her and that she needed to sign papers while they brought it up the stairs. She was perplexed but obeyed their instructions. When they got the crate into her living room, which was sparsely decorated, they uncrated the painting.

Again they were surprised. The theme of the oil was an angel reaching out to two boys seemingly lost in a forest. This painting had been slightly damaged and all that could be made of the painter's signature was Tinta.......... The brothers hung the framed canvas on the street side bare wall so that sunlight would not further damage the oil colors. They were offered tea and sat with the widow to admire the masterwork now hanging on her wall. They gathered that she was just managing to provide for her family. She hurried the brothers because she had to prepare for her evening job at the university where she did library research and cataloging for various professors.

Sig and Ted had many unanswered questions, but for now they only dared to gently probe. Over the ensuing years they kept an eye on Maria Gutta and her children. Funds and various forms of support or influence were given to her. Some were furnished through Paul, their former plant manager.

Sig and Ted knew that they could never resurrect the family industrial complex from the rubble pile at their old plant. They were aware that manufacturing heavy equipment in an environment dominated by Soviet communism was unlikely to succeed and even less likely to be profitable. The brothers now had capital from the recovered loot and they searched for a cottage industry where the resources in Hungary could provide a base of operation. They decided to go into the cosmetics trade. There was ample opportunity to convert some of the recouped gold into Hungarian currency. With this money they hired women, dispersed about Budapest and the surrounding countryside, to prepare cosmetics. Through a network they were able to sell these skin care products to a dealer in Vienna, who in turn marketed them to supply houses in London, Paris, New York, Chicago, Los Angeles, and Dallas.

After several years the business was consolidated and some of the middlemen were eliminated. The brothers established a school for cosmetology, which even became a government-accredited degree granting institution. Most of the students were young, very attractive females who were taught how to behave in a sophisticated manner. In addition to dermatology and cosmetology, they were taught French, English, economics, psychology and philosophy. They came as young ladies and graduated as worldly women. Many were aided in immigration to the West. When these women reached a suitable city they apprenticed themselves to some healthcare, spa, or salon in order to learn about and develop a clientele. After a few years, funds were made available (mostly borrowed from the brothers) to start up their own treatment centers. The brothers retained a portion of the ownership but most of their repayment came from the purchase of supplies. Each of the centers ordered most of their skin care products from the Budapest plants. It was often said that if the Hungarian supply were to dry up, a mask of beauty would be taken from the world. The brothers became multimillionaires in many currencies. Their money resided in Swiss, Israel, London, New York and Hungarian banks.

The time passed quickly. The brothers tired to ignore the political upheavals and only paid attention when the bureaucratic rulers interfered with their business. Selected bribes with dollars or merchandise often greased the tracks.

In October of 1956 Sig and Ted were awakened by the sound of explosions. The Hungarian Freedom fighters had blasted several Soviet tanks with Molotov cocktails. At first the city was in a state of jubilation but within days several armored divisions rolled into the city. At first the fighting was heavy, but the Hungarians were no match for the superior firepower of the 60,000 invading Soviet tanks. Several buildings were demolished. Paul, their former plant manager, informed them that his building took a direct hit and that Maria was killed. Werner was caring for her children, Tomas and Robe.

Quickly the brothers arranged to have Werner take the teenage boys out of Hungary while there was still anarchy and the borders were open. Thousands of Hungarians were fleeing. Contacts were made and monies sequestered to place Maria's children into boarding schools in Austria. The orphaned boys were told that their mother Maria's family had left them a trust fund that would be used to provide for them and that during their break from school they would stay with Paul Werner. All the needed papers were sequestered and the boys were told for security purposes that their new names would be Robin and Tomas Goode.

The boys were good students. Tomas was mechanically inclined and was accepted into the technical university in Berlin. Robin was interested in biological sciences and was admitted to the medical school at Gratz.

CHAPTER 12

Rolfe was moved by the 90th US Army Infantry to a small camp for displaced persons, the DP center near Salzburg in late 1945. He was quiet and reclusive during the interviews with the Red Cross. On the forms they gave him to fill out he indicated that he would like to go to the USA, Canada, Palestine, Australia, or South Africa in descending order of preference. The Jewish Victim Committee with support from the B'nai Brith had funds and resources to aid camp prisoners in finding new homes. Most of the survivors of the concentration camps adamantly did not wish to return to their country of origin. Rolfe became Avraham Lander, taking the name of his first wife Julia's second cousin and gave his home address as Kazinczy U. in Budapest.

During his stay, Rolfe studied Yiddish and Hebrew. There were many learned DPs eager to teach and exchange stories. They came from diverse backgrounds with extensive prewar education at universities and Yeshivas throughout Europe. Some had been wealthy and cultured. There were rabbis, doctors, lawyers, and engineers and there were tradesmen, such as diamond cutters and haberdashers. Some were from the Netherlands and France, but most were from Eastern European countries. There were Romanians, Croats, Hungarians, and Bulgarians, a few Germans and Austrians. Most of the Germans and Austrians were in camps further north. The common bond was suffering and survival. Some were so scared that they were barely functional and others woke nightly with nightmares and screamed out in fear or agony. The most severely affected were catatonic and stared blankly as if the world no longer existed in time or space. It was as if they were imprisoned within their own minds.

Rolfe, or Avraham as he was now known by his colleagues, was a good listener and a quick learner. The prayers and studies of the more orthodox campmates fascinated him. He attended their small congregation and became accepted by the Rebbe into the Lubvavitch. After several months he dovened in the morning and at the evening service. His beard grew, he dressed as a Hassid. Because almost none of the DPs had any of their original passports and documents, new official papers were secured for them. Avraham was now officially his name, but he managed to secure through a network of friends several sets of identity papers, including a British passport listing his country as South Africa. His picture sometimes was with or without a beard.

Avraham was still devoid of any way to have an income so he was very pleased when the Lubavitch asked him if he would like to travel and act as a courier for their organization. The Lubavitch had been scattered by the Holocaust and had ended up on all the continents except Antarctica. Many had been successful tradesmen and it was not long before they were financially successful in their new countries. There was, however, strong motivation to move a portion of their resources to banks in various financial centers. They had their possessions and monies stolen from them by the Fascists and now were trying to protect themselves and their families from this reoccurring. In some countries the export of funds was severely restricted and the Lubavitch helped to move funds to banks in Hong Kong or Geneva. The organization was not enamored of using Swiss banking institutions because of their ties to the Nazis and because of their failure to release funds to relatives of depositors who perished in the Holocaust. As soon as the Lubavitch had enough funds they bought the controlling shares of a bank in Geneva and established strong ties with the Leumi Bank in Palestine. The Swiss accounts were used as capital to finance new investments worldwide and soon the assets were in the billions of Swiss francs. The profits were used to pay interest to the accounts and to help Jews in their quest to leave Russia or DPs resettle and start new lives.

This financial empire needed couriers, to move assets, their "schleppers" as they were known had to be able to function in many different countries. They had to be facile in several languages and had to have multiple identity papers. After a month of intensive English, Avraham was sent on his first mission to Johannesburg, South Africa where the Werb family of Litvacks had established a factory for the manufacture of hats and started a chain of upscale men's stores throughout the major cities of South Africa. While visiting he was invited to the wedding of Bernie and Mary Werb. The wedding ceremony was orthodox but also included a recounting of Bernie's voyage from Vilna to Siberia to South Africa and Mary's voyage from Rhodes to Cairo to the Belgium Congo. After the vows Bernie took him to a closet which had a secret safe. The opened safe revealed at least several thousand gold coins. Each coin contained one ounce of gold.

A plan was developed to remove the gold from South Africa by melting it and pouring the molten gold into the rollers within the scrolls of a relic Torahs rescued from Vilna in Lithuania at the start of the holocaust. These Torahs were to be transported to Haifa where the gold was recovered and the diamond merchants would exchange it for diamonds. Avraham would then transport the diamonds to Antwerp, Belgium where they were exchanged for bank notes from US banks. The Hasid Avraham moved the notes to Geneva where he carried them in a canvas shopping bag into the bank and credited them to a Lubavitch investment account under the name of Werb.

This first mission took four months; it covered over 10,000 miles three continents and five countries. It accomplished several goals. First was the confidence that Avraham could travel safely and without suspicion. Second was the forging of a network of contacts. While in Palestine, Avraham was able to meet with the fledgling intelligence network, the Mossad, which would become renowned as the premier intelligence agency in the world. Also, he met members of a retribution group that was seeking out the Nazis who had fled Germany and the Nuremberg trials. He met other schleppers and learned of their ability to gather information. Avraham became his own spy; he worked for no nation. He had his own agenda.

In late 1946 he tracked Tomas and Robe to Vienna. When he saw them leaving at the train station he assumed that Maria was trying to return to Budapest. He quickly took the money he had earned as a schlepper, added a note with what he thought would give her sustenance and hope. He bumped her and passed the message and money to her in a leather purse. Avraham knew that he needed more experience and better intelligence sources before he could venture into countries occupied by the Soviet Union.

In August of 1947 he moved money from the Grisham family of Buenos Ares, who had amassed a fortune in the meat packing industry, to Geneva. They were petrified of the reported contacts between Peron and refugee SS officers and wanted to have investments elsewhere in case they needed to leave Argentina. The commission for this operation allowed Avraham the funds to obtain the necessary documents for travel into Hungry. During this operation, Avraham traveled through Spain and into France. Here in Paris he was introduced to several art dealers who were tracking and trading some of the objects d'art stolen from the Warburgs and the Rothschilds who were prominent Jewish art collectors. Michael Kuhn, whose collection was ravished, was to become a major player in the rekindled art market had many wealthy collectors and museums as clients.

By October, Avraham was ready to enter Hungry and execute his plan of redemption and retribution. The communists were atheists but were somewhat indifferent about the rebuilding of the Dohany St. Synagogue. Perhaps they had an inkling of remorse about the slaughter of the Jews in the camps and at the shores of the Danube, where even in the last moments of the war there was a carnage that stained the Blue Danube red with Jewish blood. In the Paris flea market, Avraham found some relics from a Hungarian Jew who had been given the title of Baron in the late 18th century. He contacted Rabbi Levy, a young rabbinical scholar who had been given the job of establishing a museum for the study of the history of Hungarian Jewry at the Dohany Synagogue. Avraham needed Levy to get news of his former brothers-in-law and hoped to enlist him in a plan to recover treasures stolen from the Jews.

When Avraham arrived in Budapest he met with Levy and brought him some artifacts for his exhibits. The Rabbi was unfortunately incapacitated by a fractured leg and was hobbling around on crutches. The Rabbi was not fit for a role in the planned rescue but he was an excellent source of information. He directed Avraham to a small restaurant where Sig and Ted were working. At the restaurant he enticed the brothers to join him in a covert operation. Avraham did not give them the exact nature of the mission. Avraham did not want Sig and Ted to have any implicating facts if the plans went array. Avraham used the Swiss banks where he had deposited Lubavitch monies to launder and transfer the funds and gold retaken in the rescue. Avraham held a small portion in an account in order to siphon funds into Hungry for Sig and Ted's businesses and obligations.

During the next decade, Avraham became more at home in the new state of Israel and acted as a consultant to the Mossad, the secret service there. The funds he sequestered allowed the movement of DPs from the Cypress holding camp through the barrier imposed by the British on immigration to Palestine. Thousands of Soviet Jews were saved from Stalin's reign of terror. Eventually Avraham felt secure enough to claim the right of a Jew to citizenship in Israel. He obtained an Israeli passport.

CHAPTER 13

The new cancer research building at the University of A was magnificent. The newness, bright colors, expansive and massive windows were in marked contrast to the stogy small tan brown laboratories and offices at the New York Cancer Center that Robin had lived and worked in for the past five years. The sun radiated through the glass paneled building. Everything was air conditioned and kept at 74°F. Robin was amazed how when he had to leave his car to walk the 100 or so feet to the cancer center his glasses fogged with condensation because of the heat and humidity. He had never experienced anything like it except in a Turkish bath.

When Rose and Robin arrived, they were greeted by Dr. Antonio Rigatoni, a swarthy Italian who was born in the Brooklyn but spoke with a trace of an Italian accent. Antonio invited them to his palatial home, which had porticos and verandas leading to a swimming pool fed by a waterfall. Tevia, Antonio's wife, brought appetizers of chilled linguine, portabella mushrooms and steak tidbits and an aperitif of chilled Cinzano. She was much younger than Antonio and over her bathing suit she wore a wrap around sheer cotton pareo colored with red and pink antherium flowers. Her long black hair was wet and reflected the sunlight. Robin thought that Tevia was incarnation of Rebecca, the Jewess of Ivanhoe.

The two couples sat by the pool overlooking the city and recounted their histories. Occasionally they would find people and places that brought mutual laughs. Within hours the friendship was forged. Physically the four contrasted greatly. Rose seemed Nordic, almost Wagnerian, next to Tevia, who was petite and Sephardic. Robin was a pale giant with a wiry moustache whose shadow eclipsed the smooth shaven bronze complected gray-haired Antonio. Their bonding was from mutual friends and shared experiences. The men had trained and worked with the Parsis of New York medicine. The women shared a love of art and the ability to listen to their husband's endless chatter on science and medicine.

Before the day was done, Rose and Robin had decided to buy the house next door, an antebellum home with four large white pillars. A slave wall of carefully piled stones separated the front yards, but the backyards contained gardens of neatly tailored holly bushes, roses and swimming pools beyond which were expanses of wild flowers and oak trees draped with Spanish moss or vines of ivy or honeysuckle. Deeper into the wooded areas, down a slopped expanse of huge pine trees, was an abandoned tennis court and a gazebo. Robin had never lived where there was so much colorful flora. Occasionally he would see deer and a variety of other animals including hedgehogs, raccoons, and rabbits in the forest. His first encounter with a rattler startled Robin and he soon learned to take his new golden Labrador 'Argo' and cat 'Tiger' with him when he ventured into the woods. The thrashing of his cat and dog seemed to give him a sense of safety. Although still within the city limits, Robin enjoyed this new experience in the wilderness and soon an early morning walk in the woods became a ritual. The fresh dampness of the trails mixed with the various aromas of the flowers and pines blended into a perfume which changed daily as new blossoms bloomed. This was the first home Robin ever owned. He felt the pride of possession and stomped the ground as if he were the lord of a great manor.

Rose stayed close to the house. She picked the décor and purchased the furniture at antique sales, art galleries, and bookstores. Within a year the house had the look and feeling of a country estate that had been occupied for generations. When she wasn't decorating the house, she was working to help develop the collection at the Birmingham Art Museum. Occasionally, Rose and Robin would sit in the living room in armchairs adjacent to the huge marble fireplace looking out onto the terrace and pool. Rose told Robin a few of the details of her trip to Budapest in a manner that she hoped would stimulate Robin to recollect his childhood. Each time in the conversation she would include a little more information and detail about her mission there. Robin listened intently but seemed distant in his thoughts or at least he didn't share them with Rose. About all she could learn was that Robin never knew his father. His mother said that his father had perished at the Eastern front during WWII. He wondered whether his father could possibly have survived and was at some Gulag. Robin read the Gulag Archipelago by Solzhenitsyn over and over. Robin revealed to Rose that his mother was killed during the Hungarian revolution in 1956 and that he and his brother were sent to boarding school in Austria. Rose couldn't get any more details and decided not to unveil her suspicions. Rose loved Robin but still could not get him to open up; he was shut tight like an oyster. She hoped that someday the hidden pearl would be found and freed.

Their lovemaking was sporadic but passionate but only when Robin could free himself from thoughts about his patients and his research. He was particularly ardent when he returned from a scientific conference where he had presented his work. It was as if his massaged ego was an erotic stimulation of his libido. Rose wondered whether Robin's needs might have been met by the groupies of young female residents or fellows, or even by the young secretaries in his office since he seemed only to need her bodily attention sporadically. Yet, in 1981 Rose became pregnant.

She glowed and her body grew. Occasionally she held his head to her belly to feel and listen to the stirring life within her. Robin was confused; he had no concept about fatherhood. He had never even thought about being a father. While Rose basked in her jubilance of pregnancy and felt fulfillment, Robin felt a sense of terror. Who was he? What kind of genes would he give to this child? He knew so little of his own ancestry. He almost suggested that he search for his roots, but his work kept him so busy that he never got around to it. He never shared his feelings of inadequacy with anyone. Robin felt that his façade of strength and decisiveness were important to his profession as an oncologist. More and more patients were seeking him out for treatment of their cancers. Cancer patients wanted someone who evoked confidence and who without hesitation would tell them how to deal with their tumors. Robin could not let weakness enter his character.

The reputation of the cancer center spread rapidly and patients who had previously gone to M.D. Anderson, Sloan Kettering, or the Mayo Clinic were being referred. Even the wealthy local Southerners, who previously would have gotten on their personal or corporate jets and flown elsewhere, were staying local for their health care.

One of the first was the head of a large chain of retail stores. He had started off in a small town with one haberdashery, moved to Tuscaloosa where he had two stores, then branched out through the South and Southeast. He now had 225 stores extending up to Michigan and out to California. At first he was ignored by the vests on Wall Street, but when his worth was estimated at 20 billion. He became an icon in the business world. His corporation's headquarters was a sprawling glass and concrete complex on the edge of Birmingham. It was hard to notice that Mr. Stan Wright was in town because he often drove to work in a 1950 pickup Ford truck with a bale of hay in the cargo area. His Tennessee Shit-Kicker boots had loose scuffed soles and he loved to wear faded cotton Levi jeans, held up by a wide black leather belt fastened by a heavy silver bull-headed buckle. Mr. Wright was recognized as a genius in the retail world. He had a corral full of MBAs from the ivy schools doing most of the scut work while he flew around in his Lear jet giving motivational speeches, accepting awards, including one from the President Reagan.

One day he noticed that his workday of 18 hours left him with a fatigue that he had never felt in his life. He was short of breath walking up the flip down stairwell to the Gulf Stream jet. His wife, Mary, made him promise he would go see that new foreign doctor at the medical center.

When Mr. Wright arrived at the University Medical complex in his old Ford, he was surprised to see the reception line of the Dean and Chancellor coming out in the 100-degree heat to greet him in the parking lot. He recognized them from their pictures, which were in almost every Sunday's social section of the Birmingham News. They greeted him as "Stan the Man who dresses America." He preferred to be incognito but wasn't uncomfortable with the handout boys.

Stan got a firm handshake and an arm over his shoulder from the Chancellor. The Dean always walked three feet behind the Chancellor and it reminded Stan of his visit to India where the women walked behind their husbands. The three men headed to the air-conditioned administrative offices where Stan was offered a scotch from the Chancellors well-stocked cabinet. Stan said, "No thanks. Never touch the stuff before noon, and I better be sober for the first medical exam I had since he left the Army." Stan noticed the slight tremor as the Chancellor poured himself three fingers of Glenlivet whiskey. He didn't even ask the Dean if he wanted anything and Stan sensed a look of disapproval on the Dean's face.

Dr. Goode was summoned to the VIP lounge. Robin never liked dealing with the administration and preferred to keep as far away from the front office as he could. His research success was drawing more attention and hardly a week went by that the TV cameras from CBS and NBC were not filming him and his laboratory. Robin felt like a one-man stand up show. Even if the patient was in another medical center, Robin's commentary was sought. The publicity allowed the university solicitors to get into the deep pockets of alumni and a variety of benefactors. This show was only second to that of The Bear, coach of the Crimson Tide. The money that flowed in was used for endowment funds, building drives and some even went for the fees for his services. Robin felt like he was a meal ticket for the rest of the Medicine Department and the other medical school departments. He had earned 1/3 of the revenue for the University Hospital with 1/20th of the staff. Even with this contribution Robin was expected to compete and win support from the National Cancer Institute, NCI. He had been successful in getting grant support but the price was enormous. Robin saw patients from 8 to 10, listened to residents and fellows report on their patients (which included many of the indigent patients) from 11-12, attended a noon scientific seminar from 12-1, answered phone calls and correspondence from 1-2, and saw patients when the biopsies and lab results came out from 2-6. From 6-8 he listened to reports from the research lab. He dined with Rose from 8-9 and worked in his study, writing and reviewing papers from 9-12. Four days a week he pounded the pavement, jogging for 1-2 hours after 10:30 when the heat of the day abated. Occasionally on nice weekends he and Rose rode their Yamaha motorcycles out into the countryside. The speed and flow of the wind seemed to blow away some of the tension. On occasion, he rode his antique Hungarian Maray bike.

When Robin shook Stan Wright's hand, he thought, "if I do the job, I could win some support that will allow better funding of the oncology program and reduce my begging for more hospital funds". He escorted Stan back to his suite of examining rooms. He took a careful history and then performed a detailed physical examination. He felt the armpits and groin for lymph nodes and pressed and palpated to determine whether the spleen was enlarged. Robin ordered a battery of chemical assays and an analysis of Stan's blood cells. Standard chest and abdominal x-rays were ordered as well as CAT exams. A bone marrow sample was trephined from the iliac crest. The cells were parceled out for microscopy analysis, immunological analysis, and chromosome analysis. Robin asked Stan to return in five days with his wife so they could discuss the results of all the tests.

The tests showed that Stan had a cancer of the lymph nodes with focal deposits of lymphocytes in the specimens taken from the pelvic bones. Robin assessed the type, amount, and distribution of the neoplastic cells. He thought about the options for treatment and the possible complications and prognoses. He thought carefully how he would present the findings and possible scenarios to Stan Wright. The first option was to delay treatment until the symptoms become less tolerable. The second option was to give a course of chemotherapy with cytotoxic drugs in an attempt to get a clinical remission and wait for a second course of chemotherapy. The third choice was to enroll Stan in an experimental program of immunotherapy. In this group the patients were treated with antibodies generated to react with defined surface antigens, glycoproteins on the outer cell membrane of the tumor cells. There was little evidence to support the latter option if time of survival was used as the measurement. Only a few centers had access to the monoclonal antibodies. A large facility for propagating selected antibody producing cells had been constructed at Birmingham. Mice had been immunized with human lymphoma cells and the cells from their spleens fused with tumor cells so that the resultant hybrid cell line could be selected for its ability to make the desired antibody. These hybridoma cell lines would be immortalized and billions of progeny cells could be used as factories for the antibody. The fluid media from these cells was harvested and purified. The cost of this product was enormous and on a per gram basis the antibody was 10,000 times more expensive than gold. The preparation had to be free of toxins and infectious agents such as viruses. Robin now knew that the patient he and Dr. Bluda, his mentor had treated in New York had died of AIDS from the HIV. Rod had HIV and CMV viruses in the tumor inoculum. He and Dr. Bluda had given Rod's mother Lucy the viruses from her son Rod's tumor cells.

There was almost no published data in refereed journals to support or refute the efficacy of treating patients with these particular antibody preparations. A few oral presentations at the leukemia-lymphoma section of the oncology meetings suggested that the antibodies had caused regression of the tumors. It was not clear what the toxicities of the treatment were and whether the tumor cells would become resistant. In the few patients where antibodies had been given, their appeared to be fewer side effects than that seen with the usual chemotherapy. There was no hair loss, little nausea and vomiting, and no suppression of the bone marrow with decreased red blood cell and platelet formation.

It was Monday morning when Stan and Mary Wright were escorted to the conference room adjacent to Robin's office at the medical center. The elderly couple held hands as Robin delivered the diagnosis and outlined the options for treatment. Stan asked whether he needed to have another opinion and Robin replied that he would send the slides sent to any oncologists or pathologists around the country, but that he had personally reviewed them and thought that the diagnosis was not questionable.

Stan and Mary had little training or understanding of medicine and knew even less about cancer, but the same incisive inquisitive nature that had rocketed them to the top of the business world provided them with the skill to ask extremely introspective questions about Stan's illness. The interview lasted over three hours. At the end of the session Stan knew more about lymphomas than most young physicians graduating from medical school. Mary held tears back and grasped Stan's hand. They were convinced that Dr. Goode was the oncologist they wanted to treat Stan. Robin's ability to simplify, without trivializing, the complex biology of the immune system and the elements of neoplasia and his confidence without arrogance made them choose to remain in Birmingham under his care.

There seemed to be little debate on which therapy Stan would accept. He was an active man who felt that chemotherapy would crimp his lifestyle. He had never been sick and wanted to avoid any incapacitation. Stan and Mary agreed to risk the more experimental treatment. The expense was not an issue. The $100,000 for the first course of therapy was about what he had lost at the last Kentucky Derby. Stan told Robin that for each year he could function and remain out of the hospital a substantial gift would be made to his program for the treatment of lymphatic cancers and leukemias. Robin was also told that there was to be no public announcements about his disease or his treatment because it would have an adverse effect on his company's stock. The incentive for adherence to this request was that the gift would be in stock and stock options. The university officials were to be told that Stan did not need treatment but that he would return for a complete exam in the next 6 to 12 months. They also were told that a gift of one million dollars would be made from Stan's company at the end of the year. The gift was to be free of any stipulations. A new file and identity was chosen and Stan Wright became Sam Walters.

Robin was ecstatic; this was a chance to get the financial support needed for his program. The money would allow him to hire enough staff to enhance the program he was developing. He also needed some junior faculty who could mind the shop when he left to attend meetings or give lectures. Stan's donation would give Robin the independence he needed from the Medicine Department and the University. He laughed as he thought about the golden rule of academic medicine, "Them that got the gold rule."

There was great jubilation when Stan Wright's tumorous lymph nodes went from a walnut size to a pea size to undetectable. Even the tumor in the bone marrow biopsies seemed to disappear. After six months, a few small shoddy lymph nodes became palpable to Robin's probing fingers during an examination. The antibody treatment was reinstituted and again the nodes disappeared.

At the end of a year, Robin received five million dollars for his research program. The gift was the talk of the campus. Dr. Rigatoni, Chairman of Medicine, called Robin to discuss how they would spend the windfall. Robin stood firmly in insisting that the Oncology Division retain control of the money. He was irritated by Dr. Rigatoni's demands and by his incessant smoking. Dr. Rigatoni glared at Robin, his eyes almost protruded from his plethoric face as he coughed and choked. When he left Dr. Rigatoni's office Robin felt dirty from stale smoke.

Rose was pleased by Robin's success but worried by the financial pressure and burdens. She had never seen Robin so concerned with money. She tried to be comforting but their new baby consumed her attention and affection. The baby had been almost 10 pounds at delivery and the pregnancy and delivery had drained her emotionally and physically. The baby, looked like a puffed panda or a little like Robin. The baby was named Paul. The boy was colicky and late at night Robin pulled a pillow over his own head, to mute the crying, so that he could get enough sleep to be functional at work. Rose often had to hold Paul for hours before the baby was comforted into sleep. In the early mornings when Robin arose she was often fast asleep in a rocking chair in the baby's room. The arrival of this infant seemed to be an expanding wedge between Robin and Rose. They rarely talked about his work, and sexual intimacy did not seem to fit into their agendas. Rose's erotic stimulation by Paul's suckling seemed to suffice. Robin seemed content in sublimating his desires with evening jaunts of jogging or riding his antique classical Maray 500 motorcycle. Early mornings he took a thermos of coffee and strolled with his pets around the gardens and nearby woods.

Robin was able to attract an international group of young investigators and fellows to his oncology program. Soon publications on the biological biochemical characterization of lymphomas were being produced in almost an assembly line fashion. Original papers, editorials, and reviews from his group peppered the top journals such as *Blood* and *The New England Journal of Medicine*. Unfortunately, Robin's success only provoked a wider schism between oncology, the rest of the medicine department, and the other departments in the medical school. Everyone liked the recognition and financial bonanza, but jealousy was the prevailing force.

One day during a particularly heated session, Dr. Rigatoni clutched his chest and collapsed. Robin summoned the code red team and backed away as they performed CPR. The EKG showed acute changes of a heart attack. The laboratory blood tests showed damage to the cardiac muscle. When treatment with enzymes to clear the coronary arteries of a blood clot, much the way Drano the liquid Plummer clears a stuffed drain, failed to restore blood flow, it was decided that emergency open heart surgery be preformed to replace three of the diseased blood vessels with segments of veins removed from the lower legs. The immediate postoperative course was stormy and excessive hemorrhage necessitated a return trip to the operating room to suture several small bleeding vessels. By the next day it became clear that Dr. Rigatoni would survive. Robin may have felt ambivalent but he did not feel that he had provoked the heart attack.

During the next several months Robin was somewhat sulky and took increasingly longer morning walks into the woods so that he could smell the flowers. One day Robin sat on a remnant of a stone bench at the side of the abandoned tennis court. The cracked tar surface had shoots of bushes growing up onto the court and in some places sapling pines erupted from the court surface. The post for the center court net was in place but the net cord had long since rotted away. The morning mist was streaked by the rays of the rising sun. The silhouette of a woman appeared in the path leading to the neighboring property. She was wearing a flared black skirt and a hooded red sweatshirt. Her long dark hair flowed from within the hood forward onto her chest. Her forehead was covered by cropped bangs. A plain gold band hugged her neck in the open V-neck of her sweater just above the shaded crevice between her breasts. Her eyes were wide and accentuated by a light blue black shading of mascara. Her lips were brush painted a bright red. The effect was no longer that of Rebecca the Jewess of Ivanhoe but was more reminiscent of Elizabeth Taylor's portrayal of Cleopatra. Tevia sat down next to Robin and placed her head onto his firm shoulder. Never, in the year of the two neighboring couples socializing had Robin felt the desire to hold or caress Tevia. The pressure of her petite and delicate form sent a wave of arousal through him. Energy flowed between them and Tevia increased her embrace bringing her open lips and tongue into contact with Robin's mouth. She guided his hand to the flesh below her skirt where she was warm and moist. No lingerie impeded his probing. The forest echoed with primordial moans as they entwined and lay on the stone bench. The orgasmic crescendo was followed by calmness. The stillness was only broken by the thrashing of his cat, Tiger, clawing at an s-shaped serpentine form fleeing into the forest. The streaks of sun were erased by dark clouds; claps of thunder followed the flashes of lightening in the nearby woods. The rain pelted and mingled with beads of sweat to soak their bodies. They pulled their clothes around themselves and looked deeply into each other eyes and each ran up the path leading to their respective homes. The encounter in this Eden encompassed a gambit of emotions, needs, desires, guilt and fear had transpired in less than 20 minutes. The sudden squall had smashed any attempt at rationalizing away this forbidden event.

When Robin reached the backdoor of his house, the dog and cat raced in front of him and shook the rainwater from their bodies. Robin followed and pulled his wet jeans and T-shirt from his body. He put his shorts and socks in the washer and ran to his bathroom for a scalding shower. He felt the need for cleansing. While in the shower, Robin thought about his mother. She had told Robin and Tomas that a clean body was a prerequisite for a clean mind. Her fastidious attentiveness to hygiene was part of her puritanical philosophy. To her, dirt was the symptom of a soiled soul. Even though she rarely practiced any form of organized religion, she had an intense respect for the concept of a soul. All her moral teaching related to the purity of one's soul. The tenets of her belief blended Hinduism with western religion's commandments. Her teachings included prayer of thanks for the privilege of existence. Her material wants were never intermingled with her spiritualism. At the age of 48, Robin pined for the wisdom and goodness of his mother.

CHAPTER 14

Dr. Mark Knife, the pathologist Robin had befriended while training in New York had remained there. Knife was now a on the faculty. He had continued his work in surgical pathology, which was his main service contribution. His research shifted from chemical carcinogenesis to molecular analysis of the genes involved in transplantation. While moonlighting during his training and fellowship years, he became interested in tissue typing. The use of blood group antigens to identify relationships in forensic and paternity cases appealed to his fantasy of identity as a mathematical concept. Reports of using the restriction endonuclease cleavage of DNA in immigration investigations in Great Britain was to lead him onto a trail older than the history of mankind, a trail that would take him from the Eden(s) to the Asian-American migration, through the diaspora(s), the migrations from Europe to the America's and the enslavement and deportation of Africans to the New World. The folklore and fables, the conjecture of the anthropologists, and archeologists could now be validated by the construction of mankind's pedigree. All that was dead was now alive again. The DNA encrypted more than information for human development, it held the unwritten history of the humanization of the planet.

These studies so consumed Knife that after his routine daily work he studied and wrote long into the night. He sometimes only realized that it was a new day when the secretary told him that there was a resident physician waiting to check out his cases with him. The schism between his home life and his work was oblivious to him until he came home to find a note from his wife, Toby, stating that she had left for California with their children and the principal of the Hebrew School where she worked. Knife didn't even know that she was working. The note went on to say that dinner was in the refrigerator and that the divorce papers would come next week.

Knife scratched his balding head and heated up the dinner in the microwave. The quiet of the apartment gave him a chilly feeling but he allowed in only a tinge of sadness or remorse. While eating the chicken soup he pondered which has a greater effect, genes on society or society on genes. The question was related but not identical to the debate on euthenics versus eugenics. He thought about a lecture by Sol Spiegelman at Columbia University about how DNA's ultimate purpose was to divide and propagate and that the spread of DNA on the earth and into space was part of this process. Sleep finally quelled his intracerebral debate.

In the morning Knife decided to open some of the letters stacked in his in box. Most of them were of no interest and were tossed into the trash. The envelope from the University of A., which he at first thought was another announcement for a cruise with professional tax-deductible continuing education, turned out to be a letter from his former colleague Robin Goode. He sliced the envelope open with a scalpel. The letter invited Knife to Birmingham to give a guest lecture and to interview for a position. Robin wrote that he had tried to contact him by email and telephone but had not received a reply. The invitation was for a date of Knife's choosing and asked him to call in order to schedule the visit. Knife thought back when he and Robin were in training. He reminisced on their shared intensity. Few of the present day trainees had the same dedication; many put in their shift and went home. Some were even unionized. Several mistakes in patient care with adverse or fatal outcomes had been blamed on resident physician fatigue. As a result shifts were limited and maximum work hours established. The shortage of house staff led to the hiring of young staff for clinical coverage. This was also driven by the changes in reimbursement; insurance companies which would no longer pay if an attending only signed the resident's notes. The whole system was changing in the name of managed care. Sometimes when forced into accounting for his time and productivity, Knife thought that he was lost and doomed by this new medicine. The paperwork and required documentation of policies, licensing, credentialing, competency, EEO (equal opportunity) and harassment training and protection of patient privacy were consuming greater and greater amounts of his time.

Born and bred in Brooklyn, Knife had almost never considered living anywhere but New York City. His only extended period away from N.Y. was his two years of residency at the University of Colorado in Denver and a two-year stint in the Air Force in California during the Viet Nam War. After each of these excursions, he and his wife returned to the security of the city, their families and friends. Even when Knife went to a meeting in Vegas or New Orleans, he felt somewhat uncomfortable, sort of like a fish out of the water. The shows in Chicago and the Chinese food in San Francisco didn't match up to those in New York. Even with all this, it was probably the move of his parents to "New York South", Miami rather than the absence of Toby and his children that weakened his ties to the city. He accepted Robin's invitation.

When Knife arrived in Birmingham, Robin greeted him at the airport with a hand shake and a hug. Kiddingly, he squeezed Knife's bicep and said "need to pump more iron you are getting soft." He drove him around Birmingham to show him the high spots. At the medical center, Knife met with the staff of the C team. He was very impressed with the savvy and the esprit of the cancer center. The international composition of the group was impressive. Publications, and grant awards evidenced their productivity. They were well on the way to winning the National Institute of Health's coveted designation as a Cancer Center. It certainly was not backwater medicine and science. When he visited Robin's house he noted that he hadn't felt so much in the "wilderness" since his overnight excursions to Boy Scout camp in Alpine, New Jersey as a young teenager. The expanse made him realize how compressed and crowded his existence had become.

His lecture on the use of mitochondrial DNA markers to assess maternal ancestry was well attended because the first 100 attendees got a free box lunch. There were several astute questions on the effects of selective pressure forces, the rate of homogenization with racial mixing, and the role of mitochondrial genes in carcinogenesis. Robin invited Knife to his office where he shared with him why he had asked Knife to consider joining the C team. Robin explained that the oncology unit was going to embark on combining immunological tumoricidal techniques with chemo and/or radiation therapy. This toxic therapy would be followed by bone marrow transplantation. Our team needs someone with an interest in immunogenetics for tissue typing and matching." Robin enticed Knife with the proposition that in the time when he was free of the oncology work he could pursue his interests in anthropology. He said "In fact, some of these studies might have great implications in assessing and assuring successful sustained donor recipient transplantation engraftment." Robin said "The institution would supply salary, space, computer and laboratory support for a startup period of three years, after which grants and clinical income could be expected." Knife told Robin that he was impressed with the oasis of intellect he had assembled but he wanted to think about the offer. He had always supported himself by service work in anatomical pathology and his writings in the area of genetics had been an unfunded academic pursuit. He was not sure that grant writing was his forte. Robin countered that the center had a crew of grant (ghost) writers who would work with investigators to prepare the NIH applications for support. They had been very successful in obtaining grant funding. Knife never asked what his salary would be assuming that Robin would pay well.

Knife felt that his ties to New York had weakened and he told Robin that he would be able to join the C team in the late spring after he finished his teaching obligations. There was little else to bind him to New York.

CHAPTER 15

Robin and Rose flew from Birmingham to Atlanta where they unpacked the stroller and wheeled the baby onto the shuttle train and up to the International Delta Lounge. Robin knew the Atlanta Airport well from all his domestic flying, but this was the first time in over seven years that he was returning to Europe. He had telephoned his brother Tomas, who was teaching at the Engineering School at the University in Vienna, that he would be arriving on an Air France flight from Paris. Tomas was excited. He had not seen Robin for seven years, and he had never met Rose and his nephew, Paul. Tomas had never married and had become somewhat of a recluse after the death of Maria, their mother. Tomas was to meet them at the airport and was to drive them to the Vienna International Hotel.

The high tech seats on the airplane had Robin fidgeting. For a while, Rose slept with Paul spread eagled across her chest. Soon the drone of the jet engine lulled Robin into a dream state. He was so exhausted from his work, especially during the last few weeks before this trip, that he fought sleep out of habit. To the right of the plane the porthole windows were completely dark, while on the left, Robin could see the aura of the summer sun cast north of the polar route they were flying. The clouds below appeared as a Madonna-like figure reaching skyward, arms extended as if beckoning. The symbolism of the apparition fuzzed in Robin's brain as he fell into a deep sleep. The overhead movie played to an audience of sombulants with earphones saddling their heads.

Off the coast of Ireland the aroma of pancakes with maple syrup, bacon with eggs, and freshly brewed coffee filled the cabin of the 747. The reflection of the bright dawn sun on Paul's upturned face revealed a smile as the baby stared at his father. Robin reached over and the baby grasped his index finger pulling it to his suckling lips as if it was a nipple or a pacifier. The rest of Robin's fingers reached out to caress Rose's breast, along with the tender touch of his son's hand a binding ring of energy flowed.

While Rose went to freshen up in the lavatory, Robin fed Paul apple juice from a bottle. They finished their breakfast just before arriving at the DeGaulle Airport. The Goode family walked out into the crowded terminal and crossed over to where the Air France connection for Vienna was to depart. Shortly after gaining altitude they could see the snow capped Alps. The flight was quick and at the Schwechat Airport Robin recognized his brother Tomas in the crowd behind the glass plate barrier just beyond the immigration checkpoint. They waved to each other simultaneously.

After they picked up their baggage from the carousel and passed through customs, Robin and Tomas embraced. When they broke, Tomas put his arm around Rose and welcomed her with a kiss on each cheek. Even though he had never met Rose he recognized her from the wedding picture and VCR tape Robin had made when Paul was born. Rose noted that Tomas was slightly taller than Robin and dressed in a more casual but somewhat flamboyant manner. He was much more effusive and physically affectionate. He said to Rose "You are far more beautiful than the pictures Robin has sent." His English was very good but was occasionally peppered with German. They wheeled the baby carriage and the bags to the parking garage. Tomas had rented a Mercedes 500SE because his gull winged 300SL could not hold all of them and the luggage

During the trip from the airport to the hotel, Robin revealed his planned excursion into Hungary. Both Rose and Tomas were taken by surprise. Rose almost gasped when she heard that Robin had chosen to drive to Budapest. He told them that he had researched the entry and exit visa regulations and that since the Soviet troops had withdrawn there would be no problems. He was now an American citizen and Americans were visiting Hungry on a regular basis. Robin told them "I wish to visit the grave site of our mother, Maria Gutta Havas." Rose was astounded, her mind was racing but she did not express any support or objection.

They parked the car in the hotel lot and the concierge had the luggage taken to their rooms. Tomas had taken leave from his position at the

University and was going to accompany them during their travels. The Vienna Intercontinental Hotel was in the center of Vienna. It had been recently remodeled and was modern. It was elegant. They had reserved the luxurious Belvedere suite. The suite was on the tenth floor and when the porter drew the drapes they could see to the northwest the Gothic towers of Stephenson. The church spires reached high over the city and oriented the skyline of the city. The gold tiles on the roof glittered. Tomas had already registered and was situated in the second bedroom of the suite.

After unpacking and resting for several hours they decided to walk to the center of the city. They were still sated from all of the food on the flight over and only wanted a snack of Austrian pastries and some Viennese coffee.

They left the hotel, turned left onto Schubertring following around on Kartner Rign and right onto Kartner Str. at the Opera House. By now their appetite was growing at the thought of strudels and cream cakes. At the Sacher Hotel they ordered three Kapuziners, coffee covered with whipped cream sprinkled with chocolate, and tortes. During the stop they made plans for the rest of the week. It was decided that after Robin gave his presentation they would spend one day touring around Vienna and then proceed to Budapest, which was a three-hour drive.

The brothers pushed the stroller while Rose window shopped in the fashionable stores lining Kartner Strasse. Out of the corner of her eye she watched Robin and Tomas trying to reacquaint themselves and filling in the seven-year hiatus. It was a good feeling for her. She had not seen Robin so animated in any relationship. A brief reflection of an old man walking parallel to them in the store window caught her by surprise. She remembered the feeling she had in Budapest of being watched. A bearded man who seemed as a shadow blended into the crowd. She wondered whether she was paranoid.

The next day the three decided to visit some of the tourist spots of the city. They drove to the Schonbrunn Palace. It was a quick trip and they luckily found parking on a street along the periphery of the grounds. The main buildings formed a 1441 room baroque complex whose construction had begun in the 1500s. A hunting lodge and zoological gardens were added in the 17th Century. The Empress Maria Theresa made the palace her residence in the 18th Century. Fountains, an obelisk, simulated Roman ruins, a triumphal gate, a theater, and an enclosed botanical garden were subsequently added.

The brothers removed and unfolded the stroller, Rose tucked Paul in and hung a basket onto the rear. Tomas loaded the basket with the provisions Rose had gotten the hotel chef to prepare. When they got to a shady area near the Neptune fountain bordering the formal gardens, Rose spread a blanket on the lawn and laid out the lunch of pounded thin slices of breaded veal, topped by egg slices, chicken breasts caked in a pepper mustard sauce, cups of sliced potatoes in a spicy creamy vinaigrette dressing, and small dark rye rolls. They toasted their reunion with plastic cups brimming with a chilled Liebfraumilch. Robin and Tomas talked about their work and Rose listened intently. She tried to see if she could learn more of their family history.

Paul was angled in the stroller so that he could see the park. There was a small crowd gathered in the field nearby. All their attention was focused on a teenage boy performing an acrobatic dance with a soccer ball. The white ball bounced off the boy's body in a cadence that onlookers marked by clapping. His forehead, knees, and feet worked with machine-like precision to keep the ball aloft. The performer grew more enthusiastic with the accompanying applause. A Shepard darted from the crowd and the dog leapt into the air as to vie for the ball. The ball hit the boy's temple and angled out, bounced and smacked the startled Paul on his nose.

First a trickle then a constant flow of blood washed over his upper lip and down to his chin. Rose grabbed him as he smeared his hand through the blood and onto his blue shirt. She called Robin to get tissues from her purse. Robin gently tried to tamponade the source of the hemorrhage. He kept Paul's mouth and airway free of blood, but he looked at his wife Rose and they knew that their fears had come true.

They ran to the car and drove with Tomas' hand clamped on the blaring horn to the University Hospital. Robin held his son tightly and rushed him into the emergency care area. He quickly told the resident the precipitating events and pertinent family history of bleeding. As this was done, an IV was placed and blood was drawn for testing and for a type and crossmatch, in case a blood transfusion was needed. Paul's nose was packed but still was bleeding. Calls were placed to the pediatric otolaryongologist and pediatric hematologist on call.

When the pediatric hematologist arrived, Robin immediately recognized him as a colleague from medical school. Quickly, vasopressin was administered through the IV catheter. The bleeding stopped as if a spigot had been turned off. The ENT resident was able to constrict the bleeding and repack the nose.

Robin felt a release from the intense anxiety of the last thirty minutes. He thought about his fear that his child might aspirate blood into his airways or that he would exsanguinate. Robin had taken care of many very ill and terminal patients, but he had been away from pediatric care so long that he was uncomfortable with treating infants. He also realized that in his arms and care was a life that meant as much, if not more to him than his own.

The conservation between the doctors was all in German, and it took a few minutes for Robin to readjust to speaking without thinking in English. When the excitement abated, Robin thought about his own emotions. He had never felt the intense fear of losing someone close, as he did when Paul was bleeding. He did not remember the death of his mother who was annihilated by the blast from a Soviet tank while he was at school. Robin and Tomas never viewed her body because they were told that the corpse was beyond recognition after the explosion and subsequent fire. The funeral was hurried because their neighbor Werner said that the boys must escape while there was still confusion and a wave of migrants was fleeing Hungary into Austria. They had no belongings and slept in a church shelter the evening of her death. Tomas, the older brother, comforted Robin while they waited for Werner to return. Werner arrived about 4:00 a.m. with a dilapidated VW Beetle. The three sped westward and even with their rapid departure were trapped in a morass of trucks, cars, vans, and even some horse drawn carts at the border. After several hours of crawling traffic they were waved into Austria. The Hungarian border patrol sat smoking and talking. The Austrian immigration officer seemed overwhelmed and somewhat discombobulated. The officer tried to corral the Hungarians into immigration checkpoints but Werner turned out of the convoy and sped westward. That day's events, the escape from Hungary, seemed a million years ago.

Now seeing the pediatric hematologist sparked Robin's reminiscence. He had been a classmate of Robin's in medical school. Like Robin he was also a Hungarian who fled the country, but he had waited until 1959, three years later than Robin's flight. His escape was attempted only after careful planning. He told Robin that he had hired a beautiful well endowed, curvaceous woman, with enough exposed cleavage to engage the border guards, while he hide under the back seat in a false compartment. They counted heavily on the licentious behavior of the officers. Indeed, the creativity of young Hungarians matched that used by young people fleeing other communist bloc countries for freedom in the West. Homemade helicopters, hot air balloons, mini-submarines were all tried. Some attempts ended in disaster while the successful were almost comical in their creativity and audacity.

Robin was raised from his reverie when Tomas and Rose entered the treatment cubicle. Robin introduced them to the pediatrician who then assured them that Paul was out of danger, but he told them that they would have to exercise caution with Paul since he was a "bleeder." The boy had inherited the gene for vonWillebrands disease from Rose. They would have to restrict some of his activities and protect him from trauma as much as possible. They would have to carry a vial of vasopressin with them when they traveled. With some precautions, Paul could lead a reasonably normal life and could live to "a ripe old age."

Rose wept, for all through her pregnancy she had thought about the stories of bleeding in her cousins in Finland. She remembered going to the church cemetery with her cousins and constructing a genealogical tree; charting her mother's family back at least ten generations. She could not help but notice how many of her ancestors had died just after birth or in infancy. The affliction seemed sporadic and some escaped the disease. Rose had taken a course in genetics in her senior year at Welsey. After her trip to Scandinavia she pulled the old genetics text down and tried to construct a pedigree that would reflect the recessive or dominant nature of the bleeding trait. She could not fit the mode of inheritance into any classical pattern and decided that there must have been some hanky panky on those long northern nights.

Tomas, a bachelor, was at first a little awkward with his new family. His life had been untethered by any enduring relationships or commitments. The death of his mother, Maria, left him at age 20 adrift emotionally. Paul Werner, the neighbor and friend who raised the brothers, treated them as if they were his responsibility. He clothed them and provided an apartment for them, but he never became involved in their personal lives. Werner managed the trust funds that the boys were told was left by their mother Maria until he died. Then, Werner's will was found. His estate left them enough money to complete their education and travel. Werner had also taken care of securing documents that gave the brothers Austrian citizenship under the name of Goode. When the boys were in boarding school they would return during the holidays and stay with Werner, but after the university when they went on for graduate studies, Werner decided to return to Budapest. He would correspond with Tomas and Robin. Werner found work in a prosperous cosmetic business. He became a manager of production. The owners of the business allowed him to have a small suite of rooms in their townhouse. It was here the owners, two brothers, found him after he died peacefully in his sleep. Werner's employers wrote that Werner had been extremely frugal and had accumulated a significant nest egg, which he bequeathed to Tomas and Robin. The inheritance was in a Swiss account. When Tomas and Robin used the account codes to withdraw funds for their sustenance and tuition they were baffled on how Werner could have amassed so much money in the four years of his return to Hungary. They were clueless. Werner was an enigma. They missed his caring and good humor. He was never a father figure but acted more like an uncle, friend, brother, butler, and custodian. Perhaps someday they would unravel the mystery of Werner their guardian.

When the Goode family left University Hospital, they returned to the Vienna Intercontinental Hotel. Room Service brought a luxurious meal to their suite and after dinner Robin went to the writing desk to put some finishing touches on his lecture notes. The telephone rang and Rose was surprised to hear the gruff voice of the Dean of the medical school. In an anxious voice masking his stutter, he asked to speak with Robin.

The Dean told Robin "your patient, Stan Wright, is in the intensive care unit." Stan had suffered an anaphylactic reaction to the antibody preparation Robin's team had injected. The Dean was snappy and irate. He told Robin that he was furious that he had not been kept informed that Stan Wright was being treated at University Hospital. He yelled at Robin to "get your ass back to Birmingham."

The following morning Robin gave his presentation to the International Leukemia and Lymphoma Society. The title of the plenary session was "Advances in Immunotherapy." The audience of several thousand oncologists gave him a standing ovation. Robin answered a few questions, shook hands with the symposium organizers and rushed back to the hotel room where Rose, Tomas, and Paul were waiting. He didn't have his usual post-lecture "high."

Robin told Rose "I have to return home as soon as possible." He didn't give her the details but told her that she and Tomas could continue on the planned excursion to Budapest. Robin was going to have to fly to Paris and take the SST Concorde to Dulles. From there he would fly to Atlanta and on to Birmingham. Rose stone faced her disappointment. She had been fantasizing and playing the scenarios of the reunion of Robin and Tomas in Budapest. She didn't know exactly what she could expect but she was certain that she was going to witness an emotional eruption in a man normally cold as steel.

She saw beneath Robin's normally stoic face that he was under stress and knew that she needed to go home with him. She packed quickly and booked her plane reservations. She was not going on the Concorde SST but would use the return tickets they already had. While she packed, Tomas drove Robin to the airport for his flight. Tomas then returned to help Rose with the luggage and Paul. They had several hours to kill before her departure, so they drove around the city and talked. In a discrete manner, Rose probed Tomas about his recollections of growing up in Hungary. Tomas told her that he vaguely had an image of their father as a tall man with a moustache. He remembered seeing him in a gray-black uniform holding him and his brother in each arm. They had moved often and he had a distant memory of a train trip to Budapest with his mother and brother. Tomas had no pictures of his father and was told that he had disappeared at the very end of the war. Tomas, Robin, and Maria lived a very cloistered life. He always wondered whether he had any relatives but Maria said that only very distant cousins managed to survive the Allied bombing. He remembered that his mother was a beautiful blonde and figured that he and Robin must have inherited their coloring from their father. He told Rose that his mother worked in the late evenings and that a neighbor, Paul, had watched over them while she was at work.

When it was time to depart, Tomas got Rose and the baby situated on the airplane. She invited him to visit them in the US and made him promise that they would all go to Budapest some day. He kissed Rose on the cheeks and said "I always had wondered what a sister would be like." He was genuinely intrigued with his sister-in-law. He felt that she was deeply interested in him and could feel her love and caring for his brother and nephew. They hugged and she squeezed his hand tightly as he retreated into the crowded terminal.

CHAPTER 16

When Robin rushed into the hospital room, Stan was setting up scoffing down some grits, links and eggs. Robin had driven right to the hospital only stopping to grab the chart from the nursing station. He was relieved when Stan said, "What's all the fuss? I just got dizzy, hot and itchy after the last treatment. The next thing I know I got white coats all around pounding on my chest."

Robin wiped the sweat from his face and read the notes. Stan's EKG had been flat lined for 2-3 minutes before they got the defibrillator and restarted his heart. He shook Stan's hand and greeted Stan's wife Mary in the hall. She said "Thank you for coming. Is he going to be alright?" She looked as if she had aged a lot since their last meeting. Robin replied "He is over the acute danger from his allergic reaction but we will have to change the therapy."

During the next several weeks, Stan started to show remarkable enlargement of his lymph nodes in the axilla or armpit. Robin told Stan that he could no longer use the antibody treatment and would have to begin a more standard chemotherapy regime. Even with aggressive treatment, the tumor was growing. Within the next month Stan died. Mary was very appreciative for the sensitive and intense care Robin had given her husband, and she had his estate donate ten million dollars for the construction of laboratories and clinics. In deference to Stan, Mary, herself a private person, asked only for a small bronze plaque commemorating Stan. Soon after, Mary moved out of the limelight of society and returned to the country outside Birmingham where she had grown up and felt comfortable.

It was the end of an era for Robin. Stan had been his first great benefactor and had given him courage to ask wealthy patients for contributions. Stan had given Robin more than just a handout; he had given him bravado, the balls to ask for support. Robin felt the loss of Stan's annual support. The pressure was now intense to provide for all the medical and research personnel that he had hired to expand the oncology division.

Robin began to establish a research base to put his group at the cutting edge and to put the university in a position to compete for a coveted NCI designation as a Cancer Center. These centers had to have both clinical and basic science components in their program. Even more difficult was satisfying the requirement that the center show evidence of collaboration between the clinical and basic scientists. Most of the senior scientists were prima donnas. Sharing the success of their research was incompatible with their standard modus operandi. Only the carrot of increased space, funding, graduate students, and post docs could tempt them to work together. Often agreements on the order of the listing of authors on research papers were discussed before the experiments by groups were even undertaken. Everybody knew that the secret to grantsmanship was to have enough preliminary data to make the reviewers consider the proposal a sure success. Very few of the grants awarded that led to major breakthroughs in basic principles or quantum leaps in technological approaches were awarded for the designated goals and aims in the initial application. The world of life science research was actually very conservative and often shunned radical ideas and approaches.

Robin recalled a conference he attended as a student in 1967 in Edmonton, Canada, where a young Turk, Dr. Howard Temin, reported that his experiments on RNA tumor viruses suggested that the information in RNA could be converted enzymatically to DNA, integrated and replicated with the host cell's DNA. This contradicted the prevailing dogma. The young scientist was mocked with words equivalent to an audience throwing rotting tomatoes at a performer. As it turned out, the work was one of the most significant scientific advances in biomedical research. That meeting and the reception left an indelible imprint on Robin. The awarding of the Nobel Prize to Dr. Temin was symbolic irony for many true free thinkers.

Another force was beginning to bear on the field of medical research. Basic research was producing promising major new methods for diagnosing and treating diseases. In 1980 an editorial in the Yale

News stated that the avaricious and entrepreneurial behavior of scientists was unethical and immoral. One of the scientists mentioned was the cofounder of a biomedical company six months later. Almost all the major scientists were being recruited as consultants almost as intensively as baseball and football stars. The signing bonuses were often huge stock options and consultant fees. The income from these ventures dwarfed their salaries from their universities. In some institutions the scientists were brining in paychecks larger than the deans or chancellors. The Wall Street Journal or Barron's was often found on the desks of professors and it was not infrequent for the advances or "breakthroughs" to be announced in the newspapers before publication in refereed scientific journals. Medical centers and universities set up committees to protect their intellectual property and facilitate patenting. There were debates and arguments on whether life forms could be owned, whether postdocs should be included on the patents when they were working on the inventions under the tutelage of a thesis advisor, or whether DNA sequences for undefined functions could be patented. The subspecialty of patent law for the biological sciences flourished. Sometimes it was hard to recognize borders between corporate and academic institutions. Some drug companies tried to franchise whole medical schools, hospitals, and research institutions. There was manna, greater than the government grants, in the private sector.

It was apparent to Robin that the outpouring for research would flow downstream to the clinicians. For these clinicians would have to evaluate the products generated in the basic science laboratories. Clinicians also knew enough about vertical organization of industry to realize that the most advantageous position was to be involved from discovery, to testing and evaluation. This created a moral quagmire in which the patient's medical history, clinical data, and therapeutic responses could be 'sold', a direct conflict of interest at times with optimal patient care. Clinical research often brought huge amounts of monetary support even before a product was ever brought to market. Large pharmaceutical companies and the frenzy of investors willing to gamble on start-up biotech companies were pumped up and armed with an enormous amount of capital. Venture capitalists practically shoved to be in front of the line for the bonanza of biomedicine.

As Robin turned into his driveway he stopped to pick up his mail. A voice from an curvaceous derriere protruding from a rose garden adjacent said, "You forgot to have your mail stopped, so I picked it up." As Tevia turned she stared at Robin. Tears welled as she walked toward his car. She told him to wait, as she had to get his mail from her house. Time seemed to drag until she reappeared with a Saks's shopping bag filled with magazines and letters. He could see her face with tracks of trickling tears and smears where her muddy hands had tried to wipe them. He reached out of the car and lifted the bag onto the seat next to him. He said "thank you" without making eye contact. As she was about to mouth words he shifted and sped up the driveway. He never heard the words, "I'm sorry" nor did he see the note in her outstretched hand.

As Robin entered the house the stillness and silence reminded him that it would be almost another day before Rose would return. The calmness reminded Robin that their dog and cat were at the vet. He got back in his BMW ZX coupe and drove two exits down the highway. When the vet brought Argo out, his nails scratched the ceramic tile on the office floor as he tried to get traction to race to Robin. The dog jumped up and licked Robin's face like he was a scoop of ice cream in a cone. When the vet brought out the cat Tiger, she shrieked a long gleeful meow at the sight of Robin and Argo. She had a leather leash attached to her collar and she tried to shake it loose for she had never been tethered to anything. As they drove home, the dog waved his nose out of the window to catch the breeze while Tiger nestled on the floor trying to avoid the wind and wagging dog tail.

After Robin unpacked, tossing his dirty clothes in one pile and the dry cleaning in another, he used a letter opener to slice open the bills and tossed the junk mail into the trashcan. He winced at the American Express bill balance of 23,438 dollars and mentally deducted the airplane ticket amounts of 6,339 since the Oncology Society would reimburse him for them. The rest of the bill was mainly for antiques and home furnishings Rose had ordered. He made a good salary but he needed to rein Rose in at times. She never looked at the bills.

The dog and cat were pawing at the rear door begging to go out into their garden. Robin threw on a pair of faded jeans, sneakers and a polo shirt. As he unlocked and opened the door the animals raced out into the yard. They seemed to smell familiar memories. They tracked towards the woods and the overgrown path to the abandoned tennis court. The trees were covered with climbing ivy and purple wigelia vines. The trees were a mix of pines and oak, here and there were some dogwoods. The ground was soft and soon Robin's footsteps topped the imprints of a smaller shallower imprint. The dog and cat stopped, the dog seemed to point with his nose and tail outstretched; his left front leg was raised and flexed. In the clearing on a stone slab was Tevia. Robin stood at the edge of the court as she motioned him to join her at the midcourt bench. He felt awkward and didn't know how to retreat. As he approached, she patted the bench as a sign for him to sit down, which he obeyed. Before he could clear his mouth of its sticky dryness she told him to be quiet and give her a chance to speak.

She said that she wanted to try to explain her behavior. Tevia said that she had chosen Robin for her lust not because she loved him. She said "I needed you." She explained that Antonio, her husband, had become so jealous of Robin's success that he seethed with anger. This resentment and jealousy had made him physically ill, impotent, and abusive to her. She said that Antonio was distancing himself from everyone including her. When she had tried to initiate physical intimacy he claimed that she was trying to kill him. When she suspected that he was having arousal difficulties she checked with his cardiologist and found the Viagra was not contraindicated. She bought some and suggested that he might want to try them. This offer caused him to fly into a rage. In retaliation she called him a "wet noodle" and flew from the house. It was then that she saw Robin in his garden and her rejection and wanton desire to be held by someone, took control. She appeared to present her case as if she was not asking for forgiveness or understanding but as if she wanted to be treated clinically. It was as if she was presenting herself as a patient in desperate need. She presented her desire as if it was a malady seeking the cure and he was the chosen doctor. Robin thought about how the payment for medical treatment with sex was forbidden in the Hippocratic Oath. This was not payment and this was treatment prescribed by the patient. Robin wondered whether he was dreaming while trying to rationalize away his guilt with the needs of this woman.

Tevia asked Robin not to judge her harshly. She did not ask for forgiveness, but rather for understanding. She told Robin that at one time she loved Antonio as no other but she did not know how long she could be mentally abused and isolated from her needs. The one favor that she warned Robin that she might ask was if she had to leave Antonio, could she work in the Cancer Center labs? She had to have some means of sustenance and she had a degree in molecular biology and immunology. After the request she stood, gently kissed Robin on his cheek and turned up the trail toward her house. Robin looked down he was embarrassed. He said "I will see what I can do to help you." He was nervous and anxious to get away from her. He whistled for Argo and Tiger to retreat from the tree trunk where they had treed a squirrel frightened for his life with nuts still bulging in its cheek pouches. The three headed home to prepare for Rose and Paul's return.

~~~~~~~~~~~

Rose flew home thinking about her son Paul and his bleeding disorder. She was strong and felt confident that she would be able to protect him without smothering him. During the return trip, Rose was also replaying the interactions of Tomas and Robin. She mentally sorted and stored all of the reminiscences of the past week. Her mind was computing in a manner she had not experienced since she left the investigative unit of the CRA. She then thought back on her trip to Budapest. She was almost sure that Maria's sons, Tomas and Robe Gutta (Goode), were the nephews of the brothers Ted and Sig she had interviewed seven years previously. Rose was disappointed about the aborted trip to Budapest. She had hoped that the trip would have allowed a natural unraveling and solution to the mystery. This incompleteness of her studies on the missing loot from the train at Salzburg still left her perplexed and frustrated.

At the Birmingham airport Robin greeted Rose with a bouquet of roses and a kiss so hard and deep on her mouth that she fleetingly wondered what had transpired in his psyche during her absence. She had to calm him as he tossed Paul skyward and hugged him tightly. She loved Robin deeply but he was still a mystery to her.
~~~~~~~~~~~

CHAPTER 17

Robin persisted in his belief that the reason certain patients got cancer was their innate loss of the ability to inhibit, reject, and destroy the numerous aberrant proliferating clones of cells that arose in everyone. This process was either a failure of a natural clock and rheostat that limited the repair responses to tissue "wear and tear" or a defect in the surveillance normally preventing foreign genetic material from surviving or multiplying in the host. He knew that indiscriminate non-selective chemotherapy was only a temporary strategy that would eventually end in either the cancer cells escaping or in death of the patient from the injury to vital non-cancerous tissues and organs.

Even far back in the evolution of life, organisms had developed multiple strategies for containing and destroying foreign or aberrant cells, bacteria or viruses. Life forms developed a panoply of approaches, which include molecules that bind, poison, or digest life foreign to "self".

In the past century, medicine had focused on either direct methods to kill pathogens such as antibiotics, or on vaccines to enhance the organism's ability to mount an antibody or immune defense to a known pathogen. The key, Robin thought, was to devise enhancements of the defenses against diseases where the pathogen was either undefined or unknown. Robin decided to look for the chinks in the natural armor that allowed the growth of tumor cells in cancer patients. He outlined some of the places where answers might be sought. There was a comparison of those who got cancer with those who did not. There was the possibility of finding patients who had either destroyed or neutralized the offending neoplasm. There was the analogy of pregnancy where the mother was able to sustain the presence of foreign cells, even if it was for a limited time.

One of the research projects that Robin decided to pursue was based upon an interaction with a scientist he had met during a flight from Denver to Chicago after a site visit to the University of Colorado. Mike McNaught had told him that he had been working on trying to purify, from the urine of pregnant women, human chorionic gonadotropin and that HCGH seemed to have suppressive effects on the ability of killer T cells to attack a variety of tumor cells. Robin corresponded with Mike for several years and they would get together for a beer when they found themselves at the same meetings. McNaught had moved from Ireland to England as a lad during WWII. He had an impeccable pedigree. At Cambridge he earned his doctorate. His thesis advisor went on to win two Nobel Prizes. In the ensuing years McNaught had been on the faculties of MIT, Yale and Johns Hopkins where he had taught a multitude of graduate students and colleagues the science and art of protein purification. He was legendary in the field of protein purification; his techniques had opened the doors for structural protein chemists and crystallographers. His work in protein sequencing and identification of mutations led to the validation of the genetic code and to the molecular approach to biology and human genetics.

McNaught was always around to teach and to BS. He smoked so much that when he ran out of fags he found a few puffs in a butt relit from the overflowing ashtray. His house was littered with beer cans, the microwave splatted with exploded remnants of "nonmicrowavable" cooked foods. To the grad students, McNaught was an old hippy. To him research was an avocation rather than a vocation. When he ranted about the idiotic reviews on his grant applications he always ended up saying, "Well, I guess if you can't take a joke you shouldn't be in this business." The NIH stopped sending original critique pink sheets because McNaught had shown everyone how to disperse the inked over priority scores with Clorox. Eventually McNaught gave up his nocturnal activity of grant writing and ran his research on handouts and rummaging. His pillaging got so bad that grad students coded their reagents so that they wouldn't disappear at night.

Other than failing to obtain grants, most of McNaught's life had been a success. He had been a star athlete at Cambridge and even gone to the Olympics as a contestant in the 10,000-meter race and a team member in the relays. His thesis on the active site of serine proteases was a classic. Only recently had McNaught entered into a quest that had him up against the ropes. He was befuddled on how to deal with his wife Mary's breast cancer. She had been his pal and lived only to protect her eccentric husband from the banality and cruelty of the real world. McNaught talked to everyone who would listen about how he thought that the breast cancer was masking itself from the attack of the immune system. He always refocused on the analogy to the maternal-fetal interactions.

Robin had invited McNaught to relocate from Baltimore to Birmingham because he needed someone to guide his team on the isolation and purification of potentially unique tumor protein antigens. What Robin did not know was that McNaught was removing some of the antibodies generated and injecting them into his wife Mary. This was a tragic soap opera where a scientist, stymied and confused by the complexity of cancer and desperate to save his mate, purposely ignored any codes governing or limiting human experimentation. McNaught probably knew the inevitable outcome but refused to passively permit her demise. His battle was part of the din of gossip that so often serenades academic institutions. In this case, the rumor mill was not of the usual derogatory malicious nature but was rather sympathetically sweet and poignant.

CHAPTER 18

Shortly after Robin's abruptly aborted trip to Austria, a call came from a former fellow who had returned to Bergamo northeast of Milan to practice oncology. There was a patient who wished to come to the US for treatment of his lymphoma. The next day, Senor Vincente Morella arrived in Birmingham on his private jet accompanied by his oncologist, a nurse and his wife. Robin reviewed the case and after meeting with Morella decided to present this case to the oncology clinical and scientific research group. In short, Morella was in his late 50s and had a widespread stage IV lymphoma with enlarged lymph nodes and bone marrow involvement. The tumor seemed to be growing rapidly. Morella was a very successful businessman who had parlayed his father's seed and veterinary supply company to one of the largest biotechnology companies in the world. Morella had hired literally hundreds of PhDs to engineer products that could enhance the quantity and quality of meat, poultry, and fish. The annual revenue of his companies was more than 10 billion dollars, and negotiations were in progress to acquire a petrochemical and pharmaceutical corporation.

Morella told Robin that he had a grandchild due in several months and that he wanted to see, enjoy, and spoil this child in a manner he had not been able to do with his children. Prior to coming to the USA, Morella had shopped for treatment. There was no histocompatible match for a bone marrow transplant. He was now willing to try unconventional approaches to therapy. Cost was not to be a factor in designing the therapy.

The cast of the big "C" group, as Robin's oncology group was nicknamed, was diverse. Sven Sorensen was from Sweden. He had some of the attributes of Schwarzenegger in the Terminator and dealt with terminal patients so often that behind his back he was called "Dr. Death." Heifity was an Israeli studying cell death who had come from the Haddash University in Jerusalem. Son of Polish immigrants he had been an Israeli commando on the Entebbe rescue mission and had fought in Lebanon. Dr. Sidiqqui was a Syrian who had studied immunology in Paris and specialized in infections in immune suppressed patients. Dr. Vermai, a serine, gorgeous, sari clad Indian was a clinical pharmacologist who worked closely with Dr. Pillich, a German from the Max Plank Institute, who held 46 patents on chemotherapeutic agents. His friend called him "poison pill." Shawn O'Brien, a Celtic hard-bodied thirtyish blond pushing 5'4, ran the clinical immunology laboratory when he wasn't on his Harley Davidson. Conversely, when he wasn't working, he was riding, sometimes on dirt bikes. He knew every pub for three states and they knew him. Occasionally Robin rode with him. The females found Shawn an enigma. Dr. Fen Chen was a molecular biologist; she had been an MD in China but decided to do science. First, she went to Amherst and studied embryology and then to MIT where she became a leader in the field of angiogenesis, the formation of blood vessels. She was internationally known for her development of methods for localizing protein antigens in cells. She was an artist in her work. She had been married to a Chinese physician who could not stand to be second fiddle to her and divorced her to marry his receptionist. Science was now her love and life. Males were only distractions.

The cast occasionally changed over the past five years, but most had remained with the "C" team. Two thirds of their lives were spent in labs along common corridors. They rarely socialized outside of the cancer center. They were loyal to Robin and vied for his attention even as they matured into independent senior scientists. Since most did not have conventional family lives, Robin became their surrogate dominant parent figure. As bizarre as they might be normally, he knew when they were hurting. Occasionally, though not often, the oldest of the group tried to reciprocate with advice for Robin. After all, they were all high-pressure people. Beyond the main group were the post docs, fellows, technicians, and secretaries. The sustenance of the substructure was essential for productivity. The branches of the team had so many limbs and leaves that Robin yearned for the simpler approach which he had with his mentor Max Bluda in New York. The variables to be considered and monitored when a team became this large approached the complexity of a medium sized corporation. There was a fine line between dilettante creativity and chaos. Freedom of expression and interpretation were handled democratically but focus was often provided by Robin. Robin did not take the addition of Tevia, Dr. Rigatoni's estranged wife, into the "C" group lightly. Tevia's credentials were very good, but he always felt a pang of guilt when she passed in the hall or rode in the same elevator car. More than once the crowded elevator forced them against one another. He did not know what to say or think as their eyes made contact. Her brown black eyes only mirrored his reflection.

The team proposed to try to prepare a monoclonal antibody to one of the proteins on Mr. Morella's tumor. Again they would have to remove a sample of tumorous tissue. They would dissolve the membrane proteins in a detergent and separate them on the basis of their net charge and size or stokes radius. At the end of the analyses the proteins were separated using two dimensional electrophoresis and stained so that at least 400 silver stained proteins could be separated from each other. The processing of candidate proteins from cancer cells for cellular uniqueness was performed by comparisons to proteins from non-malignant tissues.

The pattern on the electrophoresis gels was studied the way astronomers study the sky. The common features became lampposts or navigational buoys in the topographical analysis. Robin looked at so many gels that he saw their patterns like scotomata or dark spots on his retina. After several months and 1800 gels, it was apparent that there were at least 30 dectable differences between the proteins from normal lymphoid tissue and the tumor. Some proteins were enhanced and some were diminished. The focus was on the enhanced expression but it was hard to tell whether the differences were due to alterations in the primary amino acid composition or to secondary modifications.

The strategy was to isolate a candidate protein and analyze its peptide components using a mass spectrometer. In seconds the computer analyzed the patterns generated, then a laser was used to desorb the fragmented peptides. The structural and synthesis group decided to focus on peptides 8 amino acids in length that were charged but adjacent to the hydrophobic core of proteins embedded into the lipid membranes of the cells. The fragments were analyzed and recreated using solid-state syntheses. Eight candidates were chosen for generation of synthetic polymers. These synthetic polymers were then used to generate polyclonal antibodies in innoculated rabbits and then monoclonal antibodies in an in vitro hybridoma cell culture system developed at Cambridge University.

The resultant antibodies were tested for their strength of binding to their natural antigen in its cellular form. Also, panels of other adult embryonic and tumor tissue were stained with the antibodies to see if there were any unexpected cross-reactions. The candidate antibodies were genetically manipulated so that portions of the molecule were deleted and replaced with peptides that didn't cause immediate host reactions and destruction of the antibody.

The tour de force was the placement of a toxin on the end of the antibody molecule that was not necessary for cellular recognition. Mike McNaught's team was assigned the task of covalently binding the antibody with the toxin that would wreck havoc on the target's cancer cells organization and cause these cells to die. The killing portion of the hybrid molecule was a lectin prepared from castor beans. It was the same lectin, ricin, that the Bulgarian secret police used to kill Markov, a defector during the Cold War. A prick from a needle point on an umbrella had been rapidly affected in broad daylight on the Waterloo Bridge in London in 1978. It seemed that the binding and uptake of two molecules per cell would be enough to cause massive interruption of cellular protein synthesis, complete dissolution of the cytoskeletal-membrane organization and subsequent cell death. However, the C team knew that the window for killing the tumor was short since the body could mobilize defenses against this antibody-toxin.

Working day and night the team prepared a "killer antibody" in 2.5 months. There was teamwork and plenty of night shift work. The last step before trials on the tumor cells was the conjugation of the antibody with ricin molecules and the separation of the unbound ricin and unbound antibody.

McNaught activated the antibody and after the incubation he placed the mixture on a sugar affinity chromatographic column. He separated the modified from unmodified antibody. The product was concentrated, resuspended into an appropriate buffer solution, and filtered to remove and destroy any bacteria or any endotoxin that could make the patient sick.

A test of cytotoxity using varying dilutions was run on a multi-well tissue culture plate. Dr. Fen gave the brew her good housekeeping seal of approval. The crew all left for the night except for Mike. He had to see to the proper labeling of the product. He worked late into the night; he stacked, relabeled and placed all the tubes in the steel refrigerator.

The morning of July 7 was a hot humid day but the air was free of agra haze. As Robin dated the order sheet 7/7, he thought this represented a lucky permutation. He went over the risks with Mr. Morella who barely glanced at the consent form before he signed it. They inserted a PIC line into the deep veins in Mr. Morella's forearm. They didn't want any of the drug extravasiating into the tissues. A nurse would give the drug with Shawn O'Brien in attendance. Within one minute of the injection, Mr. Morella became contorted; it seemed like every muscle and went into a rigor. People scrambled, a code was called, and an injection of atropine was administered. He was shrunken into a curled ball without any vital signs within three minutes. There was not enough time to do anything but a perfunctory resuscitation.

Immediate post-mortem samples were removed and the remainder of the vial of the reagent was secured. A recording of the procedure was made and sent for transcription. Only then was the body taken to the morgue for an autopsy. The autopsy suite was in the basement of the medical center. It had just been remodeled. Instead of being a bleak, dingy room with a table and assorted knives and scissors laid out on a corkboard with jars of formalin, it was now space age. There were two rooms connected by a sealed glass partition, a hermetically sealed door keeping the pressure negative in the actual dissection room. The suits for the pathologist and assistant were sealed and reminiscent of those of astronauts or deep-sea divers because the tubing for the sealed suit had a phalange, which locked into either a tethered tube or a backpack canister, allowing air to be delivered. The gloves were fine-chained mail, like something medieval knights would wear in combat. There were moon boots with disposable covers. On the exit side there were special containers for the soiled or potentially contaminated clothing and an area to sterilize any specimens that were to leave the autopsy room for further studies. The rooms were all bathed in ultraviolet light when the suite was not in use. All of the renovations had been made because of the fear of the spread of diseases such as AIDS, hepatitis, and rare brain degenerative diseases. It made one wonder how the pathologists and deaners of the past hundred years had ever survived.

Physicians who went to observe autopsies rarely went inside the dissection area. They usually were behind the glass partition and could see the finer details on a color monitor suspended from the ceiling. They were connected to the prosectors by a two-way audio system so that they could ask questions.

The autopsy on Morella was not difficult because it was obvious that his red blood cells had aggregated and lysed. The burst red blood cells had released their pigmented hemoglobin. Also, there were microscopic clots in blood vessels throughout the body causing pinpoint hemorrhages on the surface of most of the major organs. Blood samples were analyzed for the presence of the ricin toxin. In addition to analysis for the acute cause of death, the pathologists documented and measured the extent and spread of the lymphoma throughout the body. They found the pearly white rubbery deposits of tumor in lymph nodes along the abdominal aorta, in the groin, in the porta hepatis adjacent to the liver, in the spleen, around the surface of the heart and in the peribronchial nodes in the lung. Even Robin was surprised at how extensive the tumor was, but that did not assuage his remorse about the adverse effect of the immunotoxin injection.

About two days after the autopsy, the pathologist came to talk with Robin and told him that there was almost surely free ricin toxin in the post mortem blood. He had injected one tenth of a milliliter into a rat and it had died within several minutes. These findings confirmed what Robin had suspected but had subjugated until now. Robin took the elevator to his 8th story office and stared out the tinted glass windows at the city and the surrounding hills. He could make out the iron statute of the Vulcan in the distance; this locked his gaze towards the direction where he knew his home was. His brief reverie was interrupted by the sounds of shouting from the hallways.

Robin stepped into the corridor and ran toward the laboratories. He pushed through the small crowd of white lab coats and found Mike McNaught sprawled on the floor, lips tinged a bluish shade. His extremities gave a few spasmodic contractures. Robin bent over and caught the heavy aroma of almonds. He whispered his goodbye and stood to prevent an excited nurse rushing in to attempt mouth-to-mouth resuscitation. He knew that there was a chance and that her life would be at risk. As Robin stood he saw the amber shaded reagent bottle labeled sodium cyanide on the counter. He screwed the lid back on tightly and replaced it in the reagent cabinet. The attendants had placed McNaught on a gurney and strapped him in for the hurried trip to the emergency room. Robin followed at a slower pace and by the time he reached the ER, the on-call resident physician pronounced McNaught DOA. He walked back to his office and after he closed the door he cried. He had lost a dear friend.

The funeral was attended by at least a hundred of McNaught's friends and colleagues. Some even flew in from other universities. Robin gave the eulogy. Mike McNaught had truly been a great man. With all his personal sadness, he still brought joy to all around him. Even with all his education and knowledge he was a man who took the time to taste and feel the world around him. A jovial mask hid his fears and frustrations. The wake was not a somber occasion; there was no wailing or remorse. There were a series of limericks, the poetry of Mike McNaught.

> "There was an old man from Dublin town.
> He walked around with a wrinkled frown.
> Cause there was a young lass from Cork
> Who thought he was just an old dork"

The verses went on and on and after each stanza a raised arm and glass held high toasted the departed scholar. Their speech began to slur as the whiskey worked to keep them from becoming maudlin. Taxis were called to take them to the cemetery. The phone rang and O'Brien answered it saying, "McNaught's Den of Iniquity". He handed the phone to Robin. Rose told Robin "Mary, Mike's wife, had died peacefully in her sleep."

The next day as Robin sat still, somewhat dazed and dulled from the post-funeral festivities. He thought about McNaught and without malice cursed his foolishness. His trusted friend had let him down. The extent of Morella's lymphoma and inexorable outcome were of little solace to Robin.

Robin awoke with a dry cottonmouth and a dull throbbing headache that resulted from "tying one on" at the wake. Even he with all the years of insulating himself from death found it hard to weather all the dying that had occurred in the last 48 hours. He hoped that they had buried this spell of misfortunes. Robin had already made plans for assuring quality control of any future experimental therapeutics. He would have log books with records of synthesis purification testing, and each entry and reagent bottle tag would have to be signed by two senior members of the "C" team. The reagents would be stored in locked cabinets, refrigerators, or freezers. He would have to move from the open access lassez-faire mode to a structured secure system. After Robin got out of the shower and gargled one more time to get rid of his last night's foulness, he dressed and lightly kissed Rose and Paul goodbye without awakening them and then rushed off to work at 5 a.m.

Something had been gnawing at him and he decided to stop by the security police and check it out. He asked Sgt. Reily, a burly ex-city cop who covered the graveyard shift, whether the security cameras recorded the entry and exit of all personnel and visitors to the cancer center. Reily said that the cameras were mounted above all the exits and that the recordings were kept active for the previous six-month block. Robin asked him if he could have access to the 7/6-7/7 night record. He took the tape to his office and rolled in the VCR from the departmental library. With a pen and pad, he recorded the names and times all persons who entered or left the center. At 12:15 a.m. Mike McNaught left; he even stopped to light a half-smoked butt as he walked out. Just as Robin was about to flip off the machine he saw a figure in a black raincoat with a buckle tied around the waist. The face was indistinct. The collar of the coat was upturned, and a dark brimmed hat sat low on the figure's head. Forty-five minutes later the same hurried figure left the building. Robin replayed the tape several times. He wasn't sure who the figure was but he had a strong indication that who ever it was, they were up to no good. The night of the 6-7th had been rainy and cool so the clothing apparel was not inappropriate enough to arouse attention from anyone, including the security police at the control TV monitoring station. It was not unusual for the research fellows to come and go when they had experiments or work that ran throughout the night. Robin made a mental note to request a security identification system that required a bar-coded photo ID card for entry into and exit from the building.

After replaying the security film several times, Robin decided to catalog every fact about the clandestine figure that he could discern. He projected the image onto the wall with an overhead optical apparatus used for their oncology conferences. He adjusted the size of the figure so that they were life sized by calibrating with his own image at 6'2". He then projected images of his staff whose height he roughly knew. He figured that if he needed more accurate measurements he could get it from their personal data sheets on file. He knew Shawn's height to be 5'4" because he had born the brunt of being the runt in frequent jokes. When he measured the height of the unknown figure, it came out to be between 5'7" and 5'8". Unfortunately the camera's view did not capture the lower part of the body and he could not tell whether the person was wearing slacks, sneakers, or shoes. In a less precise manner, Robin attempted to reconstruct the physical features such as the shoulder size and waist girth. He felt somewhat like a physical anthropologist. At the end of his observations he had only a sketchy outline of an endomorphic figure of moderate height, nondescriptly clothed.

The sun had risen and it was now 8:10 a.m. Robin turned off the lights, closed up the library conference room and returned to his adjacent office. Other workers were arriving and he didn't want to arouse unnecessary suspicions and rumors about his activities. He sat down and began to answer his email and to dictate some of the answers to the correspondence. His secretary brought him some coffee and a bagel and cream cheese. He chuckled to himself about how the New York bagel had inoculated itself into the culture of the Deep South. At approximately 9:00 a.m. the phone rang and his secretary told him that it was Dean Esterly's office asking him to be in the Dean's office in ten minutes.

Robin walked across the bridge connecting the cancer center to the University Medical School Administration Offices. The double glass doors opened into an emporium that was out of context with the austere décor of the surrounding school. Most of the entry way and offices were in modern glass steel and teak wood. The Dean's secretary, Martha, told Robin to go in. He entered through a floor to ceiling massive wood double door. The room was enormous compared to the other offices in the medical center and the accoutrements were dazzling in this Victorian setting. There were gold figurines given by princes from the Saudi Arabia for services rendered in setting up medical exchange programs. There were bronze plaques from the AMA for dedicated political action and lobbying for more support for medical education. There was a gold gilded shovel from the corner stone laying ceremonies for the building of the new hospital. There was a photo of the Dean shaking hands with President Ronald Regan. On the wall behind the huge 12 x 4 mahogany ornately carved desk was the Dean's diplomas, his BA from Clemson, his MD from Vanderbilt, and his residency certificates from the University of Alabama in General Surgery.

The Dean looked up and then stood up and motioned for Robin to sit in a high backed chair. The Dean came from behind his desk and sat in an adjacent chair upholstered in burnished brown leather. He did not shake hands nor make any gesture of hospitality. The chairs were set off in an alcove where the walls had tapestries of scenes of crusading knights and a carved wooden pietá. This area of the office was church-like in its serenity and religiosity.

The Dean sat with his right leg crossed over his left leg. His polished cordovan shoes reflected the light from the adjacent lamp. His hands were outstretched on the arms of the chair and on his right hand was a prominent college ring with a ruby stone and some engraving. On his left hand he wore a solid gold wedding band. His tie was solid blue with a caduceus gold tie tack. His shirt was white with blue monogrammed initials on the cuffs. His round face was smooth and a flat top of golden brown hair covered his head with a small cowlick at the rear. He removed his gold wire rimmed glasses and stared at Robin for a few moments before his pursed lips opened.

"I have had to call you in because I have received the news about the therapeutic misadventure leading to the death of one of your patients. The exact reason for this fiasco is unclear to me but I will be conducting an inquiry."

"The death of your colleague, McNaught, which was signed out as a massive myocardial infarct seems very sudden for an in hospital death and there was a reported failure to initiate resuscitative measures. I find this perplexing. The almost simultaneous death of his wife seems somewhat coincidental and suspicious."

"Your unit in the oncology department has developed a reputation of freewheeling activities. O'Brien in his black leather and adorned Harley motorcycle has been seen in every unsavory part of the city including porn shops, gay bars, and brothels. I have been told that you have accompanied him on some these motorcycle jaunts."

"By the way, we have not seen you or your lovely wife in church since the baptism of your son. You would set a better example for the medical community if you showed more piety."

Robin felt as if he was being accused of being a heathen. He had always felt more agnostic than atheistic. Growing up in a communistic society he had never felt deeply moved about organized religion. He could take it or leave it, but no one had ever confronted him on his lack of religious zeal. He had agreed to Paul's baptism because that was what Rose wanted. At first, Robin was offended by the Dean's intrusion into his personal life and beliefs, but realized that the Dean was often proselytizing. He was an elder in the church and his conversations often were sermons from his Sunday school teaching. Over the years Robin had learned to tune out the preaching and ignored it so that it was impersonal and inoffensive. The present encounter was so pointedly directed at him that Robin was beginning to feel uncomfortable. The comments no longer dealt with lack of religious fervor and knowledge, but broached a chastisement for immorality.

The Dean's next comment confirmed Robin's concern. The Dean said that it had been reported that Robin had an illicit affair with another faculty member's wife. This affair had disrupted a marriage and was sinful behavior on Robin's part. He said that he understood human frailty and even confessed to having lustful thoughts at times in his life, but he suggested that Robin needed to repent and atone for his sinful behavior by reaffirming his religious obligations.

Robin was completely caught off guard. He had no inclination that anyone knew or suspected of his liaison with Tevia. His face flushed for a moment. He then regained his composure and told the Dean that he had no idea of what he was referring to. He told the Dean that he would tighten up the security and scrutiny of this group's professional activity, but that he could not be responsible for their social activities. He never made any reference to the personal accusation not wanting to give them credence or confess to them. Inside, Robin was fuming. Never in his life had he felt so berated. Never had his social life intermeshed or impinged upon his professional endeavors.

The Dean got up out of his chair as a signal that the conversation was ended. Robin walked out. He put his lab coat in his office, had his secretary cancel his day's appointments, drove home and put on his leather-riding outfit. He jump-started his Magada motorcycle. A bust of black smoke from the exhaust filled the garage. He pulled the black helmet over his head and pulled down the plastic visor. He headed out onto the highway. The speedometer flicked between 100-120 KPM. The hefty cycle gave him a feeling of his Hungarian heritage. Something about the bike, of the four that he owned, gave him a feeling of courage. It was as if the cycle bound him like he was a charging knight at a tournament fighting for his pride and life.

CHAPTER 19

Avraham Lander (Rolfe) had amassed a substantial amount of money from his money laundering activities. He had never touched any of the capital from the recovery of the treasure nor from the sale of the artwork. That money had been used for his former family and ex in-laws, for resettling DPs and for excavating and resettling persecuted Soviet Jews. In between his work and travel, Avraham made excursions in Austria and Israel where he spied or checked up on his family. His did not reveal his identity to them. Occasionally he would do some reconnoitering for the Massad. The missions were only observational in nature and were never truly covert operations. Nevertheless he did have a few brushes with the police in Hungary.

In the 1980s, Avraham spent most of his time in Israel where he became involved in establishing a computer company that eventually branched out into a web informatics service. He also helped found a company that manufactured medical laser equipment. His main activities were in Haifa and Tel Aviv, but he maintained an apartment in Jerusalem. Whenever his business drew him to Jerusalem he would walk to a café from which he could see his ex-wife Julia's house. He kept tabs on her and over the years watched her and her family. He saw her son grow and leave home. He watched her beautiful black hair turn gray. He was at the funeral services for her second husband, Myron Katz. He watched her reorganize her life so that charitable activity and creative stitchery filled the hours of her days.

Avraham yearned so much for a reunion. As old as he was he would have palpitations when he saw Julia. One day when she was having a glass of tea and sewing an image onto a framed cloth at a café, he sat down at an adjacent table. He glanced over and saw her weaving a Matisse. It was the image of a woman whose head was covered by an ornate embroidered shawl. With his heart pounding, Avraham commented to Julia on the extraordinary beauty of her stitchery and struck up a conversation about Matisse and art. He could feel the sweat in the palms of his hands and held the arms of the chair to keep him from shaking in his excitement. Julia invited the old bearded man to join her. Their conversation strayed from art to travel and to her. He artfully maneuvered the topics so that she was the focus. After an hour he excused himself saying that he had a business appointment but not before he asked if he could meet her again the next day for tea.

Avraham left and went to his apartment. He undressed, showered the nervous perspiration from his body and lay down. He noticed a lumpy discomfort under his left arm. A peaceful wave of relaxation rolled over his body and he fell into a deep sleep. The memories of Julia, Maria, Robe and Tomas wove together. His dreams mixed up time and people and places. A reoccurring scene was at a ball with glittering chandeliers. The guests were all were dressed formally. The women wore beaded glittering gowns and his boys wore silken suits. The orchestra played as they danced. He twirled Julia while Tomas and Robe whirled off with Maria. As the music grew louder and faster, the drum beat exploded as if artillery shell. Avraham awoke to a new day.

Julia felt a warm tingle. She had put on a new floral silk georgette dress and checked her face in the mirror several times before leaving her house. She had added a touch of blush, combed her hair and let it fall loose out of the bun she normally wore. She put on a diamond pendant on a gold chain that she had brought when she fled Budapest almost 50 years ago. She carried a tote bag with her stitchery. Her lips parted and a smile spread acrossher face as she locked her door and faced this new sunny day.

Julia sat slowly sipping her iced tea. She wondered if the old man would return. She glanced at her watch and realized that she had arrived 20 minutes early. This was unusual for her and she felt as if some internal force was propelling her. She had a premonition that today was going to be new and different. She had slept well but was awakened with reminiscing visions of her family in Budapest before the war. The dreams had ended without any conclusion and they vanished into a mixture of fleeting memories.

The Hassid who Julia had met the previous day seemed changed as he approached her table. His beard was trimmed, his clothes seemed to have a freshness of being cleaned and pressed, and he stood taller and straighter as he approached with his silk black hat in his hand. He was well over six feet and had grayish black hair. He had on stylish aviator sunglasses.

They spent the next two hours discussing art from the impressionists to the modern and post-modern. Their favorites seemed to be the sculpture of Rodin, Moore, Epstein, Brancusi and Calder, and Modigliani. The conversation was focused on art and was definitely diverted from personal revelations. They seemed to psychologically dance with each other without venturing into revealing who they really were. It was as if a boundary was in place to keep these flitting mating moths from entering a candlelight's treacherous flame of revelation and destruction. Even with this subconscious gate, an intimacy seemed to be emerging. Neither was ready to probe further. After several hours, Julia found herself wondering what the magnetic attraction was that drew her to this old man.

They committed themselves to a third meeting and an outing to view the Chagall stain glass windows in the Synagogue of the Hadassah-Hebrew University Medical Center. The day was dry and sunny with only wisps of powdery white clouds sailing off to the Southeast. He had hired a taxi for the excursion. They crossed the city and chattered about how expansive the city had gotten. She reminisced on how when she first came to Jerusalem from Tel Aviv they could only go to the Mandelbaum Gate and that in order to view the Wailing Wall you had to keep your head low so that snipers didn't use you for target practice. She had become interested in medical research and she and her husband wanted to be near their son who was working in molecular immunology at the Hadassah University.

The ride took about 35 minutes. When they got there they walked around and looked at the magnificent colored glass windows depicting the biblical stories of the 12 sons of Jacob who gave rise to the 12 tribes of Israel. They strolled into the adjacent park and she unpacked her small canvas bag. She had prepared polystyrene cups with a Hungarian goulash, which they ate with plastic utensils. She had a thermos of iced tea. The taste and smell of the heavily spiced meats and sauce sent Avraham into an oliphatory stupor. He closed his eyes and squeezed the lids tight to keep him from losing his composure.

Julia watched this man dressed in a new silk black suit and white shirt. She was overcome with a feeling of familiarity. The sudden squall blew her hair like it had when she stood on the deck of the ship that had brought her from Limassol, Cyprus to Hafia in 1939. The sky darkened, thunder echoed off the hills, and a few bolts struck in the distance. A drenching rain suddenly pelted them. As they scrambled and hurried to the waiting taxi, he took off his coat and held it over her head. His soaked shirt stuck to his chest and arms.

Once in the small Fiat cab and on their way toward Julia's house, she rung out his jacket and he wiped the water from her forehead. Her light eye shadow and rouge ran. Her elderly face had a majestic but surreal and comical image. When she caught sight of herself in the rear view mirror of the taxi, she began to laugh. Avraham joined in. He had not laughed like this for almost 50 years. He reached for her hand and held it gently.

When they reached Julia's she told him to pay the cab driver and come in. He obeyed. The scene had played and replayed in his head for decades. As they walked up the flight of stairs, Avraham could not avoid looking at her figure from behind and he thought that she was pretty svelte for a woman of 75.

When they reached the second landing, she passed the bundles to Avraham as she fished in her purse for the keys. The apartment was a Co-op and had a dining room/living room that opened onto a terrace balcony, a small kitchen and two bedrooms. The furniture was modest but the artwork was spectacular. The eclectic collection had many of her own woven paintings and clay sculptures. The colorful décor and plethora of potted plants reflected a love of nature.

She closed the door and began to help Avraham remove his wet shirt and hung it with his water logged jacket on a plastic hanger in the bathroom. She said "take off those silly sunglasses the sun has gone away." She seemed to have completely forgotten her normally modest demur. She went into the bedroom, slipped off her dress and put on a terrycloth bathrobe and slippers. When she returned she brought a man's robe from the spare bedroom closet. As she held it out for Avraham, she saw the faded crude tattoo on his forearm. The arms and chest gave her a chill because it all looked so familiar, but she thought that she was hallucinating. Perhaps her dreams were invading her waking state. She thought perhaps she was entering senility. She closed her eyes tightly as if to clear them of the illusions before her.

They both sat at a small kitchen table as she prepared and served tea with lemon. Julia asked Avraham where he was from and he answered

Budapest. She laughed and said in Hungarian, "What street and district did you live in?" He answered, "The Pest VII district Erzebetvaros, Kazinczy U. 177."

Julia's eyes opened wide, her lower jaw dropped every slightly. She walked to the far wall and took down a leather photo album. He watched as she removed a faded photo of a young woman standing in front of a townhouse with three men, two in suits and one in a military uniform.

She said this is the house at the address you have just given me. He did not answer. She reopened the album and removed another photo, larger than the first but it was the full body portrait of an officer in a formal uniform. She held it up and said, "Do you know who this person is?" Avraham looked deeply into her eyes.

His eyes were the wrong color, hazel color; his hair was black not brown, his nose was slightly hooked and did not have the slightly bent deformity the soldier had earned in a boxing match. She squinted at the general head shape and the distance between the orbits of eyes and mouth shape and size were the same in the photo and in the man across the table.

She asked, "Where did you get the concentration camp ID?" He answered that he was interred in Austria near Hallein.

Then Julia remembered the scar that her husband Rolfe had from a skiing accident when they went to Innsbruck. They had been jumping moguls and had collided with her pole piercing his subscapular region. The pole punctured and gashed upward leaving a linear shallow wound that bled and bled, healed slowly and subsequently scarred.

Julia in an audacious move got up, walked around Avraham, and lifted his white tee shirt. She bent over and kissed the scar. He turned to reciprocate when she slapped him hard.

She said, "Now that you have decided to come alive, broken and mended my heart, you have an eternity to unravel, Mr. Twisted Ghost, who has decided to metamorphose and crawl out from the shadows. Take your time; you have the rest of my life. But first where are my babies," she cried.

CHAPTER 20

A mixture of bliss and anger, love and resentment peppered the relationship between Julia and Avraham. He shaved and went back to wearing the usual informal attire of an elderly Israeli. Questions were asked and answered. Some things were broached but left unknown. They moved in together. Partially clad they held each other at night; their dreams melded. One would hum an old tune and the other would smile and tears would well up in both their eyes. How could the world have ever separated these two lovers?

At night she became aware of the discomfort he had under his left arm. He tried to hide his tenderness and the growing swelling. She asked what was wrong and he said it was nothing. His psychic energy was exuberant and he was elated. However, he noticed that his physical vigor was waning.

They planned a trip to Hungary. Together they would try to mend the broken branches of their family tree. They flew El Al to Rome and Air Italia to Budapest. Avraham had arranged for a driver to meet them at the baggage claim area and to drive them around the streets crowded with cars and motorcycles. They held each other's hands.

The couple got out of the taxi and walked through the wet snow. The flakes on Julia's hair glowed with light reflected from the street lamps, quickly melting into a wet sheen. Their home no longer existed; in its place was a contemporary three story attached brick and glass townhouse. They walked down the street and stopped in front of a taupe stucco house with large black shutters that were closed tight. This was the house Julia had indelibly etched in her childhood memories. The structure seemed much smaller than the mansion in her memories. A gas lamp flickered. The unshoveled snow showed no evidence of human entry or exit. The only prints in the fresh snow were from the paws of a stray cat.

Julia rang and the chimes resounded. She thought she could recognize the first notes of Beethoven's Ninth. She held Avraham's gloved hand. She rang again and the doors were opened. A white-haired old man holding onto a carved ornate wooden cane with his left hand stood before them peering over bifocals perched on his nose. He said, "What … is that you Julia?" His right hand went up and crossed over onto his chest over his heart. Almost fifty years apart, yet their recognition was instantaneous. Julia had not written ahead nor had she informed Ted of any of the events that had occurred in the past several months. She had told him nothing about Avraham's return.

Julia and Ted embraced. He held her so tight that her breath was forced from her with a gasp and she feared that he might break her bones. Ted, even though he was stooped, still was much taller than Julia and he bent to kiss her forehead and cheeks. It was then that he realized that they were still in the cold doorway and that there was a man standing behind her holding a suitcase.

Ted brought Julia into the foyer and motioned for her escort to come in also. He had them remove their overcoats, scarves and gloves. They all shuffled into the living room where there was a blazing fire. Both Julia's and Avraham's eyes opened wide. The room had been restored just as it had been before she left for Palestine. The portraits of her parents and grandparents hung on the wall leading to the dining room. On the mantle was a silver menorah. The Matisse of a fresh bathed woman, brought back from Paris by her father, was in a gilded frame on the west wall. The bookshelves were filled with leather-bound books. The piano, the cello and violin formed a ring on the east wall, as if they were waiting for musicians out on an intermission break. Julia walked over and gently caressed the violin she had been given by her grandfather when she was 12 and she slid her hand on the smooth shiny wood of her brother Sig's cello. The three had serenaded the Glucke family many nights when they were teenagers. In her head the Mozart Einekleine Nachtmusik played while she inspected the rest of the room. There was an empty space on the north wall where a small Degas ballerina had resided during her youth. She knew where the painting was. It had been delivered to her in Tel Aviv in the early 1950's by two Israelis who said they had orders to give the rolled up canvass in a cardboard cylinder only to her. When she wrote about this to Sig and Ted they said that the painting had been lost during the war and that they had no idea of how it was found or who returned it to her.

While Julia was reacclimating herself, Avraham looked about the familiar room. Ted followed them both with his eyes. Then he asked Julia, "Who is your friend?"

Ted had sensed familiarity but he was not sure who the man was.

Julia in a flip manner said, "Oh, don't you remember my husband, Rolfe?"

Ted pushed his glasses down on his nose and peered over the top of the frame. He walked over closer to the stranger and stared at him carefully. He painted an imaginary beard on the man's face. He turned to Julia and said, "He looks more like a man who called himself Avraham and who came to pay Sig and me a visit many years ago."

Ted said, "Who are you? Avraham, Rolfe, or both?"

Julia turned to face the two men and asked, "Who is this Avraham you are referring too?"

Ted answered Julia and said that several years after the war a Hassid had come to the restaurant where he and Sig were working. This mysterious man had led them on a mission into Austria to recover much of their family's stolen fortune. He recounted the story in great detail. Ted even went on to tell about the visit to Maria's building and the delivery of the Tintoretto. He paused when he got to the details about Maria and her family. The attention shifted back to Avraham. It became clear that he had disguised himself and had been involved with Israeli agents in reclaiming the stolen money and works of art.

Ted said that he had a lot of questions but suggested they sit at the table and he asked Julia to go to the kitchen and see what provisions were there. He apologized for the lack of help, but he had given the housekeeper the evening off.

Ted turned to Avraham and asked him why he had never identified himself and why he had not gone to get his two sons.

Avraham answered that he could not reveal himself because through contacts with the Israeli secret police and Interpol he found out that Rolfe Havas was a wanted man. He was a fugitive not only from the allies and Russians but from a cadre of underground Nazis who believed that he had stolen the Nazi gold and artworks. He believed that the Russians were watching Maria the boys and that any attempt to make direct contact would have ended with his execution or imprisonment and banishment to a Gulag in the North or Eastern Siberia. He explained that the best he felt he could do was to restore most of the family's stolen money and art. He had hoped that Sig and Ted would realize who the boys were and would take care of Maria and his sons. For a long time Avraham did not dare to spend much time in Budapest. He was always afraid that someone might recognize him.

When Tomas and Robin left Hungry he kept up with their growth and education but only from a safe distance. He knew where they lived, something about their careers and he knew of his grandchild. He had caught a rare glimpse of Robin's wife and child in Vienna. He even recognized Robin's wife as an agent for the CRA, who had been trying to find the loot which he, Sig and Ted had recovered. He had great trepidation about any interaction with her. Avraham explained that he had watched Julia and only in the past few months, after the death of her second husband had he gotten the courage to speak to her. After his revelation and after her surprise and anger they had decided to return to Hungary and see if they could retrace and rebuild some kind of a life from the rubble of the past.

When Julia returned from the kitchen with some sandwiches and coffee the three of them spent hours filling in the details on the lost years. Julia listened intently and only asked only a few questions. She wanted to know why her brothers Ted and Sig did not go to Maria and try to get her children back.

Ted answered that they were afraid. They felt that anything that could raise their profile would put them at risk for scrutiny or punishment by the Soviet rulers or by their puppet communist regime. Also, they had no proof and were not absolutely sure that Maria's sons were their nephews. If they went to her and she raised a fuss they could have lost everything they had regained. They decided that the best course of action was to provide support through a third party. Ted described how their former assistant, Paul Werner had watched the boys. After the revolution and death of Maria, Sig and Ted quickly got Werner to take Robin and Tomas to Austria. Werner was given money for transportation for their papers, and money was sent for living expenses and tuition in boarding school and university. After the boys went off to college, Werner returned to Budapest. He was given a position in their cosmetics business and lived in their house.

After Werner's death, Ted and Sig arranged for a Swiss bank account for Robin and Tomas. The account was funded from money they had put into Werner's estate. After Sig's death Ted had only a few scattered reports on the whereabouts and lives of his nephews. He added that two years ago Sig died from a hemorrhage suffered after cardiac bypass surgery for blocked coronary arteries

The conversation went on through most of the night. Avraham became extremely tired and went to bed. He thought a thousand thoughts and planned and planned. First he would go to the cemetery and see Maria's grave. In the morning, he would go and see that the plot was cared for as she had cared for his children. It was chilly and foggy so Avraham took the electric trolley to the end of the line. From there he walked almost three kilometers to a small cemetery on the edge of Pest. He went to the care keeper's house and found the lot number and position of Maria Hanka Gutta's gravesite. He walked between the rows of low grave markers until he came to one small granite stone engraved with the name of Maria Havas Gutta 1911-1956, beloved mother of Tomas and Robe. He sat on the wet grass and said goodbye to the woman who had waited and wept for him. He thanked her for the love and care she had provided his two sons. He hoped she would forgive him for not having returned. On his way out he placed a stone next to the one that already sat on the top of the headstone. Avraham looked at the adjacent headstone and was surprised to see the name of Paul Werner, 1918-1972, who looked after his sons, buried next to his ex-wife, Maria. He realized that the gravesites must have been planned and paid for by the Glucke brothers. On his way out he placed a wad of US dollars into the grimy hands of the attendant and asked him to keep the two graves neat and well manicured.

After returning to his brother-in-law's house he asked Julia to remarry him. They went with Ted to the Dohany St. Synagogue when in a very private ceremony Rabbi Levy pronounced them man and wife. Avraham gave the Rabbi a thousand dollar check as a donation for the synagogue building fund. When they left the temple the sun was high and the three of them went for lunch. During the celebration Ted toasted the couple with mazel and nakis (luck and health). Avraham felt the lump under his left arm; it was larger and more discomforting than ever before. He was weary from his long journey but inside him there was contentment. He and Julia decided to tour the sites of their long departed youth and innocence. Julia visited the graves of her mother, father, and brother in a small Jewish cemetery. She had the vandalized tombstones straightened and washed them free of the painted swastikas. She placed the stones of remembrance on the ledges. She said a few kind words to the memory of each relative as tears fell from her eyes. Avraham and Julia left hand in hand. As they walked out of the cemetery, Avraham stumbled and Julia held him. She knew he was ill. As she grabbed him under his left arm she felt a lump and said nothing.

During the next several weeks, Julia, Avraham and Ted toured the sights of Budapest. They went to the spas and baths along the river shores. They even took an excursion to the summer home at Lake Balaton. They basked in the sun and took long hikes into the surrounding hills and forests. They probably overexerted themselves for they were reliving their lives of 50 years ago. One morning when Julia and Avraham knocked on Ted's bedroom door there was no answer. They waited several hours and postponed their planned picnic brunch, which was to be at the shore of the lake. At 10 o'clock they knocked again and this time they pushed open Ted's door. The large man lay still on his side in a fetal curled position. His eyes were closed. His face was slightly bluish. He did not respond to their calling voices. Ted had died peacefully at the age of 82 in his sleep.

Julia and Avraham took care of the burial details. They arranged for Ted to be buried the next morning in a gravesite adjacent to Julia's parents and brother Sig. The ceremony and eulogy were brief. In essence Ted was praised for his determination to survive. He and his brother endured the hardships of the war and together they built a very profitable cosmetic business. They were charitable and they gave extensively to organizations supporting the poor. After a brief shiva at Ted's house, Julia and Avraham hired a solicitor to see that the will was executed. The fortune was divided giving Julia 50% and her sons 50%. There were a lot of technical details and there was a limit on how much could be removed from the country. They decided to hire a manager to continue running the business on an interim basis.

The couple would return to Israel and try to find Avraham some medical attention and begin the search for their children.

CHAPTER 21

The Oncology Service at the U. of A was expanding rapidly and attracting patients from across the U.S. and from some overseas countries., Robin had hinted to Rose that he would like to go to Europe for a vacation. He was emotionally, physically, and mentally exhausted. The C team had enlarged and Robin knew that a short vacation would not impinge on the care of anyone coming to the center. While he was to be away, Dr. Knife would be in charge of the C team. Paul was left in the care of their Nanny. Even with all the planning, Robin took with him a cellular phone, worldwide pager, and a laptop computer that would connect through a modem to the Internet. He could teleconference with the C team from almost anywhere there was a satellite was in the sky. While the other laptops flashed colorful solitaire or battleship games, Robin used the flying time to write and proofread manuscripts and grant applications. Rose called home to check on Paul at each stop of the trip.

When Rose and Robin arrived in London it was the early morning. Tomas Robin's brother met them at Gatwick airport. They flew to Budapest on Lufthansa and got a limo to the Sheraton Hotel.

It was 32 years since Tomas and Robin had last seen the city. For Robin, the images seemed to come into focus, like the focusing of a camera on pictures already taken. The black and white fuzzy negatives imprinted in his brain turned into colorful live action. He went to the window to open the drapes and slowly scanned the skyline. Tomas talked a jag. Do you remember this or that, must be a new building, or remember when you, Mama and I went to the circus in that park over there?

The mention of his mother yanked Robin from his visual orgy back to the here and now. The three decided to go out for dinner and to plan what they would do during their stay. Rose had a dilemma.

She wanted to go to the court offices to look for certain records, but she also wanted to be with her husband as he recaptured some of his childhood memories. She had to pick and choose which excursions she wanted to go on. She also wanted to give Robin some time alone with his brother. When the brothers talked about going to the Rudas baths at the riverside and taking a svitz or steam therapy the next morning, she decided that would be a good time for her to meander and search for the data she wanted. Rose told the men that she would go shopping while they "washed away their sins at the baths."

Rose remembered the city from her visit in 1974. The change that impressed her most was the colorful western clothing, the rampant commercialism, prosperity, and upbeat enthusiasm. All this was contrasted to the grayness and sober attitude, which prevailed during her last visit. News stands were filled with papers and magazines from many countries including the United States. The shackles of communism had been removed and an exuberant euphoria had swept the city.

Rose walked to the old nineteenth century courthouse, most of which was remodeled. She asked a young clerk where she could find records of birth and marriages. She was directed to the third floor where she faced a young woman in her twenties behind a desk; Rose asked where she could find the records for births in the mid 1930s. The woman said that at the end of the war, bombs had landed on the building and these had burst the pipes. The old record repository had been in the basement and had been mostly destroyed by the subsequent fires and flooding. All of the records post-war were kept in a sealed section of the building. Rose asked what people did for passports and other documents. The clerk told her that everyone was reissued papers during the communist regime. People were allowed to come in and register and they were given new documents. The validity was often only as good as the memory of the person requesting IDs. These records were on a microfiche film reader and could be searched only by the last name and date of filing. Rose asked "Could I see those for the name Havas, Maria Havas." There were several listings but one seemed to fit the age of the woman she was looking for best. The data she got was Maria Havas-Gutta (Naé Marie Gutta) born in Prague in 1911. She found where Maria had registered Tomas and Robin Havas-Gutta. She listed their father as Rolfe Havas, MIA. Rose figured that Maria had to have these IDs in order for her sons to enroll in school and for her to get employment. There was no falsification but there was minimal data. The birth dates for Tomas and Robin were correct but their place of birth was given as Lenz, Austria. Rose wondered why Maria had changed their place of birth from Budapest. Could she have anticipated that this would facilitate their move into the West someday?

Rose had one other place to visit. It was the Dohany St. Synagogue. She remembered exactly how to get there. As she went in she remembered where Dr. Levy had his study and climbed the stairs to his office. She asked the secretary if she could visit with Rabbi Levy. Rose sat and waited until the Rabbi finished his morning prayers. When she entered his study, she saw a man appearing to be in his late 60s or early 70s, who stood to greet her. She introduced herself and reminded him of her visit here almost 20 years earlier. He said "time had unmeasurably altered her" and laughed. He extended his wrinkled hand and escorted her to a chair. He asked "For what great deeds am I bestowed two visits in a lifetime from a Nordic princess?" Rose blushed and reciprocated by saying "The well of knowledge and wisdom needs to be visited as many times as possible in order to see the truths of life." The two danced with words for a while when the Rabbi asked, "What can I do for you?" Rose answered, "When I came here last time you had me visit two brothers, Sig and Ted Glucke. Can you tell me where they are now?" The Rabbi answered by pointing upward. He said, "I assume since they led good lives that they went to the place where the good go after life. Physically they are buried in the Rakoskereszturi Jewish cemetery. Sig died 8 or 10 years ago and Ted died two months ago. Sig's sister, Julia, and her husband were here for the funeral. I presided over the graveside service." Rose felt a little frustrated. She had hoped that they could help her put some of the pieces in place. She asked the Rabbi for the address of Julia. He went to his appointment and account book and thumbed through the worn pages. He then remembered something else! "By the way," he said, "Julia Katz nee Julia Glucke has been in several weeks ago with this older Hungarian man." Rabbi Levy said that he had performed a brief wedding. The vows were made and the ceremonial glass was wrapped in a cloth napkin and crushed after they each sipped the wine from it.

Rose's eyes opened wide. The trail was not cold. It just led in another direction.

"Who was the new husband," she pondered. She copied Julia's address. Then she asked the Rabbi if he kept copies of documents from weddings he had performed. He said that he made three, one for the couple, one for the government and one he kept in his files. Also in his file was a copy of the Ketubah, the marriage contract. Rose was allowed to look at the Rabbi's copy. She found the name of Julia and the other name was difficult to read. The fist name was Avraham and the last name was scribbled and illegible. The print was like chicken scratches. Rose asked if she could make a copy on the Xerox machine in the receptionist's area. He allowed her to photocopy the certificate.

Rose was not sure which way the trail was leading but at least it wasn't cold. She went to the hotel and called home to check that her son Paul was behaving and staying out of trouble. The Nanny who worked for them while Rose worked at the hospital said everything was fine. Robin and Tomas returned to the hotel about 2:00 p.m. The brothers decided that they would go to see the gravesite of their mother. The three boarded the trolley and went to the cemetery. They walked silently to the caretakers hut and found out where Maria Havas Gutta was buried. When they arrived at the small headstone they were surprised to see two grave plots neatly tended in marked contrast to the surrounding sites. On Maria's marble grave stone there were two small stones. They looked over and were surprised when they saw that the name on the adjacent grave was Paul Werner, who had cared for them during their teenage and college years. One stone sat on his marker as well.

Rose stood to the side as Tomas and Robin each bent and silently seemed to pray. The sight was unusual because both brothers were not religious. Each seemed to apologize for not having come sooner. Each thanked their mother for the teachings, values, and kindness she had bestowed upon them. There was somber silence as each stood and said their goodbyes again. Then the brothers went over to Werner's grave each said a few words of remembrance. They thanked him for being a fine guardian and a faithful friend.

Rose watched silently. She wondered why these graves had been singled out for special care. On their way out of the cemetery, Rose stopped by the watchman's hut and thanked him for his extra special care at the two sites. He told Rose that an elderly gentleman had come about two months ago and that he had paid for the extra trimming and care. Laughingly, he said, "Not that it matters to the buried bodies." She gave him several coins and told him that he was doing a great service to those buried and their living relatives. She also got him to describe the elderly man who had paid for the extra gravesite care.

After dinner the three strolled past the site of the house where they had lived. They walked to the school they had attended. The next day there seemed to be a change in both Robin and Tomas. They were more jovial; almost a joie de vivre had replaced their serious intenseness. The closure with their mother seemed to lift a burden from both of them. Perhaps, thought Rose, this is a closure that these men needed. The three flew to Paris where they toured the town and had dinner at Pavillon Dauphine in the Bois du Boulogne. Rose danced with both of the brothers. Robin held her tightly and gave her an unusually romantic kiss after the last dance. He said "You are the most beautiful woman I have ever held in my arms." She rested her head on his shoulder and thought about what a wonderful man her husband was. Rose, Robin and Tomas cruised the Seine on a glass-enclosed boat and rode the elevator to the top of the Eiffel Tower. The next day they went to Charles de Galle Airport and the brothers embraced and hugged goodbye. Rose and Tomas kissed each other lightly and Robin and Rose flew home.

CHAPTER 22

When Robin went to work he reviewed the daily roster of patients. He noticed that there were 16 new patients. Six were residents of the state, eight were from other states, and four were from other countries. One patient was from South Africa, one from Greece, one from Italy and one was from Israel. Robin worked late into the evening reviewing the referral records the present admission examination, lab, X-ray and biopsy reports.

He rounded at 7:00 a.m. with the residents and Heme-Onc fellows. They finished at 8:00 p.m. Robin's energy level was very high. The vacation had made him more intense than ever. He wanted to call the pathology resident back in to go over the biopsies from the patients but decided that the review could wait until the morning. The pathologist didn't really like to get called in the evening. Anyway, he decided that he would like to spend some time with his son. The Paul was nearly ten and was quite precocious.

Even with all the protective precautions that Rose took, Paul had become an outstanding swimmer. Rose would not let him participate in any contact sports for fear of severe bruising or bleeding. She insisted on Paul playing the violin but he really didn't want to practice. The boy loved to hike in the woods with Robin and became very adept at identifying the flora and fauna. With Robin's help, they had built a terrarium and were trying to construct a mini biosphere that would require minimal external nutrition or water. It was a tricky project that led to philosophical debates on the nature of nature, God, the universe, creation, reproduction, existence and death. The interaction between father and son became almost a religious rite for Robin. The bonding with Paul filled a void in his own life. There was a transcendental quality to their interaction. No Mr. Wizard on a TV tube could mimic this relationship. The discoveries were not that of a teacher-student. The pair was learning together of and about the world, about each other, and of and about themselves. There was no course syllabus, no guidebook, and no encyclopedia for this type of filial relationship. The more Robin mentored, the more he became the learner. Rose watched this awesome dynamic duo and only intruded with diner. She sensed that in seeking the elements of his own history Robin had found a need to create a bonding with his son. It was as if a genetic force, a heritable trait, drove this transmittance and assimilation of knowledge.

In the morning Robin often left the house before dawn. During his drive to work he dictated several memos and letters for his secretary Sheri and a list of "to do's" for his administrators Diane and Dee. This crew kept the world from intruding on his schedule and kept his trail free of detritus. This morning as he drove his car with the top down, the wind blew cool moist air on his face. He could see the fluffs of fog and the grayish plumes rising from the few remaining chimneys at the steel mills. Traffic was light so he revved the car up to 80 on the interstate. He pulled into the empty lot adjacent to the cancer center and pushed the button to activate the convertible roof. As he walked into the center he said good morning to Sgt. Reily. He walked the stairs, two at a time to his eighth floor office. Diane was already in and there was a poppy seed bagel with low fat cream cheese and a Diet Dr. Pepper on his desk.

A pile of emails lay on his blotter. Each was labeled in red if he had to act or yellow if it was FYI only. Robin turned to the computer on his right and typed only a few short replies. He was a lousy typist and anything that required an answer longer than two or three sentences was either dictated or handwritten for response by the office staff. One of the other tasks was to check the financial status of the bills sent for care. In particular he had to check when insurance companies had denied payment. He also had to check that international patients, who were not covered by US insurance carriers or Medicare, had a deposit draft for expenses incurred for their care. This could be as high as $100,000 if transplantation was part of the therapy. The hospital, which was a state institution, required that the care of out-of-state patients did not lead to an unrecoupable loss. These chores were what Robin liked least about his job. Robin read several journals, which were piled on his desk and waited for the residents to arrive.

At 8:00 a.m. they gathered in the conference room and the cases were presented with slides of the biopsies shown by the pathologists. The lab results were reviewed and the x-rays, CAT scans, MRIs, PETs and special radioactive scans were described by the radiologist. A working plan of action was presented for each of the patients. Some of the patients were in hospital beds but a significant number were housed at a nearby hotel that had suites so that the patients and their families could be chauffeured over for diagnostic tests or treatment. Only the very sick or patients undergoing intense treatment were kept as inpatients.

Later that day Robin scheduled the new Israeli patient, Avraham Lander for a consultation. Robin introduced himself to Avraham and to his wife Julia in his office. He had an unusual feeling as he shook their hands. It was a sense of familiarity and an ill-defined intimacy. Robin glanced at the already thick chart and saw the patient's residence listed, as Jerusalem, Israel, but his place of birth was Budapest, Hungary.

The ice was broken when Robin said "Jo napot" (hello) and welcome to the United States. He also told them that he had been raised in Hungary and lived there until he was seventeen. Robin asked why they had come to his group for treatment. It was Julia who answered. They had gone to the Hadassah Hospital in Jerusalem and after an aggressive round of chemotherapy the tumor had not shrunk and continued to grow. She said that they first went to the internet and then Avraham had used his contacts from his medical laser company to get him passes to the American Society for Hematology (ASH) meeting in Orlando. At this meeting they had listened to the plenary sessions and had perused the posters. The 12,000 attendees and 6,000 posters and presentations had left them perplexed. Julia said when they got to the poster from the group from this cancer center that they were impressed with their vigorous and aggressive attempt not only to debulk and treat lymphomas, but to achieve survivals considered to be curative. Robin noticed that Julia's reply almost seemed rehearsed.

The discussion lasted over the scheduled time of an hour and often lapsed into Hungarian. The intake interview left Robin with an intense desire to help this couple. For some unknown reason this case felt very personal. He told the couple that he would review the case and that they would have to get a new biopsy so that they could better characterize the type of lymphoma they would have to treat.

Also, a battery of tests including a bone marrow examination would have to be performed. A variety of radiological procedures would be done to evaluate the extent or stage of the cancer. After the tests, Robin would meet with the couple and discuss the therapeutic plan.

CHAPTER 23

Two months after his threats to Robin, when the Dean had developed amnesia about his anger and threats, a Turkish shipping magnate showed up at his office with his personal physician, nurse, wife and four children looking for the oncologist Dr. Robin Goode. He had already been to Paris and London for treatment. He was prepared to endow the center with a very large fund if they would treat his lymphoma. His name was Kadir Yassif. He was an international shipping magnate and he owned a fleet of 40 supertankers. It was said that he bankrolled his initial fleet by smuggling Jews from Cyprus to Palestine on his fishing boat. Some of the funds came from American Jews, some came from the remnants of the client's fortunes, and some came from retrieved Nazi loot. He had worked hard and tried to stay out of the conflicts between the Turks and Greeks on his native Cyprus.

At the age of 55 he was just beginning to enjoy the comforts that his wealth provided when he developed kidney disease. He had a transplant and was doing well with immunosuppressive therapy. At 60 he noticed that he had "swollen glands" in his neck. These persisted after a course of antibiotics. His physician took him to the Institute Pasteur in Paris and to the Hammersmith Hospital in London. They made the diagnosis of a B-cell lymphoma. Kadir asked his physicians who was doing the most promising therapy and all the assembled lists had Dr. Goode's name.

Dr. Esterly, the Dean, called Robin. He was informed that the US State Department had called to facilitate Mr. Yassif's enrollment for treatment. It seemed that Yassif had a lot of influence in the Mideast and the CIA had a vested interest in keeping him functional and friendly.

Goode brought Yassif to the cancer center for his intake interview, lab tests, and routine x-rays. The tumor would have to be rebiopsied and characterized. The C team held their initial briefing. Robin reviewed and discussed the observation that lymphomas had developed in patients after transplantation. This had been reported as early as the late 1960 and 1970s by the transplantation team at the University of Colorado. Some of these tumors regressed when the immunosuppressive therapy given to prevent the rejection of transplanted kidney was reduced or eliminated. No one really understood the mechanisms involved.

There was evidence that certain lymphomas were circumstantially linked to infections by the Ebstein Barr Virus (EBV), a DNA virus related to the herpes family of viruses. The EBV infection was most strongly related to carcinomas of the nasal and pharyngeal passages, which occurred most frequently in southern China. The virus was present in lymphomas of the jaw frequently seen in Africa. The EB was also seen in the lymphocytes of patients with infectious mononucleosis, which was usually benign, and a self-limited disease. Another immunodeficiency condition where lymphomas were being seen was in patients with human immunodeficiency virus (HIV) and again in these patients there was a strong suspicion that a human herpes virus might be the culprit.

In the discussions with his staff, Robin told them that he wanted all possible immune titers for EB (Epstein-Barr) viral antigens and stains with molecular probes for EB DNA performed on Mr. Yassif's blood and tumor tissue.

Several days later, Heifity reported that he had been able to detect EBV in Yassif's blood using methods that amplified the DNA signal from the presence of a few copies, millions of times. He then prepared fluorescent probe, which he and Dr. Chen had used to stain and detect viral nucleic acids in the cells of Kassif's excised lymph node.

Robin asked Yassif and his wife to come to his office. He said to Kassif "your tumor would most probably regress if we reduced your immunosuppressive medication however, you might loose the function of the transplanted kidney." The patient told Robin that he trusted him and would follow his recommendation. Within several weeks after lowering the cyclosporine immunosuppressive therapy the tumor masses started to disappear. They watched the functional status of the transplanted kidney and to their amazement that kidney continued to function.

Yassif left the hospital and left its coffers with $10 million and a promise of an additional $30 million for research expansion of the cancer center. Dean Esterly called Robin to his office and told him that the money would have to be used to bail out the nearby insolvent medical center. He told Robin that his success had not bought him a "pass" and that the investigations about the allegations of Robin's personal and professional misconduct could still lead to punitive actions or even dismissal. Robin felt devastated. He felt blackmailed and speculated on who might have engineered these attacks. He wondered how to smoke out his accuser.

~~~~~~~~~~~~~~

Paul was growing and Robin was learning how to enjoy parenthood. Rose was a little fidgety from tending to Paul on 7/24 basis. She decided to start work as an assistant to Mark Knife in the immunogenetics laboratory. She would work on setting up the files and computer databases for the tissue transplantation program. She had a strong interest in genetics and thought it would keep her intellectually alert. They arranged to have the nanny fulltime so that Rose could go in to work three or four days a week.

Knife was a good teacher and he appreciated her help in starting up his laboratory. They talked about his anthropological interests. He explained how DNA analysis was not only useful for identifying genetic diseases but was being used in forensics to identify victims in mass disasters. The large number of informative gene sequences made the establishment or refinement of filial relationships statistically reliable. He told her that any doubts about the validity of the interpretations could only be related to the identity and integrity of the tissues or DNA analyzed. The chain of evidence was as critical as the actual analysis of the DNA markers.

Working alongside Knife, Rose got to know him a lot better. He was hard working and intense, but he also enjoyed good intellectual and social interactions. His alliances and friendships seemed to be focused on the arts and natural sciences. Within weeks of his arrival, his rental house became the meeting place for the University of A. free thinkers. He carried a whole lot of baggage from the Beat generation, but drugs were now not in vogue. He invited Robin and Rose and several of the C team to soirees at his home. Robin found himself more interested in these gatherings than when he had gone to Knife's place in lower
~~~~~~~~~~~~~~

Manhattan. Robin actually had become a little less intense and so singularly focused on his science. He seemed to be trying to develop an appreciation for the beauty of God's earth and creatures. He actually even thought about genes and DNA in a context not related to cancer. Knife's philosophical approach to the understanding of creation and the evolution of mankind were becoming a surrogate for a religious perspective. Although Robin thought laughingly that this was probably not what Dean Esterly had in mind for him when he insinuated that Robin needed religion. Watching his son grow up stimulated Robin to develop a more humanistic approach to medicine and life.

In appreciation for Knife's guiding them to a renewed appreciation of humanity, Robin and Rose reciprocated by taking Knife, city born and breed, into the beautiful southern countryside. They taught him to truly "smell the flowers.", but only after introducing him to a nasal inhaler with topical steroids. Knife seemed to be allergic to anything that grew in soil.

One day while setting up the auto downloading from the DNA sequencer to the computer, Rose asked Knife what he knew about von Willebrands Disease and whether they could analyze her son, Paul's bleeding defect. Knife said the next time Paul had blood work done she should also try to get a sample for DNA analysis. He told her to get samples from any and all blood relatives. She wrote to Tomas and got him to send a sample. She got Robin to give a blood sample. Rose had learned to prep the samples for DNA. As she learned more and read more, Rose realized that DNA from a variety of studies could be obtained from envelopes licked before sealing, hair if it was plucked, and lipstick. She remembered the gold lipstick case Robin kept in his jewelry box that he told her was from his mother, Maria. She cut a sliver off, extracted the DNA from one-half of the sample and saved one-half. All the samples were sent to the University of Michigan for RFLP (restriction fragment length polymorphism) analysis and for specific mutational analyses.

After several weeks without any answers, Rose ran the human identity PCR kit on the samples. It was no surprise that her son Paul was a mixture of hers and Robin's genes. No mix-up at the hospital. Rose didn't know why she wasn't surprised that Maria's DNA from the lipstick had almost no matches in informative alleles for either Robin's or Tomas' DNA. Rose filed the results.

When the studies came back from the coagulation genetics lab at Michigan they were more detailed than she expected. It seems that while they were studying the vonWillebrands gene at Michigan, a collaborating group in Israel was studying vWF mutations. The samples were sent to the Hadassah Medical Center genetics study group. Studies on the distribution of Factor XI mutations in Jews recapitulated the diasporas. In addition to the vonWillebrands disease inherited from Rose, Paul had a mild factor XI deficiency, inherited from Robin. This combination of mutations accentuated Paul's bleeding when he was injured. This type of XI mutation alone would have little symptomology if Paul had not had the other mutation(s) in the vonWillebrand gene. The report was very technical and she went over it very carefully with Knife until she felt she understood the technical details and ramifications. She drew and redrew her family's pedigree.

Two questions were obvious (1) Who was Robin's real mother? and (2) Was the XI mutation indicative of a progenitor with Jewish genes? The only person Rose showed the results were Knife and he was sworn to silence. All of the DNA samples were frozen and catalogued in the freezer and in the computer files. Alterations or deletions would require the electronic signatures of two senior staff members under the new tightened security measures.

Rose loved the genetic studies and working in the lab. She began to help Knife in his studies on mitochondrial maternally transmitted genetic markers. Knife showed her a study on which he was a collaborating co-investigator. Dr. Goldstein at University College London had traced a strong linkage between the Cohen lineage of high priests in early Jewish biblical history and a Y chromosomal genetic mutation. This allelic distribution was used to show that a black tribe, the Lemba, deep in southern Africa, that had practiced many Hebraic traditions and decorated their religious paraphernalia with the six-pointed Star of David was truly genetically descended from the Cohen clan.

Knife was extending these studies to mitochondrial genes. He had developed informative markers for maternally transmitted mitochondrial genes. One day Rose saw the mitochondrial analyses on the samples from Robin, Tomas, Paul, Maria, and herself. She ran them alongside of known Cohen positive and Cohen negative samples. Knife's DNA analysis matched the Cohen positive control.

The results showed that both Robin and Tomas carried the Cohen mitochondrial mutation. She and Paul were negative. Again, there was the question of who was the true mother of Tomas and Robin. Rose tried to correlate the genetic studies with the facts she had gathered in Budapest. She decided, however, to give the studies a rest until she had more information on where or who were Robin's real mother and father.

CHAPTER 24

The laboratory tests on Robin's Israeli patient, Avraham Lender showed that the low-grade indolent lymphoma was transforming into a high grade more aggressive cancer. New smaller lymph nodes in the cervical areas were beginning to become palpable. There was a slight enlargement of the spleen but no evidence of lymph node enlargement in the chest or abdomen. There was no sign of intestinal involvement. The bone marrow was markedly depleted of the normal hematopoietic cells but they could not detect any cancer cells.

Robin studied the reports from the hospital in Jerusalem. The therapy had been aggressive and the combination had damaged the normal blood forming cells precluding the use of stem cells from Avraham's own marrow in an autologous transplant. If a suitable donor could be found, an allelogenic transplant could be performed. Other than the ill effects from the lymphoma, Avraham was in good shape. His robust cardiac function would allow the use of very potent chemotherapeutic agents that would have a side effect of destroying cardiac muscle cells.

Robin would use a combination of local radiotherapy and extensive chemotherapy to destroy the large lymph node in the armpit area, to destroy other local lymphomatous nodes and to destroy any distant metastatic tumor. This would deplete Avraham's remaining bone marrow. His blood forming cells would be destroyed and he would be anemic. His white blood cells, the neutrophils and lymphocytes would be destroyed and he would be susceptible to infection. His platelet count would drop because the marrow precursors would be destroyed and he might bleed or even exsanguinate. All of these side effects could be controlled with transfusions of blood cells, platelets, and antibiotics or antifungal agents, but these would only work as a stopgap measure. A compatible bone marrow donor was needed if long-term survival was to be accomplished. The key to the success hinged on the effectiveness of Dr. Knife's immunogenetics group in finding a suitable donor.

Rose entered the hospital room and greeted Avraham and Julia. She scanned the chart and said "Shalom," one of the few words in Hebrew she knew. She scanned further and found the history of Avraham's Hungarian nationality. She had picked up a few phrases from her trips to Budapest and from listening to Robin teach their son Paul. She greeted the couple in Hungarian, but she explained that she was not very fluent.

Avraham stared at her. Julia looked at this attractive woman who appeared to be in her 40s. It was difficult to tell exactly how old she was. She had an ageless beauty. She reminded Julia of Candice Bergen the model and actress who had seemed not to age for decades.

Julia looked up from her crewelwork and peered out the upper half of her bifocals so that she could better examine the woman in the white laboratory coat sitting on the edge of Avraham's bed. It was then that she read the nametag, Rose Goode. She asked Rose if she was related to the doctor taking care of Avraham.

Rose answered, "He is my husband." Avraham's head bent to better focus on Rose. He had never seen her up so close. With a smile he said to Julia, "I knew he was an aesthetic."

Rose and Julia seemed to bond. They talked about places and things. Much of the early conversation focused around Europe and Hungary. Rose told Julia that she would like to spend more time with her but she had to draw some samples of blood from Avraham. She explained that she was working in the immunogenetics laboratory and that they were entering in a genetic profile on all patients and their families so that they could find the best matches for patients who needed transplants. Before she could draw the sample she needed to get Avraham to sign a form called an "Informed Consent." In essence, the patient was allowing the investigators to analyze the DNA for any markers that could be used to find compatible donor-recipient matches and to analyze the genetic material for markers of genetic diseases. The investigators would not provide any outside agencies with materials or the data from the analyses without encryption that protected the subject from being identified. In fact, a double encryption with fire walling of the computer records had been added for privacy protection. Avraham scribbled his signature on the document. Rose put a tourniquet on his arm an inspected it for the best site for the venipuncture. She mentally noted his somewhat faded crude tattoo. She thought that it was from internment at a concentration camp but she didn't say anything. She inserted the needle and drew about 10 cc of blood into a syringe from a prominent vein in his forearm. She carefully labeled the tube checking the name against his ID on his hospital bracelet. Rose turned to Julia and asked "would you also consent to have a sample drawn so that we can enlarge the DNA database."

Julia hesitatingly consented and signed the forms. It was a little more difficult to obtain the blood from her arms because the veins were smaller and seemed to roll and collapse as Rose tried to pierce them. It took Rose several tries to get a good blood sample. She apologized to Julia for the extra stick and the bruise. She put a Band-Aid on the needle puncture site. Before Rose left the hospital room, she made a date to have tea with Julia. After Rose left, Julia went over to the bed and held Avraham's hand; they quietly looked at each other. Each had something to reveal but neither was sure how to broach their revelations. It had been a long trip from Tel Aviv and Avraham was exhausted from all of the tests. He closed his eyes; Julia fluffed the pillows behind him and placed his arm, where the biopsy had been performed, on some supporting pillows. He dozed off and she propped up a pillow in the armchair in the corner of the room, pulled a light blanket over her and she also fell asleep.

About two hours later, Julia, scrunched in her chair, heard some voices. At first she thought that she was dreaming because the conversation was in Hebrew. Instead of waking she listened without moving. She opened her eyes to a squint and tried to observe the figure in front of her without putting on her glasses. It was a young attractive dark complected woman with long black hair, wearing a lab coat talking to Avraham. The woman was of moderate height and build. She was facing Avraham and had her back towards Julia. She was telling Avraham that she needed to draw blood for additional immunological studies. Her Hebrew was that of a native Israeli, a sabra. Avraham told her that he just had blood taken, but she was relentless in her request for another sample. Julia had not heard her introduce herself and could not see her nametag.

While the blood was being drawn, the woman told Avraham that she had gotten a Masters Degree in Israel and was working on her PhD in New York when she married an Internal Medicine Fellow who was doing a fellowship in immunology research. He had become well recognized for his work in autoimmune diseases and had been asked to chair the Department of Medicine at the University of A. For several years she focused on building their home and had become an avid gardener. More recently she had returned to doing laboratory work and had joined the oncology unit.

Julia feigned sleep and continued to examine the woman. When the sample was obtained, the woman put her paraphernalia on a tray with a carrying handle and left. Julia found her glasses in her pocket book and put them on. She also took out a pad and pencil. She wrote down all the features she could remember about the woman who had just been in the room. Her height, hair color, build, skin color. Her hands were thin with long pointy fingers. Julia could not distinctly see her face.

When the woman left the room Avraham asked Julia what she was doing and she replied that the technician had looked so familiar that she wanted to have some notes so she could think about where and when she might have met her previously. Julia had a pretty good memory and usually didn't forget a face. As she got older it was a little more of a struggle to connect the face to a name. It wasn't that she forgot, but it just took longer for her memory to make the connections and associations. Julia was sure she knew this woman.

It was getting close to dinnertime and the nurse brought a tray for Avraham. After Julia helped him get situated she told him that she was going to the cafeteria to get a bite to eat. Julia took the elevator to the rooftop where the dining area, enclosed by glass on three sides, faced out on the surrounding countryside. Julia looked out and thought about how green and fertile the surrounding rural areas appeared.

Julia got a tray and went down the serving line where there was a choice of meats, vegetables, desserts and drinks. She chose a meat loaf, some black-eyed peas a dish that she had never seen before, a small salad, a sliver of pecan pie, and some iced tea with a sliver of lemon. She hated cafeteria style dining because your eyes were always bigger than your stomach. As she turned to carry her loaded tray to an uncrowded seating section she noticed the dark haired woman who had drawn Avraham's blood sitting in a distant booth with a younger blonde man. She was very attractive but in a mature fashion and she seemed to be older than her companion. They were not holding hands but in the short while Julia observed them she frequently fondled his hand. Julia sensed a clandestine nature to their relationship. They seemed to be engrossed in each other. Julia wanted to have a better look at this woman but she didn't want the woman to see her, so she chose a table where a pillar obscured her. She continued her covert observation. When Julia glanced around the pole she could see the woman's profile. Julia was pretty sure that she knew the identity of the woman. A chill went through her body and she thought the world was truly remarkably small.

During the next several days the pace of testing slowed and Julia and Avraham were told that they could wait in a guesthouse rather than stay in the hospital. Before they left the hospital Julia ran into Rose and invited her for lunch. She even asked her if Rose wished to bring her son with her. The request didn't sound too strange because it was on a Saturday afternoon and Rose had mentioned that she had to pick Paul up from swim team practice. Julia had asked in a manner that did not convey her intense desire to see the boy she believed to be her grandchild.

When the time came for the planned rendezvous, Julia practiced being calm. She dressed in a flared gray knit skirt and a charcoal knit blouse open at the neck. She wore a strand of gray Mikimotto pearls. Her gray hair fell on to her neck and back. She looked much younger than her actual age. Avraham remarked on how beautiful she looked and kissed her before she left the hotel room. He was to stay in the room and rest.

Rose stood by her black Lexus 300 SUV and waved when she saw Julia. As Julia approached the Lexus, she was disappointed that Rose did not have her son with her. Rose seemed very animated and opened the door for Julia. She explained that her son's swim practice had been extended and they would pick him up on the way back from their luncheon. Rose drove to an elegant small restaurant where they sat outside at a table covered by a large umbrella. They each ordered a drink. Rose ordered a Martini and Julia ordered a Mai Tai. The ordering of liquor, which was unusual for either, seemed to portend the seriousness of the meeting and planned discussions.

Rose began with a toast. She said as they touched glass to glass "to revelation." Julia's eyebrow rose in a quizzical manner. She tinkled her glass against Rose's "to reunion and redemption." Each chuckled. The two women looked at each other. Just then the waiter came to take their orders. The meeting was awkward for both women; each had an agenda but no opening move. Finally Julia said, "You go first."

Rose said, "I am sorry that I did not acknowledge that I recognized you. It was many years ago when I visited your family in Tel Aviv. It was at a Seder. As we toasted the angel Elijah, the door blew open and we glimpsed an old bearded man who disappeared into the night. I have thought back about you and your family many times."

"When I worked for the CRA I was teaching lost art and came across a filing from a Julia Katz, but the return address was Jerusalem not Tel Aviv. Was that you?"

Julia answered, "Yes."

Rose asked, "How have you been?"

Julia answered tearfully, "I still miss my son, David. You may know that he died in an unexplained laboratory accident while working at the Institute for Molecular Biology." She took out a tissue and wiped the tears from her cheek and eyes.

Rose replied" I am so sorry. He was a fine intelligent and sensitive young man. I am truly sorry that we did not have time to know each other better. In those days I had little time for anything except my graduate studies and career."

Rose then became more inquisitive. She asked, knowing the answer beforehand, whether her husband's patient, Avraham, was David's father.

Julia answered, "No, David's father died last year."

Knowing the answer, Rose asked naively, "Who is Avraham, the man you have brought here for my husband to treat?" This was the credibility check, the trademark of Rose the investigator.

Julia parried the question by retorting, "Who do you think he is?"

A smile formed on Rose's face. She answered, "If Avraham was not Robin and Tomas' father, then he was the elusive double everyone fantasizes exists statistically, if not literally." To lighten the intensity of the moment, Rose said, "He is the reincarnate or ghost of Robin's missing father. At first the physical features suggest that they are dissimilar but intense scrutiny of the genes and markers used in forensic DNA identification shows that they are 50% identical with those found in Robin's DNA. The odds were greater than a billion to one that they were first order relatives." Rose noticed that Julia did not flinch at this news. Rose immediately understood that she already knew and that was why she and Avraham had come.

Rose became suspicious. Did they only come because they now needed help; possibly they knew that this was Avraham's last chance for a bone marrow transplant. Rose decided to lay down a card. She said that the analysis of Julia's DNA had shown a match to Robin and that it was certain that Julia, rather than Maria, was his natural mother. She informed Julia that she had also matched her to Robin's brother, Tomas' DNA. The analysis revealed even more information.

At this point Julia's stoic façade failed and she began to weep. Rose signaled the waiter and had him charge the bill to her American Express Card. She helped Julia to the car and drove to Paul's swim practice. They picked up Paul and drove to Rose's home. Rose brought Julia into a solarium and had the housekeeper bring some ice tea. Paul was excused to do his homework. Rose said to Julia that she felt that it was time to lay down all the cards so that she could decide how to untangle this family's Gordian knot of relationships. Was there a reason to restructure, reconcile and to reprogram the past?

The wrestling match ended with the two women embracing each other. Now Rose was holding back tears. The conundrum that puzzled her for almost two decades suddenly became clear. Rose wanted to shout, but regained her composure and equilibrium.

She held Julia who was still bawling and somewhat spasmodically sniffling. It was an eternity of minutes before the women said anything. Then it was Rose who asked Julia if she wanted to tell her the details of her family's dissolution and dispersion. Rose had many unanswered questions.

She asked why Julia left her sons when she was sent away.

Julia answered that the decision was made very rapidly and that the boys were judged to be too young to make the treacherous journey. The original plan was for them to be sent out later. At the end of the war, Julia said she could not find her former husband or her children. Her contact with her brothers Sig and Ted was sporadic and they told her that they could not find any trace of Robe, or Tomas, or of Rolfe her former husband. The international Jewish Relief Organization could not find the children. Julia said that she and her second husband searched through thousands of pictures and files of DP for her children and former husband. After several years she assumed that they had perished.

Rose continued her interrogation but the questions took a quantum leap in time. Rose asked how she reunited with Rolfe.

Julia recounted the story of the old Hassid who courted her, Rolfe transformed into Avraham. She explained how Avraham had escaped and disguised himself, how he had hidden from and spied on his family. He was afraid for many years that he would be exposed and possibly even imprisoned.

Rose recollected her paranoia of being watched in Vienna and Budapest. So it was not her imagination. The father and son both shared the ability to imprison their emotions and to hide the past from the present. Both were psychic chameleons, camouflage was the armor that protected them from the world's cruelty.

After many questions Rose asked Julia what happened to her son David. Julia said that he had been poisoned. Someone in the laboratory where he was working had put acrylamide, a substance used in his experiments, into his coffee cup. He became severely paralyzed and then went into respiratory failure. The police investigated but could never find the perpetrator. The investigation lasted several months but no one was implicated. Julia said she had a strong suspicion of who killed her son but that she could never prove it.

Rose in a blunt manner asked Julia, "Why now? Why have you and Avraham finally decided to see your Robin?"

Julia hesitated and answered that Avraham had always watched his sons from afar. He took great pride in their accomplishments. In his apartment Avraham had kept school items, news clippings and a copy of every article and book Robin or Tomas had ever written.

When she learned Avraham's identity, Julia had questioned him and evoked from Avraham the complex and convoluted methods and actions that he had taken to see that the boys were cared for and supported. She recounted to Rose the recovery of the looted family fortune. She described how Avraham had gotten the art and money to her brothers and how they had indirectly and discreetly supported Maria and then Werner. She described how money had been sequestered into Swiss accounts to support and educate Tomas and Robin. Some money and art had even been anonymously sent to Julia in Israel.

Julia said that they knew that appearing into Robin's life was probably obtrusive and possibly even wrong. She explained that she and Avraham had discussed their decision to come over and that there were several reasons that they chose to come to Alabama. The first was that they needed Robin and felt that if there was any hope of Avraham surviving his cancer it lay with the skill of Robin and God's wishes. The second reason is that they were both growing older and they wished to have some contact and restoration with their children before aging or death robbed them of their ability to meet their children and grandchild. Lastly, they needed to transfer the assets from the estate of her brothers Ted and Sig Glucke. When she finished, Julia held her tissue to her face to prevent her from sobbing.

She continued and said, "I only pray that we have made a decision that will not hurt you or my sons."

Rose got up and walked out of the room. She returned in a few minutes. She placed a corroded gold gilded lipstick tube on the coffee table. She said to Julia, "In this tube lies the only memory my husband has of his mother. You and I must use great wisdom in replacing those cloistered memories with living memories of a past he has never known. Before this great revelation is made, we must plan carefully for the confusion and possible denial that may result. I suggest that we go slowly and scientifically." She added "My husband is a devotee of science."

"Before I take you back to your hotel I must explain to you that Robin is under tremendous psychological stress. One of his patients died mysteriously on an experimental therapy. Another associate of my husband committed suicide thinking that the mistake in therapy was his fault. The Dean has threatened to have Robin not only removed from the faculty but is threatening to have his medical license revoked. Please give us some time to deal with these professional problems before we give him the psychological jolt of his life?"

Julia asked, "Before you take me back to the hotel could I please have another brief look at your son, Paul?" They stood up and Rose took Julia to an alcove to the den where they watched Paul practicing. The way he held the instrument, tucked under his chin, his bow and body movements, reminded her of herself when she had played the violin. After a few minutes Rose took Julia to the car and drove her to her hotel. When she entered she found Avraham napping. Julia sat quietly and watched his breathing.

As she watched Avraham, her mind drifted like a time machine. In front of her was a dashing officer in a blue ceremonial uniform trimmed with red cuffs and capped with gold epilates. On his chest was a slate of colored ribbons and several dangling silver and bronze medals. A sheathed steel sword hung from a leather belt. A red silk cummerbund encircled his waist below the braided buttons on his low cut jacket. Bushy brown hair and a burly moustache bordered the tan face fixed with a broad smile.

She was in a full-length white brocade dress with elbow length gloves and wore only a smooth skinny band of gold around her neck. Her long black curled hair flowed along her neck and fell onto her chest.

Together they danced. She held his hand tightly. They orbited the floor. Julia reached out and the old man came to life. When he opened his eyes she kissed him on his dry lips.

He said, "What have you been up to? You look like you swallowed a canary or even two canaries." Julia told him about her meeting with Rose. She said to Avraham, "You know she is very smart and very cunning. Rose has known about you and the last forty years of your shenanigans. She had read your genes like a gypsy fortuneteller at an Ouija board. She has our past and holds our future."

As Julia fell asleep she dreamed about her son David. He was a devoted son, devoted to his parents and to his work. He was intense, often working so hard that he was oblivious to the outside world. When Julia told him that she didn't think that his planned marriage to Tevia, a graduate student was best for him, he ignored her and it was only after Julia followed the young woman to an apartment of another man, a member of the graduate faculty at the institute that she forced David to listen. David confronted Tevia. The engagement was broken but not before the couple had an angry encounter during which Tevia threw the diamond engagement ring that David had given her into his face. She cursed him and vehemently mocked his failure at satisfying her. Less than two weeks after the blow up, David was found in respiratory failure. He was rushed to the emergency department but there was severe brain damage from the lack of oxygen. No one knew how long David had been anoxic because he was found by the security guard slumped over his desk late at night. David died in a coma. The postmortem forensic studies revealed traces of acrylamide in his tissues. An investigation by the police who interviewed the staff and students at the institute could not indict anyone. They had interviewed Tevia several times, but she had an alibi for at least 12 hours prior to the time David was found. No evidence was found as to how David might have ingested the poison. There was even some speculation that David had committed suicide. This was not an idea that Julia could accept.

Julia's recollection of David must have been conjured up by the recognition of the technician who drew Avraham's blood. During the past several years Julia had wondered what had become of that woman. Several times Julia thought that if she had not been so adamant about Tevia's unsuitability as her son's wife that he might not have died. Periodically, Julia experienced a guilt trip. She felt that she had failed all of her sons. It was early in the morning when Julia finally calmed her anxiety enough to fall into a deep sleep.

~~~~~~~~~~~~~

Rose needed someone she could trust to talk with in confidence and she needed to do it before the situation became uncontrollable. There was no way to reverse the avalanching events. She thought that with a slowing down perhaps she could better control the possible cataclysm. Rose decided to talk with Knife. After all, he already was familiar with some of Rose's genetic analyses of her family. Also, there was no doubt that he would recognize the similarity of Robin's and Avraham's DNA sequences. The comparison would be automatically drawn to his attention by the computerized best match software that Knife had written. There was no way that Rose could prevent Knife from seeing the relationships between Avraham, Robin, Tomas and her son Paul and those between Julia, Robin, Tomas and Paul.

Usually, Rose got up soon after Robin left for work. She did several household chores and left lists for the maid and gardener. She roused Paul and made sure that he had some breakfast before she drove him to school. It was almost nine before she arrived at the immunogenetics laboratory. She knocked on Knife's office door. He beckoned her in and pointed to a chair adjacent to his desk. She sat a little like a dog responding to a command. Knife said, "I've been expecting you," in a calm but firm manner.

He had several printouts spread across his desk. "Okay," he said, "Let's get past trivial explanations. I know your compulsivity well enough to know that specimen mix-up is almost as unlikely as a statistical fluke." Rose nodded. He said, "You know that I have always been interested in the stories DNA analysis could reveal but most of
~~~~~~~~~~~~~

my studies have been on historical or anthropological in nature. Now I am faced with the living history of your husband's family. For my own curiosity would you like to fill in some of the gaps?"

Rose said, "It's a long story." Knife answered, "It's a slow day. Get some coffee and let's put it down just as if we were analyzing a scientific experiment."

Rose told Knife the story of how she had been unwittingly part of Robin's family history even before they were married. She told Knife about her tracking of Nazi loot with the CRA. She told him about her trip to Hallein in Austria and her first trip to Budapest. She told him the stories that Ted and Sig had told her. Rose told him of the meeting she had with Julia yesterday and also said that she was still not completely clear on all of the events. She reminded Knife that she and Knife had already known that Robin was not genetically related to Maria. Up to now she had been able to let that skeleton remain in the closet. With the arrival of Avraham and Julia, she wasn't sure what was going to happen.

Knife reminded Rose that there were ethical and security issues. The security issues were those that he and Robin had instituted whereby no data could be altered or deleted without two senior staff members signing their recognition of the changes. In other words, the data could not go away. Rose added that it's probably true that Avraham and Julia wouldn't go away either.

When three o'clock rolled around, Rose said that she had to leave to pick up Paul at school. She asked Knife to tell Robin that there were some technical problems and that he could not go over the DNA studies on Avraham for another day or two. She said that she needed some more time with Julia in order to fill in some details and to plan a course of action. Knife agreed.

Rose knew that sooner or later she would have to untangle and straighten out the mess. Before truth reshaped the lives of her family she wanted to do some more preparative work. She wanted to spend more time with Avraham and Julia, especially before any major therapy was begun and the acuteness of Avraham's illness became the primary focus. This was especially true if the treatment did not bring his disease under control. Rose thought about the possibility of the truth being unmasked, only to leave a void if Avraham died. Another plan she prepared involved getting Tomas to come over from Austria. If there was to be unveiling of Robin and Tomas' parents it probably should be done only once. Also, if a transplant were to be attempted there would have to be a decision on who would be the most suitable donor.

That evening when Robin returned to the hospital after dinner for a meeting with the Board of Trustees of the University, Rose telephoned Tomas. It was almost midnight in Austria when she reached him. She asked him to come for a visit and he asked when she had in mind. Rose answered that she very much wanted him to come as soon as possible. Tomas sensed the urgency and asked if she, Robin and Paul were all right. Rose answered that they all were in good health. Tomas said that there was a break in his teaching and consulting for several weeks and that he would see if he could get airplane reservations to come in the next day or two. Rose told him that his visit would be a surprise for Robin whose birthday was in several days. Ironically, she said she hoped the brothers enjoyed surprises.

In the morning Rose went to the hotel to pick up Julia. They would return to Rose's house to continue their conversations, the nature of which turned from suspicious and inquisitional to congenial.

Rose again confided in Julia that the next week was going to be very turbulent for Robin. The Board of Inquiry concerned with the death of one of Robin's patients was beginning its investigation. Rose told Julia about the poisoning and about Robin's suspicion that someone was trying to sabotage him and his team. The story aroused Julia's attention but she just listened and tried to remember all the details.

After several hours of conversation, Julia casually asked Rose if she knew the Israeli technician who had come to draw blood from Avraham in the hospital after Rose two days ago. Rose replied that there were two Israeli's on the team, one was a physician, Dr. Heifity, and the other was an immunologist who had been the Goode's next-door neighbor. She had been married to the Chief of Medicine, Robin's immediate boss. She had separated from her husband and was living elsewhere in town. Her married name was Tevia Rigatoni but Rose did not recall her maiden name. Rose said that she and Tevia had been very friendly but that the relationship had cooled over the last year and was almost neutral when they ran into each other at the hospital.

Rose took Julia back to the hotel just before lunch so that Julia could take care of Avraham and so that Rose could go to the laboratory for several hours of work.

When she arrived at the lab she did not wait for an invitation into Knife's office. She put her head inside the door and asked if she could consult with him. She sat down and filled Knife in on the information she had gotten from Julia. Much of it was not really surprising to him. He told Rose that both Robin and Tomas were excellent matches as bone marrow transplant donors for Avraham and he showed her the genetic analysis as well as the information he had gotten on immunological matching. Then he threw in a fact that Rose had forgotten. Robin was positive for antibodies against the hepatitis C virus. HCV positivity was reason for excluding him as a potential donor.

Rose told Knife that she had invited Robin's brother Tomas to visit and that he would be arriving in two days. Knife said that her brother-in-law Tomas would be the best choice if a transplant was going to be undertaken.

Knife said that he had been called by Robin to come to an urgent meeting and that he would have to excuse himself. Rose left and went shopping for extra food for her houseguest and when she got home she worked with the maid to prepare the spare guest bedroom.

When Knife arrived at Robin's office, they went into the library and Robin told his secretary that they were not to be disturbed.

Robin told Knife that he needed his help. He then filled him in on his observations and speculations relating to the death of Mr. Morella. He gave him the medical examiner's autopsy report and the toxicology test results. Robin told Knife that he remembered his forensic work at the ME's office in Manhattan when they were in training there. He proceeded to show him the surveillance tapes from the night prior to the murder.

Like Robin, Knife played the tapes several times rewinding, fast forwarding and pausing at various selected frames. "Okay," he said, "First let's get some help from the image enhancement professionals. Let's see whether they can enlarge the image of the suspicious character entering the building after McNaught leaves. We can have them look for any identifying marks like labels, stains, or tears in the outerwear or hat. Possibly the stitching or weave can give a clue to the manufacturer or to the owner. We can scan other security tapes from the building and see if the same outfit has been previously recorded. It is still within the six-month active file. Get Reilly to sequester the VCRs, check with the weather bureau to see which nights were rainy. Particularly review the recordings from those nights."

He had Robin review the tapes with him focusing on different details each time. They looked at the body habitus, the spinal curvature, and the arm-carrying angle. Finally, Knife said that he would get a copy to the physical anthropologists to see if they could do a more thorough reconstruction.

Lastly, Knife had Robin focus on the ground to see if the camera had recorded any muddy footprints in the entryway. There were several hazy prints. Most of these were partials or obscured by more than one print. Since they were only pictures, the standard practices of analysis of fresh prints could not be applied but the Solenate Shoeprint Database called SICAR available from Foster and Freeman for analysis might give some information on the type and size of the shoes worn by people entering or leaving the building that night. The sex and size of the shoes' owners could probably be deduced. Knife would also contact the FBI forensic experts at Quantico with whom he had collaborated with on his DNA studies to see if they had any suggestions. Since there were a number of foreign nationals working at the center, access to Interpol databases might be important. After Knife told Robin what should be done on the investigation, Robin said that he had other professional and departmental business to discuss.

First he confided that the intradepartmental promotions committee chaired by Dr. Rigatoni had turned down Shawn O'Brien's promotion to Associate Professor with tenure. It seemed to Robin that the standards for the oncology group were set well above the other divisions of the Department of Medicine. There was a block of senior professors who seemed to vote whichever way the Departmental Chairman, often not subtlety, instructed them. This was true even if the chairman was not even at the committee meeting. If perchance the candidate got by, the Chair's supporting letter to the medical school committee would almost always sway the vote. In the case of O'Brien, the comments by the committee stated that most of his 21 papers were co-authored with other members of the C team, in particular with Robin. The committee said that they could not attest to O'Brien's individual contribution to the scholarly works. They also commented that his grant funding was from projects in an umbrella program grant and was not a RO1 grant given to individuals from the NIH. They had not even considered the high priority scores that O'Brien had been given by the scientists brought in from other institutions for a site inspection of the program. The promotions committee did not put much weight on the huge clinical load that was O'Brien's responsibility. He had billed for and personally generated more revenue than four of the other subdivisions of medicine. The man worked with enthusiasm and gusto. When he wasn't seeing patients or teaching medical students he was in the laboratory working with basic scientists. It was only occasionally that he took off for fugues on his motorcycle. Robin told Knife that he didn't relish the task of telling the volatile O'Brien that he had not been endorsed for promotion at the departmental level. Robin said that university rules would allow O'Brien to nominate himself for promotion at the meeting of the medical school's promotion committee. However, Robin would have to warn him that success with self-proposals were unlikely. He also had to tell him that this would be his seventh year and that he probably would have to find another position elsewhere if promotion was not granted. Robin asked Knife for his thoughts and Knife answered candidly that he thought that O'Brien's turn down was a rebuff to Robin and the C team. He questioned whether Robin should appeal directly to the Dean or Chancellor. Robin answered that until the investigation cleared the mystery and events surrounding Mr. Morella's death he had no influence with the administration. In fact, his interjection could have a negative connotation.

Changing subjects, Robin said the last topic he wished to review with Knife was the results from the immunogenetic testing of his patient Avraham Lander. Knife's eyebrows raised, he sucked in some air and told Robin that there had been some technical difficulties with the DNA sequencer and that he would have to wait 24-36 hours for the results. Since the results would be late Friday, he would call Robin when they were ready. Robin said that Rose had mentioned that she was having several people to dinner this coming Friday and that he would like Knife to come to their house and join them. He knew that Knife and Rose liked each other and that she would not mind his inviting Knife without consulting her.

Knife replied that he would be there and told him that he might even be able to give him some preliminary results from the anthropology and FBI consultations. In an effort to lighten things up, Knife gave a Boy Scout salute and said he would "get right on it, chief."

Rose planned a special dinner for Friday. It was also Robin's 50th birthday. The weather was warm and Rose had the housekeeper set the table set on the veranda.

Robin was working late and would not arrive home until just before dinnertime. At 5 o'clock, Rose raced to the airport to pick up Tomas. She sent a cab to the hotel to fetch Julia and Avraham. She saw that Paul dressed decently for dinner, and then she showered and dressed. She wore a silk sheathed red dress and matching jacket. The outfit was simple but elegant. The only jewelry she wore was studded diamond earrings. Rose ran her hands down the skirt, smoothed out a few wrinkles and admired herself in the mirror. She applied a dab of Channel#5 to the back of her ear lobes and went downstairs to light the candelabras and inspect the dinner table.

Robin had been delayed by a very combative meeting with O'Brien where he informed O'Brian about the lack of endorsement of his promotion and tenure. Robin did not arrive until 6:55 p.m., and Rose told him to hurry and change for dinner. She had laid an outfit out on the bed. She kissed him on the cheek and said that she would greet the guests.

As Avraham and Julia arrived, Avraham inspected the house and jokingly said to her that the "cancer business must be pretty good." She held his hand as they got out of the taxi. Julia carried a small box with a present because Rose had told that it was Robin's birthday. The date was not unfamiliar to her. They rang the bell and Rose approached to let them in. Avraham saw her coming, he gave a low lecherous whistle and Julia poked him. A few minutes later Knife arrived, the maid ushered him out to the porch and veranda. Tomas came down carrying a present for this brother's birthday. It was an original manuscript from Paul Erlich, the father of modern medicinal chemistry, and a figure that Tomas knew Robin had greatly revered during his medical training.

Knife turned back to go out to the driveway to get his briefcase from his car. As he reentered the house, he ran into Robin coming down the stairs. Knife motioned for Robin to go into the library. Knife said, "Let me give you a brief report on the investigations. The blown up image of the suspicious person in the tapes showed the trench coat to be most likely foreign made, possibly by an Italian manufacturer. There was a small rip in the stitching at the attachment of the left sleeve. The anthropologists were not 100% certain, but thought the body habitus and gait suggest the figure was a woman. The computer analysis of the remnants of the muddy shoe prints showed a mixture of tread marks. Some prints, based upon the size and fullness, were obviously from a relatively large male. There were some smaller partial prints probably from a much lighter person. Even with a partial tread the shoe specialists said that it was not from typical American footwear worn or made here or in the Far East." Knife apologized that the findings were not more definitive, but said that he would keep on trying. Robin thanked him and said that they had better get into dinner or Rose would have a conniption.

As Robin entered he was greeted by Tomas with a big bear hug. After disengaging, he was given a hug by his son and embraced by his wife. He turned and was additionally surprised by the presence of his patient, Avraham and his wife.

Rose suggested that they have a cocktail before dinner. She said that had a variety of drinks but for the special occasion she had a pitcher of blue martinis, a mixture of Starry Night liquor and vodka. Avraham and Paul opted for cokes.

After they sat, they all toasted Robin with happy birthday wishes. He was a little perplexed about the fuss and also why his patient was a guest. Rose proposed a toast to Robin, "May the back half be even better than the first. May your life be fulfilled with love and the recognition of your achievements. May health and equanimity grace you."

Robin replied, "To my family and friends, may health, happiness, wisdom and justice reward all of us."

Rose told them all to have another drink. Robin had not eaten since early in the morning and the effect of the alcohol was hitting him rapidly.

Rose said that she was going to reveal something that would change all their lives. Since the most rational way to achieve truth was through scientific observations and facts that was the approach she was going to take. She removed a gilded tube of lipstick from her purse and said to Robin and Tomas. This tube is not from your biological mother. I have analyzed the DNA left from the lips of its owner and by both analysis of the nuclear DNA and mitochondria DNA there is little in common with the DNAs I have from you or Tomas. Maria may have mothered you, but she was not your natural mother.

Both Tomas and Robin looked at her in a strange and doubting manner. He said to Rose that negative evidence was often not substantial enough to support a strong hypothesis. Robin's interjection was stated more as a fact without any real emotion. He said perhaps someone had shared or used her lipstick. After all, cosmetics were a luxury in Hungary in the early and mid 1950s. He suggested with a hint of sarcasm, that it was even possible that "a date visiting him, when he was single, could have used the tube."

For a moment the guests were quiet. Julia and Avraham looked at each other. Then Rose began speaking to both Robin and Tomas. Well, by now you have realized that we have DNA samples from all of you in the computerized DNA bank at the hospital. She then turned and faced Knife. He was caught off guard and grunted. "Look," he said, "I am in a very awkward position and before I discuss any of the DNA results I must have consent from all the adults present. I will accept a verbal consent since you are all witnesses, but I will not discuss or interpret the tests unless you all agree that you wish to have the results given in a group presentation." Each person was asked and verbally consented.

Knife said let us start with the most recent genetic events. Paul is definitely a mixture of Robin's and Rose's genes. He definitely has his mitochondrial DNA and his major mutation for his von Willebrands bleeding disorder inherited from Rose. We can go into more detail later on. Tomas and Robin are definitely a mix of genetic material from Avraham and Julia. The statistical analysis make the frequency of this pedigree occurring by random chance less than one in 4 billion or less than the number of humans on this planet.

Both Robin and Tomas were still absorbing the data. The emotional impact was probably going to take longer. Robin scratched his head and turned to look more carefully at Julia and then Avraham. He asked them in Hungarian if they understood what Rose had just said.

Robin looked closely at the elderly couple. He stared into their faces looking for evidences of him. The eye color was different; the hair color was black and the nose that certainly didn't have any similarity to either himself or his brother. Tomas had more features consistent with a heritage from Avraham. The picture was different when he compared himself to Julia. Robin found that he had several facial features consistent with her.

Just as he was about to comment on his observations, there was a burst of several shotgun blasts and the tingling of glass shattering. Everyone jumped up from their chairs and started to follow Robin, who was headed in the direction of the neighboring house. He ran between the driveways and hurdled over the low stonewall between the adjacent driveways. The others walked out, around the wall and down the drive towards the front of the Rigatoni house. Through the broken window he could hear Tevia shouting at Rigatoni. She was demanding that he give her the jewelry in his safe and give her cash so that she could leave town. In return he called her a "whore" and told her to get out. She called him an impotent pompous asshole. She stepped back as if retreating and lunged forward felling Rigatoni with some type of military karate like maneuver. He dropped the gun causing it to fire again.

As the group rushed towards the neighboring house, Knife noticed a white Ram Dodge truck with two motorcycles in the back parked at the far end of the circular drive. In it sat Shawn O'Brien obviously waiting for someone.

The front door of the house swung open as Tevia rushed out colliding into Robin. He grabbed her just as the rest of his houseguests arrived. She was dressed in a raincoat and wore steel-shank military boots, black jeans and a black tight fitting sweater. She was frenetic and agitated. He shook her. It was just then that Tevia and Julia faced each other. The recognition was instantaneous. Julia shrieked, "Murderess, you killed by son David." Tevia, whose face appeared gaunt and witch-like shouted, "Get out of my life you bitch."

As Tevia broke from Robin's hold she twisted and he saw the tear extending from under her arm to the rear of her coat.

He grabbed Tevia and pulled her off to the side of the path. He said, "I know that you killed my patient." Bluffingly he told her, "I can identify you as being present in the cancer center the night before a switch was made in the medication. I can link you and your boot prints to the crime."

Robin knew that he was stretching his proof and that his allegation was based upon weak circumstantial evidence. Tevia obviously so caught off balance and in the act of attacking her husband, yanked free of Robin. She pulled a small revolver and pointed it at him. She said, "I've been trained to shoot to kill, so get back." Robin told her to calm down, but she ran to the waiting truck and told Shawn to get going.

Robin entered the house and found Rigatoni on the floor writhing in pain. He checked to see that Rigatoni was not in imminent danger of dying. He tried to use the telephone in the bedroom but the line had been severed by the pellets from the shotgun blasts. Robin reached down for his mobile phone clipped to his belt and dialed 911 for an ambulance. Robin asked Rose to take the others back to the house. He told her that he would have to arrange for Dr Rigatoni's care since there was no one else at his house. He probably would have to ride in the ambulance to the ER and see that Rigatoni was stable. He promised that he would return as soon as possible.

At the hospital, the staff decided that Dr. Rigatoni should be admitted to rule out any cardiac injury because of his previous heart attacks. His rib fractures were not serious. The census in the cardiac unit was particularly low so the cardiologist decided to put Rigatoni in a monitored bed for the night even without any acute changes on the EKG. The house staff scurried to get all the tests run. After all it wouldn't look good if they screwed up on the care of the Chairman of Medicine. Rigatoni never thanked Robin or even acknowledged Robin's presence.

Robin called home and Knife drove over to the hospital to give him a ride back to the house. Knife, in his sarcastic manner said, "Couldn't have happened to a nicer guy." Robin ignored the comment and refocused on the evening's earlier events.

It seemed like he had gotten a double-barreled jolt for his 50th birthday present. By the time they arrived home Robin had formulated a tentative plan. First he asked to meet with Tomas, who seemed very dazed. They went to the den and Robin asked him if he was all right. Tomas answered that he was having difficulty with rearranging the few remnants of the family relationships he had ever known. But, he believed the strange tale that had unfolded this evening. He asked Robin what if anything they should do.

Robin decided to deal with Avraham's illness first. He would remain as Avraham's oncologist. He told Tomas that the best treatment would include a bone marrow transplant and asked Tomas if he would be willing to be the donor. Robin explained that he could not use his own marrow because of the possibility of transmitting the hepatitis virus to the recipient. He explained what was involved in being a donor. Tomas consented to be the donor.

Robin and Tomas rejoined the party where Rose, Julia, Avraham and a sleepy Paul were getting ready to cut the birthday cake. They had eaten a light dinner while Robin was at the hospital. Robin blew out the symbolic candle. As he did this he made his wish. The turmoil and excitement had kept him from being hungry and he turned down Rose's offer of food.

He said that he had an announcement. Robin said that they all needed more time to adjust to the new and old relationships but the first step should be the treatment of Avraham's cancer. He then announced that Tomas had agreed to be the donor so that they could proceed with the aggressive therapeutic plan.

Julia wiped the tears from her eyes.

Then Robin put his arm around Julia and said "I thank you for providing the solution as to who murdered one of my patients." I realize that the association was enough to catch Tevia off guard and allow me to confront her. I do not have enough expertise to know whether she will be prosecuted or proven guilty. I believe that I can now refute any charges of negligence and protect my position at the hospital. He raised his champagne glass and toasted Julia.

After the toast Rose said that they needed to open Robin's birthday presents. The gift of the Paul Erlich manuscripts from Tomas was opened first. Robin read the title and thanked him profusely. The second gift was from Paul and it was a special high-pitched whistle for Robin to call Argo when they walked in the woods. Robin blew it and the Lab raised his head, got up from his comfortable curled repose and scrambled to Robin. The dog put his head on Robin's knee begging for a pat. Paul came over and father and son embraced.

Next was Julia's gift. She hesitated as she handed the box to Robin. As he unfolded the silk tallis, she explained that the prayer book and the tallis, shaul were her father's and were one of the few things she had brought with her to Palestine when she had fled from Hungry. The book had been in her family for several generations. She hoped that he would enjoy it.

Lastly, everyone looked at Rose who flushed. She said that she was so busy making the arrangements for the dinner that she didn't have time to wrap her present. She told Robin that she would have to give it to him later. A faint smile graced her lips.

Robin said that it was getting very late and that tomorrow would be busy for all of them. Knife volunteered to drive Julia and Avraham back to their hotel. Robin told Knife that if he kept this chauffeuring up he would have to redo his job description and give him a bonus.

Paul shook hands with Avraham and Julia bent over to give him a kiss on the forehead. Rose scooted him off to bed saying that he had better get some sleep before his swim meet tomorrow.

When everyone had departed or retired, Robin and Rose were left in the den alone. He said, "I'll help you clean up." She said "Leave it for the morning." She walked over to him and whispered in his ear "Come up to the bedroom and get your present." She kissed him, hugged him tightly and said, "I love you."

The next morning the dog's barking roused Robin from the deepest sleep he had for as long as he could remember. The sun was already casting shadows into the bedroom. He looked over at Rose partially covered by her black silk negligee and proudly felt her radiance. As he bent to kiss her lightly she surprised him by reaching out and pulling him down for her embrace. Kiddingly, she called him her Inspector Clouseau, thinking of her favorite actor Peter Sellers.

Before going to work Robin walked Argo. He tried his new whistle several times. He planned the coming day in his head. He poked his head into Paul's room and wished him luck in the swim meet.

CHAPTER 25

It was unusual, but his secretary and administrator were already in when he arrived at his office. A bagel and Dr Pepper soda were on his desk along with a printout of his day's schedule. He knew he was going to have to rearrange several of the items on the agenda. He downed the coke and wasn't quite sure why he felt so energetic but he was wired.

He made a few notes about things he had to do. He needed to meet with Sgt. Reily from security. He needed to get the key to O'Brien's office file cabinet and computer access codes. All of the keys and codes would have to be changed or deleted. He would have to check the files and notes for information that related to patient care, treatment protocols or clinical investigations. Because of any legal importance, he wanted Sgt. Reily and his administrator present to catalog and secure the materials.

In addition to his normal patient load, he noticed that Mr. Yassif was flying in from Athens for his annual checkup.

He noted that Rose needed to get a battery of tests on Tomas, including a variety of tests for infectious diseases that had to be done before donor marrow was obtained.

Another major item for the day was the quarterly budget review.

A special note to the secretary was to clear the calendar so that he could pick up Rose and attend Paul's swim meet at 4:00 p.m. This note caught his secretary's, attention. It was unusual for Dr. Goode.

When Sgt. Reily arrived, Robin, his secretary, and his administrative assistant, Diane, went down the corridor to Shawn O'Brien's office. They emptied out his desk drawers and divided the contents into piles. The personal papers and bills were catalogued. Robin found bills for the last month in Shawn's credit cards for hotels in Mobile and Memphis, but he could not tell whether the rooms were single or double. Robin was curious about when Shawn's liaison with Tevia began. He reminded himself that they would also have to clean up and catalog the items in Tevia's office. A significant number of restaurant bills were on Shaw's credit card. Some were for establishments where Robin had an idea of what a single dinner might cost. Based upon this estimate, Robin felt that Shawn's dining for two began in the last two months. There were also charges for women's clothing purchased at SAKS and the GAP and a gold bracelet from Bailey Banks and Biddle for $700. There was a letter to Shawn from a friend in Shin Fein soliciting funds from Shawn. A crumpled yellow lab slip dated last week from the State Department of Health was at the rear of the center desk drawer. The report sent a shiver through Robin. It was informing Shawn that he was HIV positive and requesting that he either seek his own physician's treatment or report to the AIDS treatment center at the State Department of Health as soon as possible. While they were examining the documents, Reily summoned the Information Technology Security Officer who released Shawn's computer password so that they could access his files and emails. A perusal of his surfing activities revealed that Shawn had managed to circumvent the software that had been installed on all the university computers to prevent access to pornography by logging on through his own AOL account. Some of the material was hard core and had both homosexual and pedophilic content. As soon as Reily realized the nature of the material, he suggested that they impound the computer and its hard drive. Since the computer belonged to the State University, it was the best legal approach.

Robin had seen enough to place a story together, but he also realized that he did not have an official termination or resignation for Shawn O'Brien. Robin was also anxious to examine the contents of Tevia's office and computer. He asked Reily to wait a few hours. He went back to his office, dictated a letter of termination for Tevia, and had the secretary type it. They sent it special delivery to both her office and to the address on her personnel file. This address turned out to be the same as O'Brien's. After they saw the postman's attempted delivery at about noon, Robin called Reily to return and open Tevia's office. He didn't have to ask for access to the computer, Reily had anticipated the request and had secured the password. The group entered Tevia's office and essentially did a repeat performance of the search.

The information in Tevia's file cabinet included her curriculum vitae. Robin didn't remember all the details other than her training in Israel and New York City. His eyebrows rose when he saw that Tevia had served in the Special Operations (SO) branch of the Israeli Army before going to graduate school. Heifity, who had been a commando and involved in several rescue missions had told Robin that the women in the SO division were trained in martial arts and weapons usage. Heifity said that they were probably the most lethal women to have existed since the fabled Amazons. Their modus operandi in an attack was reflexive and machine-like and often deadly. This explained Dr. Rigatoni's fractured ribs and the remarks Tevia had made to him when she pointed her pistol at him. He thought to himself that it was a good thing that he didn't challenge her any more than he had.

When Robin opened Tevia's locked desk drawer, he found about 15 bottles of medications. He examined the labels one by one. One prescription was for rispiridone, a potent antipsychotic. He shook the vial and realized that it was empty. He calculated the number of tablets gotten at the last refill and realized that Tevia had probably let her prescription medication lapse. He could now understand why she had seemed so agitated and irrational when he had encountered her last evening at Rigatoni's house. Rigatoni was probably lucky to be alive.

Robin copied a few facts onto a legal pad. The rest of the materials were gathered, placed in boxes, sealed and stored in a locked bin in the basement of the cancer center. Robin asked Sergeant Reilly to pull the personnel and health files for Shaun and Tevia. He needed all the evidence he could get.

CHAPTER 26

Mr. Yassif, who had been so appreciative of Robin's care and had promised a large contribution to the oncology program, was due for his biannual checkup. The appointment had been scheduled weeks in advance for 2:15. All of the lab work and x-rays had been performed and read out yesterday. Robin rushed from his detective work back to his office and reviewed all of the results before Mr. Yassif arrived. He greeted him and was pleased when he told Mr. Yassif that there was no evidence of any tumor and that his transplanted kidney seemed to be functioning very well even with the reduction in immunosuppressive drugs.

Mrs. Yassif, who had always been quietly at her husband's side, handed Robin a gift-wrapped package. She told Robin to open it. Inside was a translation of Homer's Odyssey, which was bound in ornate embossed leather cover. She said that mythology still held her fascination and that reality was often more bizarre than those ancient stories. Robin thanked her and thought this is my week for symbolic gifts. He shook hands with Mr. Yassif and Mrs. Yassif gave him a weak hug. Robin told them that he had to hurry off to his next appointment.

The day had been much busier than Robin had planned. He asked Dee and Diane if they could come back after supper for a budget review session. They agreed and even asked if he wanted them to order Chinese takeout so that he would not have to race home and back. He said yes and pulled two twenties from his wallet for the food. He pulled off his lab coat and threw his sport jacket over his shoulder. As he was leaving, he pulled his mobile phone out and while on the elevator hit *2, which automatically dialed Rose's mobile phone. He told her that he would have to meet her at the school's swimming pool. Robin had attended very few of the school functions and was too embarrassed to call Rose again when he found himself lost. He called Diane who looked it up on the computerized map and talked him there over his car phone.

Robin ran through the school lobby and got to the poolside stands just before the 100-meter event. This was one of two events in which Paul was competing. Robin was glad he made it on time. Robin climbed the stairs two at a time, sat down next to Rose and squeezed her hand. He was a little surprised to see Julia sitting on the other side of Rose. During the last lap of the race, Robin stood up and cheered. This was definitely out of character for him, in fact, he had told Rose that he thought that the over enthusiasm of parents at their children's competitive sports events put too much pressure on their kids. He had even shown her a news article about the beating death of a parent during an argument after a hockey game outside of Boston.

Paul came in third out of eight and Robin was ready to go to him. Rose grabbed him and told him that there were more heats and events, so he had better sit down. Robin barely noticed that Julia was sitting on the other side of Rose.

Paul competed in the relay race and was the last swimmer. His performance was so good that his relay team won. This was the last event and Robin rushed down to embrace and congratulate his son. The boy looked grown up in his Speedo spandex racing briefs and swim goggles dangling around his neck. He told Paul how proud of him he was. This was something no father had ever told Robin.

Rose told Robin that she was going to take Tomas, Paul, Julia, and Avraham out for dinner while Paul went to the locker room for the team celebration and to change his clothes. Robin told Rose and Julia about the search of O'Brien and Tevia's offices. Julia listened intently.

Robin left to return to work and Rose dropped Julia at the hotel to change and get Avraham ready for dinner. After she picked Tomas up she would return to the hotel and take the couple with them to a French restaurant. Rose told Julia to take as much time as she needed because the reservations were not until 7:00 p.m. and Rose wanted to shower and change.

As soon as Julia entered the hotel room she aroused Avraham and told him the facts she had gotten from Robin's investigations. Without saying much he walked over to the night table, opened his wallet, and fished for a card with a list of names and telephone numbers. The names were types of birds like penguin, bluebird, cardinal, etc. Next to each were the ten-digit country code and a telephone number. Avraham put on his glasses and dialed. He put his hand over the receiver, as the connection was being made and said to Julia, "They owe me this one."

He spoke to the person on the other end and said, "This is pigeon. I want to talk with night owl. This is solo pigeon." After about 30 seconds, a voice said, "I thought you went the way of the dodo." Avraham answered, "You wish. Send the file on Tevia Rigatoni and all of her faces to the Atlanta, Ga. (Georgia), kangaroo, fast jump." He hung up and dialed another number. After the phone picked up, he entered another 20-digit code from memory and placed the receiver back on its cradle. He thought to himself that he should have sent this message several days ago.

Julia looked at Avraham and said, "Would you mind telling me what you just did?"

Avraham said that he had just called in a few favors. For the past 40 or so years he had supplied the Israeli Intelligence with so much information that he had been given access to certain operations officers. Because of his travel with Julia and his illness he had been out of contact so when he called in just now they had asked if he was extinct. He had asked for any files on Tevia or aliases. They were to be sent by diplomatic pouch immediately. The first conversation was a little like a game and only had meaning when validated by the second call's coded message.

Julia asked, "Are you a spy?" He answered, "No, just some eyes. During my business trips I just kept my eyes open." He did not mention what things he had looked at. Julia realized that Avraham often said little but was very observant. They dressed and went to the lobby to wait for Rose. Avraham bought a New York Times and scanned the headlines. There was nothing on the front page that CNN hadn't already reported. Julia wondered why he turned to peruse the classified ads. They saw Rose's SUV pull up in front of the hotel drive and went out to join her.

~~~~~~~~~~~

Robin dreaded doing the budget so a lot of the accounting work fell on Diane. When he got back to his office she had the spreadsheets laid out in the library. First they ate their dinner. The two women fumbled
~~~~~~~~~~~

with their chopsticks before shifting to the plastic utensils. Robin just had the egg roll and wonton soup. He washed the food down with Diet Dr Pepper.

When he started the review of the Excel formatted budget he started to get nervous. Everything was in the black but the margin was very slim. The costs for establishing human tumors in immune suppressed nude mice were skyrocketing. The university had raised the overhead tariff on all grants. The clinical revenues were still excellent, but the salaries for the staff had a state imposed mandated 4% raise. The division was quite solvent but the projected revenues and expenditures would cross into the red or deficit in nine months unless there was additional revenue.

Robin would have to make a prioritized contingency plan to forestall the budgetary crises. He would do everything to protect against riffing personnel. The first item that would have to be cut was the architectural consultants who were charging a quarter of a million for designing a new building for the cancer center. This would delay the expansion. Robin dreaded having to inform the Chancellor because building buildings seemed to be the most exciting part of the Chancellor's activities. He made a note to get an appointment with the Chancellor as soon as possible.

The budget review continued for several hours and it put Robin into a depressive mood. When he finally pulled into his driveway it was about 10:30 p.m. He took Argo out for a walk. The lights were out in Rigatoni's house and the broken windows were sealed with Bisqueen sheeting. Argo barked and chased in the direction of rustling foliage towards the woods and old tennis court. Robin was tired. He pulled out his key chain with the whistle Paul had given him and blew it to signal the dog to return. When they entered the house Rose was in her robe waiting for Robin. She offered to make him a snack, but he declined. She could feel his tenseness and led him up to their bedroom. After he shed his clothes and showered she rubbed his back and neck. He fell asleep while she was massaging him. She thought about how Robin, like Atlas, carried the weight of the world on his shoulders and neck. She wondered if he was dreaming. In all the years they were together he had never shared his nocturnal dreams. She knew he had nightmares because occasionally he shook and shouted out waking her from deep sleep.

~~~~~~~~~~~

After his appointment with Robin, Mr. Yassif had his wife schedule a meeting with the Chancellor of the medical school. He was irate because he had given millions of dollars for the oncology program and for the construction of a new building of the cancer center. During his visit he did not see any evidence that the center was progressing. He did not tell Robin that he was going to request this meeting. The Chancellor was out of town, so Mr. Yassif requested that a meeting be set up as soon as possible. Within minutes of the time Mr. Yassif called from his hotel room, the Chancellor called him from Denver where he was addressing the American Association of Medical Colleges. The Chancellor told Mr. Yassif that he would return on the next flight and meet with him the next evening. The families would have dinner together. Yassif called his home office in Athens and had his chief attorney fax a copy of the documents relating to his gift to the medical center. When the fax arrived, it was brought immediately to his hotel room. He reviewed the stipulations in the bequest.

The next evening at the chancellor's mansion just after Mr. and Mrs. Yassif were greeted, Mr. Yassif asked if he could meet privately with the Chancellor. The two went into the den while the wives went to the poolside bar for cocktails. When they got seated at a table, Mr. Yassif asked the Chancellor if he knew the condition applying to the large gift he had given the University. The Chancellor said he remembered that the bulk of funds were for the oncology service, for cancer research and for the expansion of the cancer center. Yassif replied that he had come in for his biannual checkup and in conversations with Robin found that very little of the funds donated for the C team and for the new building had been dispersed for the designated purpose. He asked the Chancellor if he knew how the monies had been spent. The Chancellor flushed and said that he had not checked these accounts but that he would get on the phone immediately to the accounting department and would meet with Dean Esterly the next morning. He assured Yassif that he would have an answer by close of business the next day. Yassif, who normally was quite guarded in his emotional response said in a somewhat intimidating manner, "I am sure that the Board of Trustees and the news media would like an update on the good things that the donation had brought about." He also said that any future
~~~~~~~~~~~

disbursements of the $40 million promised funds would be held until there was a reconciliation of the utilization of the monies with the intent stated in the original documents. The Chancellor said that he guaranteed the institution's compliance.

The two men left the den to join their wives. The Chancellor was anxious to get another drink. Mr. Yassif was a keen observer of behavior and he noted the increase in the Chancellor's tremor. He could not tell whether his speech was affected by a slurring or an accentuation of his drawl. He thought that he probably would not have chosen to socialize with the Chancellor and his wife if the business at hand did not require it.

The dinner was excellent. The dishes were a southern splendor starting with a seafood gumbo over rice. The entrée was a glazed ham steak topped by pineapple rings surrounded by radiating asparagus tips. The dessert was flaming bananas caramelized by the flames from the glowing cognac.

As they were leaving, the Chancellor gave Mr. Yassif a firm handshake, covering their two right hands with his left hand as if cementing their bonding.

The next day a quick audit of the accounts revealed that the donated funds had been ciphered into Dean Esterly's accounts to bail out the medical school whose overall collections on patient bills had been dismal for the past year. The Chancellor could not afford to have Mr. Yassif go public, so he devised a plan. First he would fire the Dean for his misuse of the funds. An action he didn't mind because he never really liked the way the guy looked at him when he took a drink. Secondly, he would restore the amount that had been diverted by using funds he could tap from departmental war chests that certain fiscally sound departments had squirreled away. Anyone who objected would be shown the university bylaws limiting these accounts to a maximum of one million dollars. He decided in fact to have the university business manager effect the transfer and inform the departmental managers of the transfer today. This way he could tell Mr. Yassif that the issue had been resolved.

The Chancellor decided to call in Dean Esterly as soon as he arrived. When the Dean got to the Chancellor's office he was shown in immediately. The Chancellor said, "I'm not going to mince words. You are fired. If you are not out of your office in an hour I will have the

State Police and the university police escort you out. If you decide to oppose this order I will have an affidavit for your arrest by tomorrow."

The Dean's face went white and after a few seconds he asked if he could have an explanation for this action. The Chancellor replied, "Fiscal mismanagement both on a personal and professional level, acceptance of very expensive gifts from entities contracting with the university is graft, and lastly, harassment of several faculty members." The Chancellor said, "Get out now before I change my mind and take legal action. Leave your office keys and the keys to the official state car supplied to you with my administrator."

The Dean stood up and asked, "How am I supposed to get home?" The Chancellor replied, "That's your problem." The Dean left the office. He was confused. He always had thought of himself as hard working, extremely competent, pleasant and well liked. How could this happen to him?

The Chancellor's next order of business was to call Robin to his office. When Robin came in, the Chancellor offered him a drink. Robin declined saying that he was seeing patients shortly. The Chancellor told Robin of Mr. Yassif's visit and of the action that he had been taken to get rid of the Dean. He not only asked Robin for his support, but also told him that he would like him to head the Search Committee for a new dean. He asked Robin if he would undertake this task. Robin agreed and thought, "The world really does turn upside down at times."

At the hotel a phone call came for Avraham telling him that his information packet had arrived. He told Julia that he needed to go out for about four or five hours. He gave her a roll of bills and a credit card so that she could go shopping. He took a taxi to the airport, passed through security quickly because he didn't have any luggage. At the gate he had his electronic ticket confirmed. He showed his passport and boarded the first class section of the 737. He was in Atlanta an hour later. He left the terminal and caught a cab to the Israeli consulate. He handed the guard the classified ads from the New York Times and asked if the circled flat was still available. This confirmed his identity. The guard handed him a thick envelope. Avraham turned around and made the trip back. He was in their room reading when Julia returned from shopping, carrying an armload of packages.

She kissed him and he grunted. She tried to distract him by trying on some of the dresses she had bought, but his attention was focused on the papers in front of him. She posed facing the mirror and asked if he liked the outfit. He glanced up and said, "Very sexy." She smiled.

When he finished studying the dossier on Tevia Rigatoni (AKA Capt. Tevia Elyan), he summarized the contents of the files for Julia.

Tevia had been born in Israel and was orphaned during the war of Independence in 1948 when she was only weeks old. She was brought up on the Allonim Kibbutz not far from Golan Heights and the border. She was a child of the Kibbutz and was raised by several families. She was very athletic and worked in the fields with the boys and young men when she was in her early teens. After high school she enlisted in the Army. Because of her intelligence, strength and stamina, she was supported through college and trained to work in special operations. During a reconnaissance mission into Lebanon she was captured by Palestine guerrilla forces. She was held for four months. When she was released she didn't show external signs of beatings or torture. The examining psychiatrist noted inappropriate affect and definite hostility, especially to men who tried to exact any control over her. She was considered a liability and was released from active service. Because of her lethal training, her file was always open but mostly inactive. There were entries relating to her education and an entry relating to a heated interview during the civilian investigation of the death of her fiancée in Jerusalem. The last entry in her file noted her immigration to the US and that her married name was Rigatoni.

At the end of the file was a hand written note from Col. Josh Epstein a psychiatrist. This woman could have psychotic behavior and because of her special military training in lethal techniques was to be considered potentially dangerous. The note asked Avraham to call them if there was any contact, especially if the circumstances were suspicious. The instructions read, "Do not confront. Potentially dangerous." This was underlined.

Avraham wondered what had triggered Tevia's most recent violent outbreak. Could she have sensed an impending danger after her encounters with Avraham and Julia? He wasn't sure. He also knew that she was most likely armed.

Avraham sat at the writing desk and composed a description of the events that had occurred. He addressed the FedEx label to Col. Epstein in Tel Aviv and took the envelope to the hotel concierge for posting. He had left his family to survive on their own for most of his life, but this time he felt preventative security might be important.

The reply to this letter came in 24 hours by telephone. Col. Epstein said the potential for damage was of the highest order. The damage could besmirch the Israeli government. Now that the problem child had erupted they would have to take measures to "erase and eradicate." Protective shields would be in place for anyone who was threatened. Please list candidates. Avraham listed Robin, Rose, Tomas, Paul, Julia and himself. The voice said, "Open line 7/24," signifying that he could dial uncoded anytime. Avraham thanked the caller. He and Julia went downstairs to the hotel restaurant for dinner. This was to be his last night out before the start of the intensive chemotherapy.

Robin left work early; he was feeling pretty good. He had gotten to spend time with his brother Tomas during the bone marrow collections. On his way home he passed a sporting goods store. He turned around the block and pulled into a parking spot at the rear entrance to the store. He went in and talked with the salesman about archery. He left the store with three bows, two 50 lb compound bows and one 150 lb reflex bow, three dozen target arrows, three straw targets on tripods, and a dozen paper bull's eye paper targets. Robin had been excited about spending more time with Paul and he hoped the family could enjoy archery in their backyard. There was a clear 200 yards in front of the old tennis courts where he could set up the range with targets on tripods. The third bow was so that Rose could join Robin and Paul, father and son.

Rose was absolutely astounded when she arrived home and saw Robin and Paul stringing their bows, from her back bedroom window. Sitting on the terrace shouting encouragement was Uncle Tomas. He called to them as "William Tell and Robin Hood." He even took a few turns at shooting.

The setting sun reflected onto the silver covered Bible lying on the dresser in Rose's bedroom. It was Julia's present to Robin. In the center was a medallion engraved with the Ten Commandments, capped by a crown, the crown of the Torah. On the back cover there were two blessing hands. Rose went to the bookshelf where she kept the art books and her reference books that she used when tracking lost artworks for the CRA. She blew the dust from the binding and flipped the pages, scanning the illustrations. She found a picture of a similar Bible cover and found that the inlay work on Robin's book was similar to others in the texts. Reference was made to the symbolic blessing hands of the Cohen, the high priests of the Israelites.

Rose opened the latches that secured the Bible. The text fell open to a page, which was in Hebrew on the right and Hungarian on the left. From her rudimentary knowledge of Hungarian, she could translate and discern that it was the 23rd Psalm. Rose thumbed carefully through the yellowed pages. On the last page and inside the cover was the Glucke-Havas-Katz family history. The dates of marriages, births, and deaths for Julia's family were carefully entered for at least six generations. Rose could not understand all the encryptions but she could make out the entries for Julia, Sig and Ted. Next to Julia's in fresher ink was the name Rolfe Havas (m.) 1931. Below this were Tomas Havas (b.) 1934, and Robe Havas (b.) 1936. Then there was a gap and an entry for Julia and Myron Katz (m.) 1948 and another for David Katz (b.) 1949, (d.) 1974.

All the dates and events that Rose had searched for in Budapest were there. Rose closed the book and put it back on the credenza and went to join her warrior clan shouting as they fired their arrows at imaginary enemy targets. Argos panted from running after the arrows that over shot the targets. Rose poured water into a bowl for the exhausted dog.

CHAPTER 27

After everyone retired to his or her bedrooms, Robin still felt energetic so he went back downstairs and took Argos for a walk. He noticed some fuzzy flashes of light through the opaque plastic sheeting on the broken windows of Rigatoni's bedroom. The dog had headed towards the neighbor's house and was standing on the stone wall that separated the two properties. It was then that Robin noticed the garage door was open. Robin thought he should return to his house and call the police; perhaps someone was burglarizing the house. He turned and called his dog to come back. Just then two figures emerged from the rear door of Rigatoni's house. Possibly there was a third person. There was a foggy mist and it was hard to see the indistinct silhouettes. They seemed to be running or chasing the first shadow. They headed into the woods towards the old tennis courts. Argos let out several barks and bolted forward but he was now secured on Robin's leash so he could not chase the strangers. Robin stood still and after a short period he heard a popping sound sort of like those made when a string of ladyfingers, small firecrackers, make when they go off. He thought about gunshots but the sounds seemed muted.

Robin and Argos went into the house and Robin dialed 911. He told the police that he thought there might have been a break-in in the next-door house and he gave his address and telephone number. He looked at his watch; it was 10:40 p.m. At 10:52 p.m. Robin saw the flashing blue and red lights of a patrol car pull into Rigatoni's driveway. Robin went out to meet the officers. He told them about the lights and the open garage next-door and that the owner of the house was in the hospital. He also told them that he saw two or three people running into the woods from the rear of the house.

The officers called for some backup. They got out their flashlights and approached the house. In several minutes two more police cars arrived. Four officers pointed their lights towards the direction that Robin had reported seeing figures. They approached the heavily wooded area cautiously. At least two of the cops had their pistols drawn. When they got to the edge of the woods, they seemed to have trepidations about entering the dense thickets and foliage. They headed back towards the houses and talked with Robin. They asked him about what he had seen and about the wooded area. Robin said there was only woods for a mile or so and that the uninhabited area went until it abutted State Hwy 280.

The officers closed Rigatoni's garage and back door and wrote up their report. They told Robin that they would patrol the neighborhood and that they would return early in the morning to continue their investigation. They also told him to lock his doors and to call them if he saw or heard anything suspicious.

Robin thanked them for responding rapidly.

When Robin reentered his house, Rose was waiting wrapped in her robe. She asked him what was going on.

Robin responded that he thought there had been a burglary at Rigatoni's house. He told her what he had seen and what had transpired. She said, "Come to bed or you will not be able to function tomorrow." He walked up the stairs behind her but he wasn't sure that he could fall asleep.

When Robin came down in the morning, the others were having breakfast. Paul was still excited and asked if Robin could go into work a little later so that they could have another target session with the bows and arrows. Rose looked at Robin. It was Saturday and he could go in at eleven to finish rounds with the C team.

They took their coffee out to the terrace and Paul and Robin began to shoot. Paul had improved and was hitting the target. Robin was still a little bleary eyed and missed by a lot. Several arrows flew well over the targets and into the woods.

After each had shot a dozen or so they went off to retrieve the spent arrows. Argos went with them. Robin's over shot arrows were difficult to find. As they neared the old tennis court, Robin saw one arrow imbedded in the ground with the red and white-feathered tail sticking up. The dog was next to the arrow sniffing something. Robin bent to pick up the arrow when he saw the shell casing. It was then that he realized that there were at least a dozen shells. He picked one up and smelled the gunpowder. He didn't know much about guns and ammunition but he knew enough to make it out as a 22 gauge. He got Paul and walked quickly back to the house. He called 911.

The officers accompanied Robin into the woods. They noted the shells, their number and position, and with a latex gloved hand placed those in a zip lock plastic baggy. The officers walked around looking for footprints. One shouted and they all went to where he was. On the ground was a substantial puddle of coagulated blood, some of it trailed off into broken bushes. One officer got on his walkie-talkie and called the homicide detectives. Robin was asked to return to his house and wait for the detectives to arrive. Robin took the detectives to the waiting patrolmen. The detectives were dressed in sport jackets and weren't really anxious to hike into the wilderness. They went back to their car and got into jumpsuits and boots. They brought a metal box with sample containers for the blood samples and paraphernalia for taking footprint casts. Pictures of the site were taken. Several additional police were summoned including one with some dogs. Robin had Paul put Argos in the house because he loved to play with other dogs, even those that didn't want to play with him.

The technician with the bloodhounds stopped at the areas of the bloodstains and then headed along the trail of blood and broken foliage into the jungle-like forest.

Robin called the hospital and told the C team to round without him. He asked them to have Knife call him. About 15 minutes later, Knife called. Robin asked him if he could come over right away. When Knife arrived, Rose set out some coffee and bagels and Robin went over the events of the last night and this morning. Paul sat proudly by his father's side.

Knife asked Robin to take him to the area where the blood had been found. Knife looked around in a nonchalant manner while they were standing to the side of the area cordoned off with yellow plastic tape. Robin and Knife could hear a voice on the walkie-talkie reporting back to the detectives.

He said that he and the dogs had followed the trail about a mile out onto Hwy 280. The trail ended abruptly at the edge of the highway. The handler asked if he could be picked up at the highway so that he wouldn't have to take the dogs back through the underbrush. The detectives said that he should wait there and they would pick him up. They asked Robin not to disturb the scene since they might have to return to examine anything they might have missed. Robin said okay.

They all headed back to the house and all the police left. Rose now had a light lunch prepared. They would have to take Tomas to the airport in a few hours.

Knife pulled Robin aside and said, "I've been thinking. It's going to rain shortly and I think we should have a few samples of the blood clots before they wash away." He and Robin took some plastic baggies and a few plastic spoons from the kitchen and headed to the roped off area. While they were out there, Knife said the events and scene seemed crazy.

Why would the burglars shoot one another? Why would they then go to the exhausting effort to drag the wounded or dead out through the woods and remove the wounded or corpse? By the way he added, "It was most likely a corpse based upon the amount of blood lost. Why were so many shots fired? By the description of the sounds you heard and the 22 caliber you described, it was an automatic like an Uzi automatic with some type of silencer. Was this an execution at a crime scene?"

Robin was amazed at Knife's analytic acuity.

Knife extracted the DNA and had the blood typed for the ABO, Rh and several other blood group antigens. One thing that was readily apparent was that the blood was from a female. There were no Y chromosome genes detectable. The DNA markers did not have a good match to any individual profile in the transplant databank. Knife considered Tevia as a possible candidate, but he didn't have any data on her. He asked Robin if there was anything in her belongings that might contain cellular material. They even went to the storage bins and sorted through her belongings that had been taken from her laboratory. The search did not produce any suitable specimens. Knife told Robin that this approach was at an impasse.

Robin wired friends at Mt. Sinai Hospital and at Hadassah Hospital to see if they could tell whether Tevia had ever been admitted for surgery or had her blood typed. All inquiries came back as negative. The employment health history at the University had not listed any disease or surgical history and there was no other useful information. Neither Robin nor Knife considered asking Rigatoni for any information.

The detectives talked to Robin again and the only information they had confirmed was Knife's speculation that the ammunition was almost surely from an Uzi automatic. This wasn't much help because black market Uzi's were becoming more popular in certain gangs, mostly because the shooters made up for their lack of precision shooting by rapidly laying down a cluster of bullets. The Uzi could deliver 600 rounds per minute. The officers were frustrated. They had dusted the Rigatoni house and found no usable fingerprints or clues. The bedroom wall safe had been opened and evidently cash and other valuables had been removed. Without a body they were not certain whether they were dealing with a homicide or not. Their attention focused mostly on whether the stolen goods might show up at pawnshops or at known fences. Their investigation was growing cold fast. They had no idea as to a motive for the shooting.

Robin forced himself to concentrate on his medical work. Nevertheless, he found that he would drift off and think about the events in his backyard. He had never been up close to a crime before. It preoccupied his thoughts and it scared him. He was concerned about his family's safety.

Tomas had returned to Austria but now called Robin or Rose once or twice a week. He inquired about how Avraham's treatment was progressing and whether the bone marrow transplant had worked. Robin found it hard not to spend extra time with Avraham while he was undergoing therapy. A lot of the conversation was low key and trivia. The conversation frequently lapsed into Hungarian. There were remembrances of places and things but it skirted issues of intimacy. Robin wanted to keep his patient in good spirits. After many years of treating patients with cancer he knew that the psychological state of the patient had a tremendous effect on the clinical outcome.

Robin still had a hard time accepting Avraham and Julia as his real parents and he could not get up the courage or nerve to ask why they never searched harder to find their sons. He almost felt that if he allowed them to become his parents that he was betraying Maria who raised him. He knew that it would take time for him to sort things out.

Julia often sat by the side of the bed weaving her pictures. Her creativity was evident even when she was copying a masterpiece. The relief effect of the stitchery gave a dimension to the reproductions that was unique. After Julia finished her rendition of the Old King by Rouault, she gave it as a present to Robin and Rose. Rose had it matted and framed in an ornate gilded frame. She hung it in the living room in her house.

Almost every day Julia had either lunch, tea or dinner with Rose. They both wanted to get to know each other better. The conversations were more open and probing then when they were altogether with Robin and Avraham. The relationship was taking on some of the characteristics of a mother-daughter-in-law relationship. There were even some of the rough spots. But the function was not that of possessiveness or turf clashes. It was clear that Julia dared not to claim anything the Goode's didn't want to give. It was not a position Julia enjoyed being in, but she had little choice. Julia almost bit her tongue when she wanted to say anything about how they should be bringing up Paul, her genetic grandchild. She felt almost deprived of the inalienable right grandparents often exert in an effort to display their savvy in parenting. The very few critiques she made were subdued and subtle.

Rose, on the other hand, was much more frank and direct. Some of her questioning was almost blunt. Rose wanted answers to questions that she had thought about for many years. Realizing that Julia was a little frightened, she backed off.

One day the two were lunching in Rose's kitchen when Rose went to her bedroom and brought down the Bible that Julia had given Robin. She made Julia go over the family history. The story was familiar. Rose had heard much of it from Sig and Ted Glucke years ago.

Julia sensed that Rose was traveling on a familiar trail. In order to test this, Julia distorted a few facts relating to the description of her brothers and keenly watched Rose's face for any evidence of recognition of the inaccuracy. The deception worked as evidenced by Rose's raised eyebrow.

Julia paused in her recollections and said to Rose, "Why am I telling you things you already know?"

Rose regained her usual poker face affect. She said to Julia, "Sometimes you have to drive down a road twice to appreciate the scenery."

The conversation turned from ancient history to the present. Rose told Julia about the events that had occurred in the backyard several days ago and confided in her that she was a little afraid to have Paul out there by himself. Julia said that it might be a good idea to either have him play elsewhere or for Rose to be nearby. Julia made a mental note of the story and was anxious to relay it to Avraham later.

Julia asked Rose if it bothered her that Robin was half Jewish.

Rose thought for a minute and replied, "I already knew." Julia was astonished and asked if she had surmised this from the linkage to Ted and Sig. Rose answered that she had suspected that Robin was related to Ted and Sig but she never had any substantial proof. "No," she said, "The answer was in Robin's DNA." Rose explained how she had sent the DNA for study and the genetic markers on mitochondrial DNA had suggested that he was a Cohen on his mother's side and not on his father's side. The mutation in the factor XI had suggested a Jewish heritage.

Julia said, "You knew all that?" Rose said, "Yes", but she did not see where revealing this to Robin would have had any importance because there were just clues without facts. It was only when Julia and Avraham materialized that she thought about confronting the enigma of Robin's ancestry. After all it was not like the cakewalk she had had with her own lineage studies in a church graveyard on a small island in the North Sea.

The afternoon had slipped by and Julia looked at her watch. She said, "I must get back to the hospital. Avraham will be getting lonely. This man, who has been on his own many years, seems so dependent upon me. He has separation anxiety." Rose said, "Perhaps the fear of losing again what you have lost before is greater."

When Julia got to Avraham's room, Robin and Avraham seemed deep in conversation. Avraham said to Julia that Robin told him that the therapy had shrunken or killed most of the tumor. The stem cells from Tomas seemed to be growing and repopulating his bone marrow, the engraftment was successful. Robin told Julia that the lab test results looked very promising. He said goodnight to them and left.

Julia kissed Avraham on the cheek and told him about the break-in and shooting that Rose had described. She asked him if Robin had told him the story. Avraham said, "No." Julia told him about the police investigators, the blood, and Dr. Knife's investigation. She told him about the spent ammo shells and the search for the victim's body.

"Is it possible that Tevia returned?" she asked Avraham. He answered that it was more than possible, it was most likely.

She asked Avraham if he knew any more. He answered that it was most likely that Tevia's past had gotten her into trouble. However, without a body it might be hard to know for sure what had happened.

Avraham told her that the dossier he had requested from the secret police suggested that Tevia had been suspected of being involved in several suspicious deaths or actual murders. Each time there was not enough evidence to indict her. There was strong indication that she was homicidal, particularly if she was romantically involved with the victim. She was as lethal as the Latrodectus, the black widow spider. Even while she was still in the Israeli Army Special Ops, a Major General linked to her had mysteriously fallen from the ridge at Masada, the site where the biblical martyrs had jumped to their deaths rather than surrendering to the Romans. He added that the Israeli secret service had a long memory and had the Islamic Modus Operandi of an "eye for an eye." To them retribution and prevention had an intricate and profound relationship.

Avraham's eyes grew tired and Julia tidied his bed so that he could go to sleep. She would take a taxi from the hospital back to the hotel.

Several weeks passed and Avraham grew stronger. The bonds grew stronger between Robin and his biological parents. Julia and Avraham told Robin, Julia and Paul about what life was like in Hungary when they were growing up. They talked about their parents and ancestors. The stories covered many generations. They took a trip as a family to Washington DC. Avraham, Robin and Paul really enjoyed the Aerospace Museum, while Julia and Rose toured the National Gallery of Art and the Holocaust Memorial.

These people, who were strangers several months ago, felt an attractive force indescribable by the laws of either physics or biology.

Robin felt a fullness in his life. He realized that roots are more than an anchor in the ground.

Julia and Avraham announced that it was time for them to return to Israel. Robin and Rose promised that they would bring Paul for a visit. At the airport they all embraced and promised, "next year in Israel."

P.S. Dr. Knife was surprisingly selected to be the new Dean of the medical school.

EPILOGUE

Lost and Found is fiction. I was working out in the gym with a Hungarian born refuge who had fled communist Hungary to become a prominent professional when his father and mother came over for a visit in 1988. His father, is the basis for Rolfe/Avraham in the story. In broken Yiddish-German and English he told me about the last days of WW II. He had been a Hungarian aristocrat and a career officer in the Hungarian Army. He was a colonel when he was mustered into the German Army. He described how his last mission in Austria just prior to the invasion and occupation by the Americans, British and Russians was to move a cargo of artworks, gold and jewels from Salzburg south to an isolated monastery where the monks hid the cache in a cave left from an old salt mine.

He had his family disrupted by the Nazis and the war and was determined to see that his future would lead to their safety and eventual reunification. The prestige and influence that he had as a successful aristocrat and the vestiges of the industrial empire of his first wife's family helped to ensure the raising and survival of his children even during the communist regimes and Russian occupation of Hungary. He died recently a very sorrowed but proud man.

The character Robin is a composite of many driven medical researchers who have worked tenaciously to make advances in understanding and combating diseases. I t was said that they had "fire in their bellies." They often worked on the cutting edge and used methods of experimentation that would not have passed scrupulous reviews of the Internal Review Boards in existence now.

The story is about some of the types of research that were tried and some that are fictional. The solicitation and competition by research groups, often in the same institutions, for government, foundation and philanthropic support is ubiquitous in academic medical research. The conflicts between individual researchers and between the researchers and the deans and chancellors is extremely common. These idolized researchers often have the same human frailties as everyone else. Egotism and jealousy often leads to feuds over power, space, money and even sex. It is not uncommon to have dismissals or groups transferring because of disagreements. Uncommonly there have even been suicides or homicides.

The mass killings, the breakup of families and the social disruption brought about holocaust and WW II still is remembered and haunts us. The tales of persecution, pogroms, expulsion and of wandering are not new to the Jews. They have been subjected to this for thousands of years during which they have been the scapegoats (Kapore) for many kings and dictators. We are still seeing the active discovery of the plundering that took place during the rule of the Nazis. A team of 345 specialists called Monument Men was assembled by the Allied Forces after the war to track the artwork looted by the Nazis. Even with this extensive effort the German government is still finding pieces of art extorted from Jewish families under duress that have been hidden. It is still estimated that there are over 100, 000 Objects d'art worth billions of dollars that have not and may never be returned to their owners. The courts are still deciding who gets to keep theirs or their ancestors belongings. Some of the art has been recovered and hangs in museums.

Although there were efforts by the Red Cross and publications of lists of the people who perished in the War and Holocaust not every family has been as lucky as the Havas and Goodes in reuniting their families and surviving.

ACKNOWLEDGEMENTS

I would like to thank my wife Pat for her support during the creation and writing of Lost and Found. The love of my daughters Sandy and Linda and my mother Pauline was most treasured.

Many thanks to Diane Sawyer, my assistant who helped organize my notes and thoughts from scribbling on yellow pads into a manuscript.

Thanks, also to David Ward who encouraged me to tell my story and to all my colleagues whose experiences helped shape this work of fiction.

Made in the USA
Las Vegas, NV
20 December 2021